Waking Up

Waking Up

A Smith Family Story

Meredith P. Beeler

Library of Congress Control Number: 2015915146
ISBN: Hardcover   978-1-5144-0777-6
                   Softcover   978-1-5144-0776-9
                   eBook   978-1-5144-0775-2

Print information available on the last page.

Rev. date: 09/14/2015

To order additional copies of this book, contact:
Xlibris
1-888-795-4274
www.Xlibris.com
Orders@Xlibris.com
720795

For Adam,
my biggest fan.
"I have found the one whom my soul loves."
–Song of Solomon 3:4

PART 1

Chapter 1

Waking Up

The rough shadows on the walls and the constant dripping of water somewhere out of my vision cause me to shrink back into the darkness. A sudden scream pierces the black, and that is when I feel the warm sunlight on my eyelids and sink further into the covers. *It was just another dream, thank God. Just a dream.* With a satisfied smile, I sit up to enjoy the rays of warmth. Instead of feeling the lingering effects of sleep, however, the first thing I feel is pain. Why am I so sore? I hate to exercise; it's never been my thing, but that is exactly how I feel—like I have been lifting weights and running hard.

As I stretch my sore muscles, I have the sensation of something stuck in my throat. I cough and try to clear it but gag repeatedly. My back arches with the effort, and I thank my lucky stars I do not vomit on the bed. I slowly reach up, and my whole body tenses as I feel a small tube running out of my nose. I follow its course and realize it is attached to my cheek by a small piece of tape. Without further thought given to the tube's purpose, I tear the piece of tape off my face and proceed to extract the tube from my nose. It must run all the way from my nostril to my stomach because it takes a good five seconds to pull the cursed thing completely out. I fall to the floor with violent dry heaves and only then do the alien-ness of my surroundings process through my hazy brain.

I do not recognize the room I am in or the bed I apparently slept in last night. It is queen-sized with two large pillows, one mashed with the effects of sleep and another which looks untouched. The bedding is soft and plain—a white sheet and a large white down comforter. This is not my room. However, I cannot conjure up the image of what "my room" looks like. I continue to take stock in my surroundings as I toss the clear

1

plastic tube, which is covered in some sort of slime as far away from me as possible. My nerves begin to build with what I recognize as fear.

The rest of the room is very modest: a wooden nightstand on each side of the bed; a chest of drawers, also wooden but more modern, against one wall; a dresser on the wall facing the bed; an empty closet. I see a large window above the dresser which helps confirm it is sunny outside. I see small vegetation and some palm trees. Where am I?

As I calmly try to assess my situation, I listen for sounds around me and hear none: no one walking around; no TV babble; no running water; nothing to clue me into what might await me if I open the only door in the bedroom. I slowly get off the floor, giving my aching body time to adjust and notice I have on a thin white nightgown made of a silky material. Although the fabric is almost see-through, the length and neckline make it fairly modest. Underneath, I feel something bulky around my waist and pull the nightgown up to reveal an adult diaper. Thankfully, it is void of any waste, and I make just as short work of removing it as I did the plastic tube in my nose.

As I make my way to the large window, I pick out small things about the room I missed before. There are some generic pictures on the walls consisting of palm trees and sea shells, a small clock, a candle on a pedestal. Other than that, the room is empty. The view out the window is what one would expect to see at the beach: lots of sunlight and the palm trees I noticed before. However, instead of seeing an ocean in front of me, I see gently rolling hills, fields—I realize belatedly—with rows upon rows of grapevines. Finally I recognize what I am looking at—vineyards. They are, as far as I can see, in all directions—to my right there is a long road, a driveway maybe, which looks to be gravel and well worn.

I look down at the small clock and it says four thirty-one. It has to mean four thirty-one in the afternoon. I stand still a couple more minutes trying to determine my next move. I have no idea where I am or how I got here. My body is even more sore standing up than when I was in bed. I am starting to panic. What should I do? I try to pump myself up, give myself a pep talk as I make my way to the door. But as I am about to open it, fear once again grips my body, and I am frozen on the spot, unable to take another step. The cause of my fear is not my unknown surroundings and the strange situation I have awakened to, well, not only that, but I suddenly realize I have no clue *who* I am.

How have I not realized this before now? I was so wrapped up in figuring out *where* I was that I didn't think I needed to figure out *who* I was. My body starts to shake, and my fingers are numb. I stumble and find myself curled into a ball on the carpet. Lying there, I start with the most basic detail, my name. I try to picture it written on a blank piece of paper. But as I go through the alphabet—A, Alice, Amanda, Allison, Amber; B, Bethany, Becky, Brittany; C, Caroline, Catherine, Catelyn—nothing sounds familiar, and I realize I could be lying here for a long time and never get an answer. I try another tactic and begin trying to picture my parents' faces—their hair color, eye color, smiles—but once again, I come up blank. I struggle to conjure up my favorite color and my favorite food, even my favorite movie, but I have no luck.

Panic begins to rise from my belly, and I start counting aloud backward from one hundred. By the time I reach ten, I have decided to take a different approach. I'm not sure how long I have been lying here on the soft carpet, but I do know I will not find out anything if I stay in this room. The panic and fear subside, and a fierce determination replaces it. I pick myself off the floor, turn the doorknob, and walk into the unknown.

It turns out the "unknown" is just a medium-sized living room with a small kitchen attached. The first thing I notice is the brightness of the room. Windows are everywhere, and all the furniture is either white or a version of off-white. The second thing I notice is how clean the place is—sparsely furnished like the bedroom, a few lamps dominate the side tables, a couple of magazines are on the coffee table, too far away for me to see their covers. The furnishings all seem to be comfortable and well worn. The kitchen is also clean with a bowl of fruit on the table, and a jar filled with utensils sits next to the stove.

I slowly make my way through it, trying to find some kind of clue to where I am *and, more importantly, who I am.* I look to the refrigerator, hoping to see pictures or cards or notes, anything really, to give me a clue. There is one of those magnetic advertisement calendars of the whole year, and from it I learn it is 2013. *At least I know something now.*

I turn to look out of a large window above the sink, and I can tell the house is in an "L" shape. I can see into what I am referring to now as "my room." To the far right of my bedroom window, the side of the house which was not visible, is another house, an extremely large house. From what I can see, it has two stories, maybe three if there is an underground basement. It seems to be the length of half a football field with a four-car garage on one side, my side, and what looks to be an atrium or indoor pool on the other. I must be standing in what is the guest house. As I stare back out the window and wonder again how I got here, the front door opens, and in stream a group of people.

Men and women, all laughing and talking loudly at the same time, file in through the door. I notice a few things about them while their attention is still on each other: there are two men, young, maybe in their thirties, and three women, two of them older, one of them younger, but all of them dressed like they just came from a country club—lots of khaki, plaid, and pastels. Suddenly, I am supremely aware of my thin nightgown as well as the fact that I am being confronted by six strangers. It seems like my uneasiness radiates toward them because at that moment, they all stop and stare at me. I have no idea what look is on my face, fear or confusion, but I do notice the look on their faces.

The older women in the front have small guarded smiles; the young woman looks like she is trying to comfort me but failing miserably and instead burning a hole through my skull. One of the young men, who has dark hair, has a smile that stretches across his face, crinkling his eyes, which are shockingly green. And then I notice the other man. He was in the back of the group but is now making his way toward me. He is average height, blond hair, and, just like the other man, has shocking green eyes.

I process all these details quickly through my overwhelmed brain, but they don't stick. What does stick is the strange sense I have seen him before. He is giving me a look like he is trying to let me know what he is thinking, and then his facial expression changes into one of overwhelming joy. His forehead ceases to crease, his green eyes open wider, he smiles at me, showing straight, white teeth. As he quickens his step toward me, he looks at me like I should know him; like he knows me, better than anyone, and I have that strange feeling again. A sensation I am unfamiliar with bubbles in my chest, and I feel my mouth turning up at the corners with a small tentative smile.

****

She's Awake

Just like the first time I saw Eleanor, I think she is the most beautiful woman I have ever seen. And just like that first time, I know she was meant for me—my angel comes from dream to reality.

Chapter 2

Andrew

Honolulu, Hawaii, Three Weeks Ago

The weather is perfect, I realize as I walk back to my hotel. The warm breeze is one of the reasons I am making my way through the bustling city at almost midnight. I only have a couple more days here, and I want to enjoy every moment I can outside of the convention center where I have spent the last two days. The stuffy, crowded, and sterile center is full of fellow doctors who, like me, would rather be outside basking in the sun or surfing the waves at one of the most beautiful beaches and oceans in the world. Instead, we are stuck inside the very dull center listening to one lecture after another describing the latest in medical technology. Before I rein in my pessimism, I give myself permission to grovel a few more minutes.

If I am being honest, I came to Honolulu to get away from doctors, medicine, and anything sterile. But being who I am, the middle child of a four-child family, I am prone to the occasional feeling of guilt. My first guilty feeling occurred as soon as I walked into my hotel. At the front desk, I was handed the conference information packet. I was tempted to dump it into the waste bin right in front of the doe-eyed young girl who was greeting each guest individually with a very cheery "Welcome to the Honolulu Hilton." Before she could continue with her prerehearsed speech of "The first lecture is scheduled for seven, following a meet-and-greet starting at five . . .", I quickly thanked her and headed straight to my room, cursing under my breath the whole time. *If she didn't remind me so much of Annie . . .*

However, I know that no matter who was handing out that packet, doe-eyed or not, I would have attended the meet-and-greet, at least to get a free meal. I was pleasantly surprised with my hotel room, not only its cleanliness and modern furnishings not my style but also still nice. But the most impressive thing was the view. If I was a betting man, which I'm not, I would have wagered I had the best view in the entire hotel. The large picture window contained exactly that, a picture. The beautiful beach with perfect colored sand and the blue ocean filled with gently rolling waves seemed so close, I stood there with my mouth hung open, knowing with certainty, coming to this conference was the best decision I had made in months.

Looking back on the past year, really, I can see the pattern of depression slowly taking its toll on my wonderful life. And there is no denying my life is wonderful. I am a member of a huge, loving, crazy, hilarious, interloping family. My job is (or should be) one of the most satisfying occupations in the world. I am reasonably healthy and active—I play basketball on the weekends with a group of friends. I meet some friends at a local restaurant after work sometimes. Like I said, a wonderful life, well-rounded, balanced. But even surrounded by friends and family and work, I was starting to get restless. I knew at some point this would happen.

After years of military service, during wartime, the life of an everyday, average joe gets to be monotonous. And the worst part was I could see the depression creeping in, and I was helpless to stop it. This trip to Hawaii was supposed to be a momentous turning point in my life: I came here to decide whether or not to continue practicing medicine. When you are a doctor, it is not only your occupation but your life. And my life had been on a downward spiral.

There were very few lectures I planned to attend while in Honolulu. The rest of my time was to be spent lying on the beach, taking stock in my life, and figuring out what I wanted to do with the rest of it. I know at thirty-five years of age, I should have decided by now. Being in the position to start anew if I so choose, I relished the possibility in front of me. I hadn't felt this excited about my future since I graduated high school.

But here I am, walking away from the second day full of lectures with not one single minute of beach time under my belt. After the meet-and-greet on the first night, I have attended each and every lecture, like some sort of information junkie. Every time someone new took the podium, I was there, at least in body. I had not scribbled one line of notes or received one handout from the hundreds of tables lining the inside of the convention center. And even now, with the fresh air blowing on my face and the smell of salt water in my nostrils, I don't know why. I honestly think sitting on that beach and facing my future is too much for me to handle. I have been in some truly horrifying situations but none more so than the life of uncertainty that is laid out before me.

At just the moment I start to mentally kick myself, I hear a strange gurgling sound coming from my right. I don't know if it's my want of a distraction or the gut-wrenching sound of something not quite right, which causes me to turn down the darkened alley.

Chapter 3

Eleanor

As the man draws closer, his right hand comes up and gently cups my cheek. His eyes show restraint, and once again, I get the feeling he is trying to communicate his thoughts to me. He leans toward me, but I stand still, rooted to the spot, frozen by his proximity. He kisses me gently, and as he pulls away, his hand lingers on my face, and his eyes burn into me. Then he straightens up, moves his hand to my shoulder, which is now covered in goose bumps, and turns us both to face the group.

"I would like to introduce you all to my bride," he says with assurance.

I am starting to panic. His bride, wait, what? I don't know this man, and now I belong to him. His words send a shot of trepidation through me. His smile is so genuine that for now, I go with it. Just so I don't appear weak and unsure in front of these strangers, I tell myself.

"Everyone, this is Eleanor." Hearing my name for the first time doesn't ring any bells, and the fear which is churning my stomach begins to creep into my limbs. The smiles on the faces of the people become a little more relaxed. The dark-haired man moves toward me and folds me into an embrace that chokes off my breath and makes my already sore body feel like it is going to crack. Somehow my "husband" realizes this and steps in, saying, "Okay, Josh, she is officially welcomed to our family" in a joking voice. Josh looks to my "husband" and grins again, throwing his arms around him and squeezing him just as tight as he squeezed me. They embrace for a second and then step apart, their posture like school boys.

"I'm sure Eleanor is tired, everyone," says the dark-haired guy. "We should leave the newlyweds to some peace and quiet." With that, everyone looks to me one last time, smiles, and heads for the door. The young woman stays with her eyes on me, but when the man named Joshua grabs her hand, she follows everyone else. The door shuts, and I am left alone with my "husband."

I instantly put distance between the two of us, walking all the way behind the kitchen table, and he does not stop me. He looks straight into my eyes, and I stare back, willing myself not to seem timid or scared.

"First off, my name is Andrew Smith, and you are safe here."

As I stare at this stranger, I feel unsure about everything. If he was truly my husband, wouldn't I feel more of a pull to him, some kind of relief at seeing his face instead of simply dull recognition? Let's say he is telling the truth, then what? What do I do with the knowledge that I am a wife? I'm starting to get overwhelmed. My legs are weak and beginning to shake.

On the other hand, what if this man is not my husband? Does he intend to do me harm? *He could be preparing to torture and kill you; he did shove a tube down your nose,* my imagination so generously supplies. I quickly clear my head and shoo away my conscious, which is becoming increasingly distracting, and continue to look at the man. I notice his eyes seem to be trying to convey again what he is thinking, but I am a little more wary now.

"If you want to take a seat, I think I can explain what you are doing here to a certain degree." I sit because of my aching knees and the fact that I want to know information, and this man seems willing to give me some. I keep my hands on the table so I can defend myself if need be.

"Once again, my name is Andrew Smith. I am a doctor at Carmel Methodist Hospital. Three weeks ago, I went to a conference in Honolulu, Hawaii. I was walking back to my hotel from the conference one night, and I heard moaning in an alley. I went to check it out and found you. You had been severely beaten, so I brought you back to my hotel room to take care of you." Andrew stops there, seeing the question in my eyes.

"I know you are wondering why I did not take you to the closest hospital, and I have no answer for you except this"—he takes a deep breath, gathering his nerves, I guess. "I had the overwhelming feeling I needed to protect you. Don't ask me why I felt that way. I just did. Call it a hunch, call it intuition or even years of experience." He braces himself on the back of the chair opposite me and continues. "The extent of your injuries had me convinced this was not the usual mugging. I knew if I took you to a hospital, your care would be out of my hands, and I had to ensure you remained safe."

He stops for a minute, giving me time to process what he is saying. That's when I realize why I am so sore. *I have been beaten.* I look down at myself, and instead of focusing on what I am wearing, I see the bruises on my arms and legs, which are just starting to turn an ugly shade of pale green. This is the most fear I have felt since I woke up this morning with no clue to where I was or who I was. I look down at my shaking hands and then back up at Andrew questioningly, and he nods his head, like he understands my confusion.

"Do you remember anything?" he asks, looking hopeful and worried at the same time.

I find my voice. "Nothing of importance."

"Everything has importance at this stage in the game," he assures me.

"I woke up so sore. I thought I had been working out, but then I remembered I hate to work out."

Andrew gives a little chuckle. "Me too. Anything else?"

I just shake my head.

How can I not remember—I almost died. If what he is saying is true, though, it may be a good thing I don't. Andrew looks pained as he straightens up and walks across the kitchen to grab something. Whatever he is going for doesn't look dangerous, so I stay seated. When he returns, I recognize what he is holding: it's an ID badge.

"This is my badge for the hospital. It has all my information. If you would like to call and verify my employment, there is a phone by the door." I look at the badge and study it quickly. There is his name all right: Steven Andrew Smith, MD. A badge number follows, and then the hospital's phone number and address are across the bottom.

Do you really believe this? I ask myself, and almost immediately, I realize I do. While listening to him, I paid close attention to his eyes. They say that the eyes are the windows to the soul, and I truly believe that. This man's eyes were filled with desperation. And my guess is his particular desperation was hoping I would believe his story and trust him. That may be exactly what he wants—to trick me into thinking I can trust him. However, why the elaborate story if he was planning to hurt me—he didn't have to tell me anything. Why would he introduce me to his family? Why would he give me his credentials and then allow me to call and check, especially since the phone is next to the door? I could make a break for it . . . even if I could manage to do more than hobble along.

I look up into his staring eyes and decide to take a leap of faith, metaphorically speaking. "I believe you." The look of relief floods his face, and he is smiling some.

"But I have a few questions: Where are we? How long have I been unconscious, and why the story about being your wife?" I recognize the sounds of a Southern draw when I speak, meaning I must be from the South. He seems relieved that my questions are fairly easily to answer.

"We are in Carmel, California. We flew from Honolulu on my parents' private jet and arrived two weeks ago. You were too sick to leave Hawaii any sooner. You have been in and out of consciousness most of the time, but because of your injuries, I have been giving you a lot of medication."

I have been unconscious for three weeks!

"The story about being husband and wife is a little more complicated but necessary, I promise you," he quickly adds. "Even though we used a private jet, I had to have a cover story about why I was bringing an unconscious, beaten woman onto an airplane headed for the continental United States. The story came out of that need. How else would the situation made any sense?" He gives another strained chuckle and continues.

"After that, I told the pilot and flight attendants the truth, or most of it, that you had been attacked and beaten while on your way to meet me for dinner. They were curious about our marriage, wondering why I arrived in Hawaii a bachelor and was leaving a married man, but I told them we had been secretly dating for months, and you agreed to meet me at the conference—I proposed to you the night before the attack." He pauses to catch his breath or his courage—I'm not sure which—and then he looks down at the table.

"Okay, I said I believe you because you do seem to be telling me the whole truth. But you'll understand if I don't shower you with gratitude. Am I really supposed to believe that you, a complete stranger, out of the goodness of your heart, would rescue me from an alley, put your life on the line to take care of me, since you believed my life to still be in danger, and then concoct a story involving a fake relationship, proposal, and wedding, just for the sake of protecting me, when you don't even know who I am?" My voice gets louder and harsher, struggling to keep the fear in check.

"I wake up in a strange house, in a strange bed, with a tube down my nose, wearing an adult diaper and hardly anything else when a man walks in with a group of strangers and kisses me!" I realize I am about to have an anxiety attack by my rapid breathing and heart rate. I try to calm down, steady my breathing so I don't appear weak . . . *But I am weak.*

I start again, this time making sure I have control of my emotions. "I'm sorry. I don't want to seem ungrateful because if you are telling the truth, you did, in fact, save my life. But you have to realize I am very confused here." *Not to mention scared to death.* I look up to see the man's eyes on me.

"Well, I didn't say my story was the most believable one! I can explain about the tube in your nose and the diaper, if you would like. You see, because you were unconscious for so long, I had to keep you hydrated, medicated, and fed, which is why I chose to place a feeding tube in your nose. It was the easiest way to take care of all your needs. I assume you pulled it out when you woke up?"

I nod my head.

"No worries. I'll throw it away. The diaper should be pretty self-explanatory. Because I wanted to avoid having to give you a catheter, I simply choose the simplest option."

Holy smokes, how embarrassing. This man has been changing my diaper for the past three weeks. *Yikes.*

"Don't worry about it," he continues, "it's nothing I have not done before."

When I do not respond, Dr. Smith takes the opportunity to keep talking. "I do understand your confusion, maybe more than another person would. Not just because I am a doctor, which gives me a medical understanding of trauma, but because I felt the same confusion when I found you in that alley, left to die. You see, since I began practicing medicine, I've seen some terrible things, things you wouldn't believe even if I told you. But there was something about your injuries, your 'case', as you will, that reeked of depravity."

The two of us are silent for a few minutes, letting the enormity of the situation settle. I find my voice again to ask two more questions. "If this is just a story concocted for the need to bring me to the States, why did you introduce me to your family, and why did you kiss me?" I wait, interested to hear what he has to say. Dr. Smith's answer is delivered with a rolling of his eyes and is not what I expect.

"Well, I couldn't keep the secret of an unconscious woman in my house for very long. I knew the secret would get out, but I am honestly surprised it took so long." Once again, he looks exhausted, and that is when I get the sense this situation has taken its toll on him as well. Maybe not physically, like it has me, but definitely mentally.

"You will come to understand I have a very nosy, interloping family. I am the middle of four children, and I have a score of aunts and uncles who live on the compound." He must see the worried look on my face when he says the word "compound" because he hastily adds, "Don't worry. It's not as menacing as it sounds, just a nickname my siblings and I came up with when we were young. You will see what I mean the longer you stay here." *He is expecting me to stay.* The weight of the revelation is too much for me to process right now. *Later,* I promise myself.

He continues, "Honestly, I'm not sure why I kissed you. I tried telling myself the reason was to benefit my family. What newlywed couple doesn't kiss every chance they get, especially if one of them has been unconscious for three weeks? But I think the real reason is I was so relieved to see you standing there . . ." His voice cuts off, and he shakes his head, like he can't explain, so he stops trying. I stay silent, not really knowing how to respond.

My next question is far more important than any of the others, so I square my shoulders and look Andrew in the eye.

"What happens now?"

He returns my serious gaze and answers the only way I think he knows how. "I don't know."

Chapter 4

Andrew

Seeing a woman lying in an alleyway left to die was shocking, to say the least. Seeing her lying in my hotel bedroom is even more so. Now that she is here, I am hit with the sudden urge to leave her and hunt down every man in the city, guilty or not, and beat them senseless. One thing is for sure: her injuries are far worse than I thought upon first inspection.

Thinking back on the past forty-five minutes, I have no doubt the big man upstairs was looking down on us. When you are in a profession like mine where miracles happen every day, you cannot help but believe in a higher power. And a higher power is the only explanation I have for getting this woman and me into a crowded hotel with no questions, curious glances, or unwanted attention. The taxi driver simply turned a blind eye to an extremely questionable situation, and it was not the first time I realized money has an undeniably positive effect. The hotel lobby just happened to be deserted—even the doe-eyed receptionist had her head down, probably texting. I didn't pass anyone in the elevator or hallways. Yep, definite "upstairs" intervention.

Now that I have the woman in my room, I have to focus on accessing her injuries and determining what kind of treatment she needs.

Why did you not take her straight to the local hospital? If anyone finds her in here, you could get into serious trouble.

Of course, my conscious is right, but I have a strange feeling about this woman. Such a horrible act of violence cannot simply be happenstance. This was done intentionally and deliberately. Her attackers might be out there, combing the local emergency rooms for her right now. I have to keep her safe and do everything in my power to take care of this woman. If I take her to a hospital, I could be putting her into more danger.

With that decision made, my idle hands suddenly clench and flex, hungry for something to do. I grab the pad of paper on the bedside table and begin taking notes on the patient in front of me.

- Female, midtwenties
- Height: about 5 feet, 4 inches
- Weight: about 150 pounds
- Hair and eye color: brown, curly hair, and brown eyes
- Identifiable markings: (At this, I gently turn the body this way and that only to find a tattoo on the right shoulder blade: "Eleanor.")
- Clothing: only underwear
- Visible injuries: extensive bruising, deep, large bite mark on breast; cuts and scrapes all over body (possibly from being dragged); scratch marks on torso

After this brief and erratic exam, I begin taking a more measured evaluation of Eleanor. I have decided to call her that because of the tattoo. Plus, it makes my job more personable—Eleanor is someone, not just a body on a table or, in this case, a bed.

I take her pulse, listen to her heartbeat, check her pupils, and begin the slow and tedious task of accessing her injuries in their fullest. As I begin, I notice once again how beautiful this woman is. Her brown curly hair is definitely her most identifiable feature—thick and long. As I run my hands gingerly across her skull, the fine texture is evident even through the tangles. I stop to make a couple more notes on the paper such as cranial damage minimum; however, large bump needs constant watch.

I take in every inch of her battered body between my fingers, poking and prodding the rib cage and torso more extensively than the other areas of her body once I have determined that she has no broken bones in her legs and arms. Once again, I send up a silent "thank you" as my fingers find a couple of broken ribs, that Eleanor remains unconscious on the bed.

I have postponed the most delicate part of the exam mostly because of apprehension. I hate to confirm what my mind is pretty sure is a certainty: rape. At the end of my exam, there is no doubt that this woman is lucky to be alive.

After the first day, it was evident that I was going to need more resources to take care of Eleanor. As a doctor, it is in my ability to write prescriptions. However, that ability does not mean the capability (or legality) to write them for myself. Most doctors can get away with it once or twice, and even then, it's usually cases of emergency.

Thank goodness the medical convention was in town because when I went to the closest pharmacy with a prescription for serious pain medication and antibiotics written for a made-up name, the local pharmacist simply asked me for my identification with a bored and slightly angered look on his face. Thinking back, I was probably not the first doctor he had seen in there taking advantage of the overflow of certified doctors in the area—they couldn't possibly research each and every person who came in there flashing credentials this week.

I hated to leave the woman in my hotel room even for a minute. The thought of her being alone terrifies me. I'm pretty sure that whoever did this to her has no way of tracing her to my hotel room, but I hurry to be there in case she wakes up. I grab several packs of adult diapers, plastic tubing, and enough Ensure to feed a person for weeks and throw them into my cart.

Finding her still unconscious, I begin making the calls to get both of us on a plane and away from Honolulu. Luckily, my parent's allowed me to take their private jet, which would make the question of my bringing a severely injured stranger on board less invasive and threatening. *If I only had a good explanation for the situation.* How could I reasonably fly myself and an unconscious woman into the continental United States and not raise any questions?

After making the necessary calls and figuring out an alibi that would satisfy even the most thorough of airport investigators, I sit in my hotel room and wait. Three times a day, I check Eleanor's progress and give her medicine through the feeding tube I placed in her nose. *Things will be so much easier when we get home*, I tell myself.

Because I am forced to play a waiting game until Eleanor is well enough to travel, there is a lot of downtime. After hours of watching TV and surfing the Internet, I begin to wonder about the woman I am trying so hard to save. The question that is most often on my mind is "Why did this happen to her?" Was she a bad person, living a life of sin, doing whatever she could to make ends meet? By her clear skin and manicured nails, I get the sense that she was not a hooker or addicted to drugs. But why then was such brutality taken out on such a reasonably young girl?

I also wonder about her family: does she have any parents, siblings, husband, children? Are there people out there right now searching for her, filling out a Missing Persons report? The not knowing is what is killing me. My desire to discover Eleanor's identity is my main incentive to help her.

Chapter 5

Eleanor

After a few minutes of silence between us, I want to be alone. I think Andrew realizes this and gets out of his chair to help me stand. I have been sitting so tense for so long that my body is aching all over—like when you get a paper cut and you can feel your heartbeat in it. My body is a huge heartbeat, throbbing with every step, every twitch, and every inch I move forward.

He steers me toward the room I awoke in and stops at the door, releasing my elbow which he had been holding for support. There is no spark of electricity like you read about in books and seen play out in movies between his touch and mine. But I feel a strength coursing through him, and I borrow some of it, hoping it will give me confidence to take on my unknown future. He looks down at me for the first time with pity in his eyes, and I have a sudden urge to smack the look off his face.

I don't need your pity.

He speaks softly. "I understand that you need to rest and that you have a lot to think through. If you need me, I'll be out here, doing some stuff around the house. Take all the time you want but know that you can rest assured—you will be safe."

I realize that this is his second time reassuring my safety. He turns to walk away but remembers something and turns back. "We will also have to check your injuries later, so try to get some rest." He leaves me at the door.

As I stand in the doorway, I am determined to figure out what is going on here. Sure, I told Andrew that it seems like he is telling the truth, and I believe that. However, I still have to figure out what happens now. Where do I go from here? How long can I stay? What happened to me? And most importantly, who am I?

Andrew's words had the effect of a lifeline and an anchor all at once. I make my way to the bed while contemplating my analogy. The two basically have the same purpose, a lifeline and an anchor. They are both used for security, but they feel completely different. And anchor is heavy, always pulling down, like Andrew's story: I was beaten, I was left to die. Whereas a lifeline is tight and a constant reminder of safety, like the facts of my rescue: I was saved, I am alive.

For the first time today, I feel settled, at ease. I am still scared to death, but I know that this man—my savior, *my husband*, can be trusted. There is another question that lingers in my brain, and its subject surprises even me: What will happen to Andrew when I leave? Because staying here is not an option, and I am realizing that it never was.

As determined as I am to stay awake and make plans, my body and my mind are too worn down from the revelations of the day. I must have fallen asleep because the next thing I know, the small clock says seven five, and it is getting dark outside. I look around the room and notice a white robe made out of the same material as my nightgown hanging on the end of the bed. Andrew must have dropped it off earlier. I throw it over my shoulders, happy to have a small amount of covering, and head out of the bedroom, struggling with each aching step I take.

Andrew is standing in the kitchen over the stove cooking something. My breath catches in my throat when I see him. He is wearing only pajama pants. His chest is bare and very tight with muscles, but that is not what takes my breath. He has scars down his back—deep, thick scars. When he turns in my direction to pick up a spatula, I see that his front is just as covered as his back. My mind is grappling, trying to imagine what type of injury would cause such damage. I draw a sharp intake of breath, giving myself away, and he turns toward me with a look of anger in his face. The look quickly turns into a smile, so quickly that I can't even be sure the anger was there, and he speaks before I have time to consider it.

"Hello. I thought you might sleep longer than you did. I wasn't expecting to see you up so soon. Excuse me while I get a shirt." He walks down the hall and comes back in a few seconds, completely covered, hiding his scars.

"I'm not much of a cook," he smoothly continues, "but I have made a couple of grilled cheese sandwiches. Would you like one?"

I wrinkle up my nose. The thought of eating anything right now makes me feel nauseous.

He sees my face and says with a smile. "What, do you doubt my cooking?"

I give a small smile and shake my head.

"You know, I could use my medical expertise to give you a lecture about trying to heal without the proper nutrition, but I'm not going to do that" He wiggles his eyebrows. "I will, however, resort to begging, hands-and-knees-type begging. But you wouldn't make me do that, would you?"

I laugh a little louder and take a plate from him. I have to admit that the sandwich is starting to look appealing. The rumbling of my stomach seconds my thoughts. I can try to keep it down, for his sake. He looks relieved that I agreed to eat, and I guess that lecture was soon to follow if I had refused.

"What would you like to drink?" he asks. "I have all sorts of stuff."

I know what I really want, but I am embarrassed to ask. He senses my hesitation and says, "Just tell me what you would like, and I'll try to make it happen."

I swallow my pride and, in a quiet voice, ask, "Do you have any chocolate milk?"

He raises his eyebrows and then gives a great big laugh, filling the kitchen with its sound. At first, I don't know if I should be offended that he finds my request so funny; but as he keeps laughing, I find that it doesn't matter. It's nice to hear laughter, especially his. It's loud and seems to fill the entire house. It also has a strange effect on me—I can feel a small smile spreading across my face. He sees me joining him and then walks to me and wraps me in his arms. His embrace is so strong that I am immediately reminded of his brother's hug earlier in the day. It's hard to not lean into him, and I'm not sure that I don't for a split second. It would be really easy to simply let all my worries and fears melt away. But reality slaps me in the face, and I carefully and quickly pull myself away from him.

"I'm sorry," he apologizes as he backs away. "It's been a very long three weeks. A couple of times I thought you weren't going to make it. On the days that you were just lying there, I tried to imagine the person I was working so hard to save. Were you a nice person? A good person? I had no idea. I just had the constant drive to keep you alive so I could find out all I could about you. I guess it's just a relief to learn something, even if it is the fact that you hate to work out and you like chocolate milk."

He tries to laugh again, but it dies in his throat, and I am again confronted with the fact that he has been through just as much as I have. He turns to walk away, and I speak, a little too loud in the small room.

"My mom always made me grilled cheese sandwiches and chocolate milk," I say, trying to get rid of the tension between us. As soon as I finish talking, though, we both pause and stare at each other, realizing that I have just remembered something about my past.

"That's great!" Andrew says excitedly. "What else can you remember about your mother?"

I feel his excitement in me—like it's contagious. And I focus on the idea of grilled cheese sandwiches, chocolate milk, and my mother. I sit there for a good five minutes, and he sits from me. Even though my eyes are closed, I know he is staring at me, almost willing me to remember something. But after a while, I realize it's a lost cause. I know I look disappointed when I open my eyes and inform him that all I can see is a blank page—no images of her, no memories of her voice, nothing.

He reaches his hand toward mine and squeezes it quickly. "Don't worry," he says as he walks back to the stove, "your memory will come back." I notice that he doesn't say when.

As it turns out, Andrew has some chocolate syrup, and I find myself drinking two glasses and eating two sandwiches. He seems relieved that I have an appetite, so I feel relieved too. *Maybe this means I am getting better.*

We sit on the couch after supper, him on one end and me on the other with my third glass of chocolate milk, and we decide watch the news. Andrew thinks it might kick-start some of my memories. I'm not as certain it will help, but I sit back against the cushions while he chooses a station. The news is full of doom and gloom. The tenor of the stories—high gas prices, low job availabilities, war, poverty, and politics—are the only things that seem familiar to me.

At the end of the program, the anchorman comes on the screen announcing a "happy spot" in the news tonight. The company, MicroCorp, has opened their new factory in Honolulu. As the report continues, describing the amount of jobs it has provided, the amount of clean energy used, etc., something inside my head sparks, like a match, burning bright at first and then tapering out. It is only when I see the MicroCorp logo and their CEO, Dan Childs's picture on the screen that the match ignites again. My brain is a furnace, and all I hear is shattering glass.

I wake up to find Andrew sitting over me with worried eyes and his hand on my wrist, taking my pulse. I blink a few times and try to sit up, which he helps me do. I feel sluggish and more than a little foolish as I ask what happened. He says that he heard the glass shatter, and then I slumped against the couch. He was unable to wake me, so he has been monitoring me for the last thirty minutes.

As I try to explain to him what the MicroCorp news report did to my mind, I find that it's hard to describe. I finally get him to understand that

I remember something about MicroCorp, and whatever that something is, it's not good.

At that moment, we hear a knock on the door. My eyes widen, and I feel the rush of fear course through my veins. It's not an unpleasant feeling—more familiar than I care to admit to myself at this moment. However, a feeling that is unfamiliar to me is also making its way from my belly to my heart—nerves. I'm nervous. Nervous about who or what is on the other side of that front door.

After my unexpected fainting incident at the MicroCorp news report, I feel what newfound confidence I had built up flagging. I look at Andrew, trying to convey that I am scared, and I know when he returns my gaze that he understands. He walks slowly toward the door with a grace that marks his every move. I wonder if it's a product of his career or if it's something else. I don't have too much time to ponder because before I know it, Andrew's hand is on the doorknob. He stops, turns, and gives me a wink of reassurance and then opens the door.

Neither Andrew nor I was expecting our guests, and I certainly don't feel dressed appropriately enough for them. Andrew's mother and father walk through the door, and I hastily cover myself with the blanket Andrew had laid across my unconscious body. There is no doubt that the two people now staring at me are my "in-laws." Andrew is a perfect mix of them—blond hair like both of them, easy smile like his father, and piercing green eyes. His mother's contribution, beside hair color, takes more than just a quick glance to detect. Her face is strong, not just in features, but in intensity, just like Andrew's. She carries herself like a woman in charge, which I get the funny feeling that she is.

There is also something else, another characteristic that her son shares. As Andrew hugs them both and asks about their recent trip, I can see his mother trying to convey something to me, almost like she is willing me to know her thoughts—a trait I distinctly remember Andrew having earlier today at our first meeting. The only difference is, Andrew was trying to give me the sense of safety. His mother, however, is only giving me a sense of dread.

Andrew motions them to enter and then hurriedly comes to stand behind me, placing his hand protectively on my shoulder. I look up, hoping to see his eyes and what they may be conveying this time, only I see the underside of his chin and grin at the stubble I find there.

"Mom, Dad. I would like you to meet my wife, your daughter-in-law, Eleanor Smith."

I do my best to look convincingly happy as I smile at them. It's funny to see Andrew's parents' posture reflected in our own: his mother sitting in the easy chair, his father behind her with his hand on her shoulder. I clear my throat, feeling the need to say something, but Andrew's father speaks before I have a chance.

"Well, it's an honor to meet you, Eleanor. I'm Sean, and this is my wife Laura. But of course, you have figured that out by now." He laughs at himself, and I smile politely back. I would hate to tell him that actually, I had no idea what their names were until just this moment, so I reply the best way I know how.

"It's nice to finally meet you. Andrew has told me so much about you." I feel a slight pressure on my shoulder, and I'm unsure if it was an encouraging squeeze or a discouraging one. I look up again, hoping for some kind of reassurance when Andrew's father speaks again.

"Well, I wish we could say the same about you, dear." I hear Andrew shifting his weight behind me, and I can tell he feels the tension in the room as much as I can. I try to save him the trouble of explaining our situation and speak again.

"I have to admit that this is not ideal, meeting like this. And both Andrew and I want to apologize. But I hope that we can put the unfortunate circumstances of it behind us. I would love for you to have the chance to get to know me." I reach up and cover Andrew's hand with my own and pray that he knows my little speech was just as much for him as it was for his parents. I can tell immediately that I have made an impression, good or bad, I'm not sure. Andrew comes to stand in front of me as he addresses his mom and dad again.

"Why don't we move into the kitchen? I could make you guys a pot of coffee. I'm sure you could use it." He laughs, a tight sound, not like before.

Sean and Laura make their way into the kitchen, and Andrew turns to help me stand. He grabs my hands and gently pulls me forward, reminding me of how you see very pregnant women standing up. I give a small "thanks", and I am taken aback by his reply. Still holding my hands in his, he brings them up to his lips and places a soft kiss on them both. A cold chill runs through my body as I marvel at the tenderness with which he treats me. I'm still reeling from his touch when he pulls my silk robe closed around my waist and ties the sash tight.

"I'm sorry you have to meet my parents dressed like this," he says with eyebrows raised. His laugh is soft but genuine, and I playfully swat his shoulder. He grabs his arm like I have really done some damage and then puts a hand under my elbow and steers me into the kitchen.

Sean and Laura sit across the table from us with fake smiles painted on their faces. Andrew is beside me holding my hand. Every few seconds, he gives it a small squeeze. *Just go with the flow. Follow his lead. You're doing good so far.* I smile nervously at Andrew's parents as they sip their coffee.

Andrew finally breaks the silence, and his voice seems a little strained. "Mom, Dad, when did you get back?"

His mother tears her eyes from me and answers her son. "Just now, darling. We were going to wait until tomorrow to visit, but as soon as we walked in the door, Joshua was pushing us out again, telling us that we had to see your surprise." She stops and looks to me again. "And what a surprise it is."

I honestly can't tell if she is truly surprised or if her expression is one of anger instead. I wonder if Andrew has ever done anything like this before—bring home a wife, or even a girlfriend, for that matter, without his parents' knowing about her. *Especially one that is dressed so minimally.*

His father just sits there with a perplexed look on his face, and every once in a while, he breaks into a huge grin, just like his son Joshua did earlier. That's when I decide that Andrew has never done anything like this before and feel a sense of pride, however uncalled for, that I was his first one. A light squeeze of my hand brings me back to reality, and I turn to smile at my husband.

"Mom, I know it is a surprise, and like Eleanor said, this is not ideal. Definitely not the way I wanted you to meet my wife but . . ." Andrew's face looks so sad and broken that I rub my thumb along his, trying to comfort him the only way I know how. And hating that I am the cause of his suffering. He gives me a grateful look and then continues.

"I have been seeing Eleanor secretly for several months now. We met at the hospital when I set her broken ankle. I haven't said anything because, well, you know me, always cautious to the extreme." When he says this, Andrew's mother winces slightly, but he continues.

"I asked her to accompany me to Hawaii, but I have to admit that the marriage proposal and ceremony was a bit hasty." He turns to smile at me now. His mother and father seem to buy his story, albeit hesitantly, so his mother, Laura, begins her questioning again, this time focusing on my recent tragedy. I feel myself relax a little because I know most of this story. It's only when Andrew starts to use medical terms I don't recognize, and I see the looks of shock on his parents' faces that I start to realize the seriousness of my injuries.

"Well, my dear," Mrs. Smith addresses me after a few more uncomfortable moments of silence, "Andrew is doing all the talking, and we would love to know something about you, especially since it seems we are family now."

"There's not much to tell, I'm afraid." *All I can do now is lie*—because I don't know anything about me. I hate not having some shred of information about my past and my present. It's killing me to think his family doesn't get to know the real me.

Andrew can tell I am getting upset, and I feel another squeeze of reassurance in my hand. I smile up at him and launch into the shortest, most generic version of a life story I can muster: I am an only child; both of my parents are dead; I have lived all over but was raised in the South; I work in sales. I can tell they are dissatisfied with my generic answers, so I add a hasty, "I hate working out, and I like grilled cheese sandwiches and chocolate milk." The truth of how little I know about myself hits me, and I have to look at the table to keep my tears from showing.

"Well, it's a good thing, since that's all Andrew knows how to cook," Andrew's dad says, slapping his hand on the table and throwing his head back in a hearty laugh.

My smile becomes brighter, and I answer back, "Yes, it is a good thing."

After our good-byes and promise of attending family lunch tomorrow, which I find out is Sunday, Andrew and I stand across one another in the kitchen. Both of us are unsure of what to say. My question will cause him pain, but I have to ask it.

"What are you going to tell them?" He knows as soon as I say the words what I mean. What is he going to tell them when I've gone? He knows I am implying I won't be here forever. He just shrugs his shoulders and walks out of the room.

Phone Conversation No. 1

Saturday, 7:45 p.m.

"Yes, sir, she's awake. You were right. She is being introduced as Dr. Smith's wife, Eleanor. According to him, they have been secretly dating for several months, and she met him in Honolulu . . ."

"No, that is all the backstory that I know."

"Yes, her injuries are extensive. Her entire body is covered in deep bruises, and I'm sure there are internal injuries as well."

"Yes, sir. I will contact you if there are any more developments or if I learn anything else."

Chapter 6

Eleanor

I think that might be the last time I will see him tonight, but ten minutes after going into a back bedroom, Andrew emerges with a black bag and a large free-standing mirror. He looks at me with reservation in his eyes and informs me that it is time for my exam. I ask how often he has done this the past few weeks, and he explains it was multiple times a day in the beginning because of the seriousness of my injuries, but since Thursday, he has done it only once a day.

He asks me to remove my housecoat and lay on my bed. I should probably be wary of the situation his requests put me in, but I know he has seen and done all this before, and he is probably just as nervous as I am. There's a big difference in an unconscious body and a walking, talking woman whom you have kissed. He takes a few things out of his bag—stethoscope, bandages, and a tube of Neosporin—and gives me a tight smile. He assures me he will be as gentle as possible.

He starts with my arms, picking each up and looking over them in their entirety. He looks closely at a couple of bruises but quickly moves on to my elbows and shoulders. His touch is gentle and again; I feel strength when he gingerly probes the bones in my arms. He moves to my legs, which are much the same as my arms, but they have a few cuts and scrapes.

My muscles are still extremely sore. When he asks me to remove my gown, I get a little nervous. He gives me a small smile and promises me that he will be "totally professional", wiggling his eyebrows as he says it—giving the indication that he won't be professional at all. I smile at his attempt at a joke, knowing that he is trying to make me feel more comfortable.

Just do it, you big chicken.

As I lift off my gown, I see his expression full of pity again. I'm not sure why he looks at me like this until I catch my reflection in the free-standing mirror. My naked body is strangely not the first thing I notice. My bushy brown hair is definitely the most striking thing about me—it's long, dark, and more wavy than curly. I notice my wide brown eyes and the olive tone of my skin second.

Then I make myself look at the rest of my body. My entire chest and torso are covered in deep purple bruises. They do not show any signs of healing like my legs and arms have. I have scratch marks that cover my chest, and I even see some bite marks. On one breast, I have a bandage that shows some dried blood. Suddenly, it makes no difference that I am standing, naked in front of a strange man that I just met this morning. Suddenly, it is clear why I see pity in Andrew's eyes, and all that I want to do is run from it.

I have been raped.

Before he can guess what I'm doing, I run out the door. I don't even look for shoes or my robe. I just run: out of the room, out of the house, and down the gravel drive until I can't run anymore. I hear Andrew screaming my name, but I keep running. I have a small head start because I surprised him, but he reaches me quickly and throws his arms around me. We almost fall to the ground, but he holds me tight. I sob into his chest until I can't see anymore, and my breathing is back to normal. He picks me up, cradling me in his arms, and walks back to the house. I go willingly, unable to think on my own and too tired to protest.

Andrew takes me into the bathroom, turns on the water in the tub, and starts cleaning the gravel out of my feet. When he leads me back to the bedroom, he makes me face the mirror again. My face is red and splotchy, and my eyes are swollen, but I can still see the damage done to my body. I look at his reflection, and his face is a mask of courage. The feeling seeps into me as I return my gaze to my ravished body.

"I know how hard this is, Eleanor, but if you don't confront it now, you will be plagued with fear for the rest of your life. Look at yourself and take in every inch of hurt and damage. Make your eyes see the things you don't want to see. Take control of your situation, and it will never control you."

I don't know if it's possible for me to do what he is saying because every time I look at another spot on my body, I want to run again. But then I remember his scarred chest and back, and I know that at some point, Andrew has had to do the same thing—confront his fear and take control of it. I make myself stand there for five minutes looking at my bruises and cuts. When I turn around to check out my back, a small cry escapes my throat because I am looking at more of the same. The scars and bruises are there, but I also notice a small tattoo on my right shoulder blade. "Eleanor" is written in a neat, thin script. Andrew looks at me and answers my unspoken question. "Yes, that is where I got your name. I'm sure it is meant to represent someone else, but it seemed to fit you."

I sit on the bed again while he finishes checking my wounds. He tells me that my internal injuries were what scared him so much. He was sure that something was ruptured, but without the proper equipment, he had no way of knowing exactly what. Once again, I ask him why he did not take me to a hospital here in the States.

"I didn't have any of your information—age, birthday, address, social security number, or even allergies. I just couldn't risk it. Plus, I was supposed to know all that stuff given our marital status. It would have looked very suspicious if I had no knowledge of that basic information."

When he finishes his exam, he sits next to me on the bed and very slowly explains that since I had been raped, he had been checking my healing progress in regard to that abuse. He informed me that since I was awake now, he would take me to a female doctor to do a follow-up. I try to express my thanks for the care he has given, but my words seem feeble. He smiles and squeezes my hand, gathers his equipment, and leaves me alone in my thoughts.

Sometime in the night, I must have screamed because when I wake up, Andrew is sitting in the floor next to my bedroom door, sleeping with his head against the wall. I shake him awake and insist that he get in my bed. He is so tired that he does not refuse, just shuffles toward the bed and collapses. I creep out the door and close it quietly behind me.

The day is bright and sunny again, and I thank God because I don't know if I could get through a rainy day knowing what I do now. The lyrics to a song come to my mind: The sun will come out tomorrow.

I find my way to the bathroom where Andrew has set out clean clothes for me: a pair of gym shorts, a few sizes too big, and a plain cotton shirt, also too big. I'm not sure of the origin of the next two items of clothing, but I am grateful all the same for the clean panties and bra that sit underneath the shirt. I shower in steaming hot water, trying to wash away some of the shame I feel. Andrew must have been giving me sponge baths for the last few weeks because the only thing that is really dirty is my hair. I spend ten minutes just concentrating on scrubbing out every inch of grease.

When I get out of the shower, I feel better, like a new woman. I'm hungry, so I set out to find something, but the second I pick a cereal and sit down at the table, someone is knocking on the front door. I hesitate answering but remember that this is supposed to be my house now. I plaster on a smile and open the door to find the same young woman who was here yesterday standing with her arms burdened with clothes.

"Please come in," I say as I step aside. I notice how wary my voice sounds—*I'm supposed to be a happy newlywed*—and try to make my smile even brighter and my voice a little more chipper.

The woman stares toward my bedroom, where Andrew is now sleeping, and I realize she is trying to figure out if she has interrupted something. I can feel my cheeks heating up, and as she looks my way again, I clear my throat and hopefully the air between us.

"My name is Nicole," she starts, "and I am Andrew's sister-in-law. I am married to Joshua, the man who hugged you yesterday." At this, she smiles, really smiles, and her whole face transforms, making her into a rather beautiful woman. I'm guessing that she is older than me by maybe ten years. Her hair is shoulder-length, straight, and very black. She's wearing a summer dress made of blue eyelet and flat white sandals. I notice that she is checking me out as well, and I find myself smiling back.

Before I can say anything, she adds, "Sorry about that, my husband hugging you. He hugs everyone, and he has no sense of boundaries. It was, oddly, one of the things that attracted me to him. That and the fact that he is undeniably the goodest person I know. That's not a word, is it, goodest? But either way, it's the truth. Lucky for you, Andrew is the second goodest person I know. But of course, I am a little biased." She stops talking long enough for me to collect my thoughts and say something back.

"It is nice to meet you, Nicole. My name is Eleanor, and I am looking forward to getting to know you, Joshua, and your whole family better." She smiles, and at that moment Andrew comes out of the bedroom. Just like yesterday, he is only wearing pajama pants; but this time, he does not cover his chest. He smiles at Nicole first and then captures me with his gaze. And just like yesterday, he walks straight to me. Unlike yesterday, though, I am prepared. I put my hands on his chest and return his gaze.

Nicole clears her throat a little too loudly, and I am pulled back into the moment where my fake sister-in-law is staring at her shoes, and my fake husband is looking at me like I have just twisted his guts out, which is not the look I was hoping for *or expecting*. I notice he is asking Nicole what she is doing here.

"I knew that you guys left Hawaii in a hurry and a bit of a wrecked state." At this, she looks at me sadly, almost like she is torn and continues. "So I brought Eleanor some clothes. I figured that might have been low on your priority list, Andy. I borrowed them from Annie, so it's really her you should thank. I guess I'll see you guys at lunch." At this, she heads toward the door, and Andrew heads to the bathroom. I stand there with my arms full of clothes, realizing I forgot to say thank you.

I sit at the kitchen table and eat my cereal without tasting it and wonder what kind of family I have stumbled into. Andrew's selfless act of saving my life is only the tip of the iceberg when it comes to the goodness of this family, *my family*. Joshua and Sean's immediate acceptance of me, Annie's willingness to share her clothes, and Nicole's willingness to deliver them paints a picture of a family that is giving. I may not remember who I am, but no matter what I was like before, I have a feeling in the pit of my stomach that I don't deserve their kindness.

Andrew comes out of the shower with wet hair and a stern expression. Even just knowing him for a day, I think I am beginning to understand some of his faces—like this one. I know he is going to want to have a talk about our little display of affection. I square my shoulders and make my expression match his; if he wants to have a serious discussion, that is fine with me. He keeps walking toward me with determination, and at the last minute, I falter. All I can do is stare at the floor and hope that whatever he wants to talk about will not hurt as much as I think it will.

I can see his feet standing in front of me, like he is waiting for me to look at him. I brace myself for what I think is going to be an argument. I look up, a retort on my lips, and then suddenly I look into his eyes, and that's when I realize that I don't understand his faces like I thought I did. This face is full of desire, regret, sadness, and a little anger. It scares me. But then his eyes soften, and I can see the man who saved me.

The man I want to save me over and over again.

He is struggling with something that I cannot fathom. I lean close, put my hands on either side of his face, and whisper the words that will never be enough, "Thank you for saving my life."

He places his hands on top of mine and replies, "Thank you for saving mine."

Chapter 7

Andrew

It seems to be more than coincidence that the very night I was contemplating my departure from the medical profession, I find a woman dying in an alley from the most extensive wounds I have ever seen on a civilian. For the past year, I have been craving some sort of sign to let me know if this is what I am meant to do for the rest of my life. I feel like if I can save this woman and find out her story, I can end my medical career with a content heart. I can have no regrets, no cause to ever look back. If I can save her, perhaps I can save myself.

Today is a big day, an important day. For not only me but for Eleanor as well. I can hear the shower turn on in the bathroom and feel relieved that I will have a few minutes to myself. *Wow, I forgot how comfortable this bed is!* The past two weeks spent sleeping on the pull-out bed in the guest room and spending last night on the floor has wreaked havoc on my back. At the ripe old age of thirty-five, I've had my fair share of bad luck in the injury department. Let's just say that Eleanor's time in front of the mirror last night was not a new experience to me. I confront my fears every day.

Hearing her sharp intake of breath behind me yesterday was like a cold slap in the face. It's been a long time since I've been around anyone new, and I had forgotten the general reaction to my scars. I couldn't keep a flash of anger from showing as I turned to see the shock in Eleanor's eyes. It kills me to admit that I never wanted her to see them, which is completely unfair, knowing that there is not an inch of her body that I have not seen. But I wanted to remain undamaged to Eleanor, crazy as it sounds. Vanity has never really been a sin of mine, but I have found, increasingly since yesterday morning when I first saw her standing in my kitchen all vulnerable and exposed, that Eleanor's presence in my life has awakened all sorts of desires and sins within me—vanity being the least of them.

A soft humming drifting from the shower has the unfortunate effect of calling up one of those newly awakened sins as I picture Eleanor's beautifully bruised body in the shower. I shake my head, trying to clear it, and wonder when Eleanor went from being my patient to an alarmingly gorgeous, vulnerable woman . . . in my house . . . in my shower . . .

I jump out of bed and fall to the floor. I reach fifty push-ups before I feel my boiling blood cool down. I go ahead and do fifty more just to be on the safe side. As I stand back up, I walk over to the mirror and begin my daily routine. I start by stripping down to my underwear. Beginning with my hands, I say something positive about each body part. Hands— strong, capable. Arms—muscular, smooth. Chest—scarred but distinctive. Stomach—ravaged but meaningful.

Working my way down, I stop at my feet, labeling them "fast." Feeling the tenderness caused by the small cuts on them, I think back to last night and Eleanor's flight from the house. I was so concerned that she would injure herself even further. By the time I reached her, I was so relieved to have her in my arms I didn't give a second thought to my father's face looking out of his bedroom window.

• •

However, I think about it now as I study my reflection in the mirror. The similarities between my father and me are shocking; not just the vivid color of our eyes, but also our hair color is the same dirty blond. We even make the same faces. But I'm pretty sure that in the thirty-five years of my life, I have never seen that specific look on my father's face.

One would think that a certain amount of shock would be the appropriate response to seeing your son chasing his naked wife down the road. Instead of shock, though, my father looked like a satisfied cat that just got finished drinking a bowl of warm milk. I don't think I will ever understand my parents, let alone their facial expressions, and I'm guessing that is the way they feel about me—alien parents and alien children.

I hear a knock on the front door and throw on my pajama pants, making a mental note to apologize to my dad for the indecent scene last night, having the feeling that an apology will not be necessary.

Seeing Eleanor come out of the bedroom dressed in one of Annie's outfits—flowing patterned pants with a matching sleeveless top—stops me in my tracks almost as quickly as seeing her in my gym shorts and T-shirt earlier this morning.

"Wow, you look amazing," I say as she looks down with blushed cheeks, brushing a nonexistent speck of lint off her shirt.

"Everything is a little tight. I'm guessing your sister is just a tad bit smaller than me."

I dismiss her uncertainties with a wave of my hand. "Nonsense."

Eleanor looks up relieved, and I make my way toward her. I can tell she is nervous, and I try to explain again that we do not have to go today. She shakes her head, and I drop the issue, grateful she is still planning to go. After meeting my parents last night and accepting the invitation to lunch, it would be a lot harder to explain our absence. I don't have the heart to tell her she has no idea what she is in for.

....

"Well, I know one thing," I start, catching her fidgeting hand in mine. "Nobody will be able to take their eyes off you."

Eleanor's cheeks pink again, and I raise my free hand to smooth the natural blush away with my fingertips. She smiles a tight smile and backs away. I mentally curse myself for the brazen act.

"I'm sorry . . . I don't know why I keep doing that." Instantly, my mind is transported back to this morning in front of Nicole. I am not sure what drew me toward Eleanor like some kind of magnet. But something was different than last night—I felt like I had to be near her; if I wasn't, I would burst. Remembering her slightly shaking hands on my chest sends a wave of heat through my limbs.

"I'm not really sure why I keep touching you," I say with a shaky voice. Eleanor just laughs.

"I assumed you were just practicing for our lunch performance today." She winks at me, and I know she doesn't really believe that. She is simply letting me off the hook. *For now, anyway.* She continues, "I know today is important for both of us, and I promise to do my best not to let you down. It's the least I can do . . . After all you have done for me."

I look into her big brown eyes, wanting to say so much but saying nothing at all. I just nod my head, deciding at the last minute that everything would be inadequate.

....

Chapter 8

Eleanor

It's noon in Carmel, and the sun is bright. As Andrew and I make our way across the driveway between the main house and our guest house, I am surprised how comfortable I feel with him. Maybe the reason is because I know he has cared for me, and we have a bond only a few people ever have: struggling for a life—*my life*. However, I remind myself to not get too comfortable. No matter how easy I feel around him, we are still strangers.

Our morning has been interesting, to say the least. Beginning with our embrace in front of Nicole to our moment in the kitchen. (I haven't had the guts to ask him what he meant when he thanked me for saving his life, but I am determined to get the answer.) Seeing him standing in the living room, dressed in khaki pants and a collared shirt, I thought my bones were going to melt. He looked as if he had just stepped out of a magazine. I don't know much about my past, but I do know one thing—I have never seen a more handsome man in my life. I felt silly in my borrowed too-tight clothes. But Andrew didn't seem to mind; he had eyes only for me. I hated hearing him apologize for touching me so much. In all honesty, however, I hated myself more for wanting him to.

We cross the separation between the houses in twenty paces. I find myself counting them, and with each step, it seems to help me calm down: One, two, three, *breathe*. Four, five, six, *be strong*. Twelve, thirteen, fourteen, *I can do this*. Eighteen nineteen, twenty, *stay focused*.

When we talked about not going to the lunch this morning after I commented on how tired Andrew looked, I appreciated the way he tried to seem like it didn't matter to him either way. But I could tell, after his declaration of, "I'm leaving the decision up to you, Eleanor. You are the one who just woke up from a three-week coma yesterday." He was worried about the impression it would send if we didn't show up. And honestly, I could not imagine spending another second in the house. I am not only itching to stretch my legs, but also looking out at the massive main house piques my interest.

As we walk into the front entrance, my breath catches as I take in my surroundings. The entrance hall is massive, two stories like I thought, and it is decorated like a palace—ornate mirrors, carvings, and staircases greet me all round the room. White marble floors polished to alarming shine make me check the bottom of my borrowed shoes for mud.

....

Andrew smiles when he sees the look of awe on my face and asks, "You don't think it's too much, do you?"

I let out a small chuckle and ask him, "What do your parents do for a living?"

His easy smiles fade a little, and his answer is very short. "They are in overseas shipping." He doesn't elaborate, which gives me the feeling it is a touchy subject, so I move onto another topic.

"But what about the vineyards?" I ask curiously.

"That's just a sideline business, my grandfather's idea actually. I guess he figured he had all this land, he might as well do something with it."

"Why do you guys call this the compound? Other than your house, I mean *our* house," I correct, as he gives me a worried look. "And the main house, I haven't seen any other buildings." He casually leans against the stairwell with a posture that portrays years of experience, which I'm guessing he has had.

"You can't know it from what you have seen, but there are over two hundred acres connected to this property. The whole area was owned by my great-great-grandparents, and over the years, it has dwindled some. My parents, along with my three aunts and one uncle and their families, Joshua and Nicole, and my other sister Lily, all live somewhere on the property. My youngest sister, Annie, whose clothes you are wearing, still lives with my mom and dad. One big happy family." By the way he says it, open and honest, I have a feeling he means it.

We make our way through the house, going past the foyer and into a massive living room. The ceiling is over twenty feet high, and a great fireplace reaches to the top. I can see the same style mirrored in Andrew's house—mostly white furniture but less cottagey here, more classical. There are couches and chairs of all shapes and sizes placed perfectly around the room—some arranged for intimate talks and others aimed at connecting the entire room. We make our way to the back porch, which is covered with a pergola. Large outdoor fans are hanging every few feet to keep the warm spring air stirring.

When we step outside, I freeze. In front of me are about seventy-five people. I was expecting a crowd, but I never expected *so many*. And all seventy-five mouths have stopped talking, and one hundred and fifty eyes have turned to look at me. Andrew squeezes my hand, and I suddenly feel a sense of panic. Something inside of me, like an internal antennae, stands to attention. My eyes scan the crowd, for what, I'm not sure—a threat, danger? The faces in front of me show an array of expressions, most of them friendly. I see several sets of shockingly white and straight teeth.

I quickly cover my own crooked smile with my lips and feel a blush creep into my cheeks. Some faces show a hint of reservation, like Andrew's mother—her smile is definitely fake. I'm guessing she was a witness to my perilous flight down the driveway last night! But my antennae are mostly drawn to the frowns on the faces of two women standing to my right. One of the frowns belongs to a girl I do not recognize. However, her green eyes identify her as Andrew's sister. She moves her gaze back and forth between my face, Andrew's face, and our interlocked hands, not trying to hide her disdain.

The other frown is on the face of Nicole, Andrew's sister-in-law. Her attention is focused, not on me but on the girl standing beside her. Before I can begin to decipher the dynamic between them, my father-in-law approaches us and folds, first Andrew and then me into hug. He is a big man, taller than Andrew with balding blond hair, but his easy smile makes him handsome. The crowd remains silent as he turns toward them and clears his throat.

"I would like to be the one to introduce my new daughter-in-law, Eleanor Smith. I hope you will welcome her with open arms like my son has. She is part of our family now."

I am appreciative for his announcement because he has no idea how lost I truly am. Andrew's family, *my family*, starts clapping and cheering, welcoming me. I can't keep a smile from spreading on my face. Andrew looks to me with a smile on his face and sadness in his eyes.

There are so many names and faces that after the first fifteen people, I stop trying to keep track. *I'll have plenty of time to learn them all*, but I have to stop myself from making plans for a future, which involves any situation in where I get to know Andrew's family better. Andrew moves easily through the crowd, never letting go of my hand and accepting hugs and pats on the back.

As we meet each person, he whispers something about them in my ear so I can seem at ease with these people that I am supposed to know. We reach a small group of people, and Andrew introduces them as his Uncle Joe, Aunt Tilly, Cousins Dave and Dan (twins), and their wives and children. As I shake hands with each person in turn and smile at the children standing close enough to see me, Andrew's Aunt Tilly gives me a warm smile.

"Oh, honey, we are so glad to meet you. And we just couldn't be happier for Andrew. You know, after all he has gone through over the years, with the accident and everything."

I just nod my head while trying to look like I have a clue what this sweet woman is talking about. I throw a quick glance to Andrew who is casually talking to his cousins. There's an awful lot of elbowing and harrumphing. His cheeks even look a little red. Dying to know what they are talking about, I have to tear my attention back to Aunt Tilly as she continues.

"I just know you will be happy here. The family is very welcoming. I remember the first time I was introduced to everyone. Whew, talk about overwhelming!" She smiles sweetly again, and I allow myself to relax a little as I answer her.

"You're right, it is overwhelming. However, I would use a different word, 'crippling', or 'debilitating' maybe." Aunt Tilly laughs, a light-tinkling sound, and I make myself really look at her now. She is petite, a few inches shorter than my five feet and four inches. Her blond hair is perfectly styled, and her makeup looks like it was done by a professional. Despite the warm weather, she is dressed in navy blue pants with a matching patterned top covered by a blue jean jacket. I don't think another woman could have looked more put together if they had walked off the cover of a magazine.

"Well, let me tell you a little secret, my dear," Aunt Tilly says, throwing a look over her shoulder at the men. "The best thing you can do is become friends with your new mother-in-law. I know the stigma of 'monster-in-law', but Laura is truly the backbone of this family. She was already established in the family and business when I met Joe. Without her, I would have been lost."

I feel a little bit of apprehension when I look across the yard and spot Andrew's mother making her way from table to table, greeting each of her guests with a pleasant smile. I look back to Aunt Tilly and raise my eyebrows, drawing another laugh from the woman. She lowers her voice, leans in close, and gently picks up my hand. "My advice to you is this—to get in good with Laura, be good to her son." The softness in her voice makes me turn my attention back to Andrew, and I realize that that is exactly what I plan to do—but not for Laura's sake.

Andrew steers me to each table, everyone eager to meet the newcomer in the family. His Uncle Arthur, I come to realize, is the "Scrooge" the family.

"Completely unacceptable, if you ask me . . . bringing home a wife no one has met, let alone approved of." His words feel like a slap in the face and bring me up short. Andrew squeezes my hand, his posture only tensing slightly.

"Uncle Arthur, that is no way to treat your new niece. I approved her, and that's all that matters." His laugh is casual as he gives me a quick wink. By Andrew's reaction, I get the feeling his uncle's harsh tone and words toward me are common. I decide to play along, not letting Uncle Arthur's grumpy mood get to me.

"I'm sorry that you never got a copy of my papers. I'll be sure to have my parole officer fax them to you, along with my arrest record." Uncle Arthur coughs on the mouthful of scotch he was about to swallow and barely catches his breath as I turn on my heel and walk away. I make sure that poor Uncle Arthur doesn't hear my laughter, but something he says catches my attention. From his stuttering reply of "Her parole officer? Andrew, what does she mean by that? Have you married a convict? What if she's here to steal from the company? Now, Andrew, this is some serious business", the word "steal" causes me to have a quick flashback of huge glass doors, the feeling of sweat running down my back, an empty street, and nerves coursing through my body.

I barely make it to a table before I collapse into an empty chair beside two children playing a portable game system. I give them a shaky smile as I try to calm my breathing. I lay my head on the table, partly because if I don't, I will pass out right here and partly to wipe the pool of sweat that has now taken up residence on my forehead. I can hear Andrew saying my name from far away, but when I open my eyes, he is squatting right beside me.

"I'm fine, just felt a little weak for a second." He doesn't seem to believe me, but I shake off his worried look and hopefully convey that what I have to tell him will have to wait until later.

"Just sit right here, and I'll get you something to drink." I watch him walk toward one of the several tables set up around the backyard. I sit up straighter and nod to the few people who are standing close by, giving me questioning looks. My head is still swimming, but I am determined to make a good impression.

As I try to calm my beating heart to a reasonable tempo, I catch Nicole's now smiling face in the crowd still standing with the other girl. On closer inspection, the girl looks a few years younger than me. She is short with pale skin and freckles and her hair is a dull red color. She is dressed very fashionably—skinny white pants with a baggy, brightly patterned tank top. Their conversation seems to be one of ease and familiarity, and I feel a small spark of jealousy. What could they be talking about? Family gossip, who's mad at who, which family member forgot to call another on their birthday, which kids are giving their parents' a little too much grief, what happened on their favorite TV show last night, what they are going to pick up at the grocery store later. I wish I could have a conversation with someone in which my life is not in jeopardy or my well-being threatened, one in which I could just be myself— whoever "myself" is.

Andrew returns with a glass of lemonade and sits beside me with a quick word to the children to "run along and play." They begrudgingly set down their games and stalk off toward the badminton net. I watch as they pick up the rackets, use them as swords, and begin chasing each other around the guests spread out on the lawn. Their play is so innocent, but at the same time mischievous I can't help from laughing along. When they barely miss whacking Uncle Arthur's scotch out of his hand, I am brought back to the present and the scenes in my flashback.

I turn my back to the playing kids with plans to tell Andrew about the details and notice a huge grin on his face. It's not directed at the troublemaking children but at me. I feel self-conscious and quickly look down at the table, feigning interest in the bright yellow tablecloth. After a few seconds, I turn my attention back to him, expecting to see the same warm smile. Instead, his face is a mask of confusion.

"What's wrong?" I ask, not sure if I really want to know the answer.

"Once again, you amaze me. Your highs and lows are so extreme I cannot figure you out."

"So what you're saying is that, basically, I am crazy?" I can't keep the defensive note out of my voice.

He laughs again, small but sincere and continues. "Not at all. It's just every time I think I'm getting close to understanding your faces, I realize I couldn't be further away."

I want to tell him I thought the same this morning. I want to tell him that I want him to understand all my faces, and I want to understand all his. I want to tell him that I want to meet each and every one of his family members, their children, grandchildren. I want to tell him I could spend every Sunday afternoon just like this one, surrounded by good people. But I know that *will* never happen; it *can* never happen. The second I realize this, I get a feeling in my chest—a little piece of my heart cracks, barely hanging on by a thread.

I take a sip of the lemonade Andrew brought me and marvel at its perfection, not too sweet, not too sour—just right. Like Andrew and his family. *But not like me.* I shake off the feeling of sadness, the heavy weight that has been sitting on my shoulders since I woke up yesterday morning. I smile at Andrew.

"I had another flashback. That's what happened. When your Uncle Arthur said something about me stealing from the company—"

Andrew interrupts, "You can't listen to Uncle Arthur. He's crazy. Nobody really listens to him."

I hold up my hand. "I didn't think anything about it. Honestly. But when he said that, I saw flashes, pictures . . . like a slideshow of sorts." I go on to tell him what my flashback consisted of, not only the images but also the emotions and the way it felt, physically. He stay quiet for the few minutes it took me to tell the story. When I finished, he didn't say anything right away, just rubbed his chin, an action that made him seem years older.

"I hate to say, this type of injury, your type of injury, is not my specialty. I know a few doctors who specialize in brain injuries. I'll give them a call tomorrow. As for now, just try to take it easy. Stay here and finish your drink. I'll make apologies for us, and we'll head home."

As Andrew stands up, I stop him with a gentle hand on his arm. "Andrew, I'm fine now, really. And I've been enjoying myself. Let's stay, please." He seems reluctant but simply shrugs.

A cousin, I'm not sure which one, calls from across the lawn and motions for him to join a group of men of the family. He turns back to me, and I nod my consent. He grabs my shoulder before asking, "Are you going to be okay?"

"Yeah, I'll be fine. There's someone I've been wanting to talk to." I look across the yard toward Nicole and the young girl. I stand up and head in their direction. Andrew sees where I am going and lets me venture on my own. As I reach the two women, I can tell the younger girl is complaining about something, and Nicole is trying to calm her down. I can also hear Nicole call the girl Annie. *Andrew's sister.* I am once again drawn to her shocking green eyes. I clear my throat to announce my presence; they both stop talking, and I get the funny feeling they were talking about me.

"Nicole, I never got to thank you for bringing me some clothes." She smiles politely, and I turn to Annie who is ignoring my gaze.

"And you must be Annie. That means that I owe you a huge debt of gratitude for letting me borrow your things. I don't think I would have made such a good impression if I had worn Andrew's gym shorts."

Annie shuffles her feet and, after a few seconds, looks up at me and smiles—a small smile but a genuine one. I feel a weight lift off my shoulders, and I continue to address her. "I would appreciate it if you could sit next to me at lunch. There are so many people to remember. I could use your help." When she looks to Nicole, I get the feeling she is seeking permission. I sense a special bond between the two as Nicole nods her head, and Annie agrees.

Nicole and Annie take me to meet some more family members. As we make our way to a table surrounded by several older members of the Smith family, I notice a very old lady sitting in a wheelchair, being dotted on by most of her companions. She is at least one hundred years old. Her skin is so wrinkled that her eyes are barely visible underneath the drooping folds of her eyelids. But beneath the wrinkles, I can tell that she was once beautiful, very beautiful. She holds herself proudly without interference from her aging body. Her hair is immaculate, her makeup too.

The people around her remind me of bees—the way drones surround the queen, always moving, always flitting about. One woman is fluffing the pillows that are propping up the older woman's arms. She quickly moves to the one between the wheelchair and her back. A man has just arrived carrying a tray of assorted drinks and timidly lowers it to the older woman's eye level. She grabs a martini off the tray and shoos the man away with a flick of her hand.

The other people sitting around her table are trying to get her attention, talking loudly over each other, and she is not paying them a bit of attention. Instead, all her attention is focused on me. Her withering look makes me feel like I am a small child about to be scolded; my hands become sweaty, and I have the strongest urge to look shyly away.

She holds both of her frail hands up, and everyone quiets immediately. This lady is, without a doubt, the queen bee in this family. Annie steps forward and then quickly looks back to me and motions me to stand beside her. I notice that Nicole doesn't make her way forward, so I do and place myself directly in front of the queen's wheelchair. Annie's voice is timid as she introduces me.

"Great-aunt Barbara, this is Eleanor, Andrew's new wife." She steps out of the way, leaving me standing stunned and alone. Unsure if I should bow or curtsey, I simply stand there and smile, hoping that my reaction is appropriate. The queen beckons me even closer, and I shuffle to the side of her wheelchair. I can smell her scent, which is a mixture of lavender, soap, and Aqua Net hairspray. The smell is oddly familiar.

"So," she begins in a rather pleasant voice, "you're Eleanor." Even though her facial expression is one of stern determination, her voice is friendly. I nod my head and wait for her to begin talking again. The rest of the family placed around the table remains silent, all their attention focused on our interaction. Great-aunt Barbara must sense my hesitation because with another flick of her wrist, the table's inhabitants abruptly stand and disperse throughout the crowd on the lawn. I turn to look at Annie and Nicole for advice, or help, but they too have moved on, leaving me alone with the queen.

"Now, my child, we can speak openly. Please have a seat." She motions to one of the newly occupied chairs and watches closely as I take a seat.

"It's all a bit intimidating, I suppose, meeting your new husband's family in this manner."

"Yes, ma'am, it is."

Great-aunt Barbara nods her head slowly. "Tell me, was being introduced like this part of the plan, or was it all a little bit hasty?" she asks, nodding toward my stomach. It suddenly dawns on me that she is asking if I'm pregnant. I feel immediately embarrassed. The bad part is that she has no idea how hasty it was, and I was not going to be the one to tell her. Instead, I answered as semi-honestly as I could.

"No, ma'am. It was hasty but not in the way you might think," I say, hoping she gets my meaning. "My introduction to the family was certainly not planned. In this way, I mean." The elder woman raises her eyebrows, seeming to sense something amiss but stays silent, so I try to dig myself out of the small hole my choice of words have created.

"I'm not sure if you know the details of mine and Andrew's relationship. We met at the hospital when he . . ." I try so hard to remember what he told his parents the night before—was it a sprained wrist, a broken finger. No, it was something to do with my leg, no my ankle!

"When he fixed my ankle," I continue as smoothly as possible. "We began dating then. When he asked me to meet him in Honolulu, I agreed. He proposed, and we were married on the island."

Great-aunt Barbara doesn't speak right away, which makes me nervous, and when she does begin to talk, I get the feeling that her mind is a lot sharper than I had anticipated.

"Well, that's a nice story. But I want to know what really happened." I give her a questioning look—full of innocence, I hope. "Child, I am 101 years old. I know an evasion of information when I hear one. That story was not something a newly married woman would tell about how she met the love of her life. I'm assuming Andrew is the love of your life. Am I correct?"

I look down at my hands, unable to lie to this woman's face, and nod my head. When I look up, I notice that she is giving me a sympathetic smile.

"I have known Andrew his whole life, of course. I know he is a good man, a good doctor, and a good family member. I also know that he has a tendency to take on projects, try to fix things. Now I'm not saying that you are such a thing to him. But let me give you a word of advice—if you want to make it in this family, the first thing you need to do is tell the truth. You'll get devoured if you can't keep up." Her voice softens as she asks, "Do you understand?" When I nod my head, she continues. "Now let's hear the real story."

I square my shoulders, clear my now very dry throat, and speak. "The real story is that Andrew saved my life. That is how we met, and that is why I am here."

Seeming satisfied by my answer, Great-aunt Barbara gives my hand some gentle pats. "I've kept you from your groom long enough. Go find Andrew. I'm sure I'll be seeing you again soon." As I stand up and turn to go, a group of family members once again flock to the queen's side. When I look back over my shoulder, her wheelchair is no longer visible.

I look for Andrew and find him staring at me across the yard. The same feeling I got the first time I looked at him bubbles up in my chest. Suddenly, the twenty yards between us is too much. He must feel the same way because he starts sprinting toward me. We reach each other, and we are the only ones there. Just like this morning around Nicole, we get lost in each other. His eyes are burning again, and I can't keep my hands off his chest. He draws me close, and our lips meet in an eager kiss.

My mind is screaming so loudly I am surprised no one else can hear it: *WHAT ARE YOU DOING? YOU DON'T KNOW THIS MAN! STOP, STOP NOW!*

My desperation to belong somewhere is joined with what seems to be sadness. Andrew is realizing that one day he will have to tell his family the truth—I was a stranger he found in an alley; he lied to them, jeopardized his future and his relationship with them for someone he didn't really know.

Because I know I will be the cause of all this hurt, I put all I have into this kiss, hoping it will be enough to say thank you. I know we will never be this way again. I know when we break apart, we will be more distant than we were before—even more like strangers. But I can't find the strength to pull away. Instead, I make the kiss deeper, and he does not object, pulling me tighter to his body. My hands find his face, and I cling to every part of him, make my body as close to his as I can as his hands stroke my back. In the background, I hear whistling, someone oohing, even people clearing their throats and laughing, and I come crashing down to reality. Andrew pulls away first, laughing a tight laugh, and then turns to his family and raises his hand as if in apology. Everyone then starts clapping as I stand there empty inside.

Andrew sees my face and squeezes my hand, harder than usual, trying to get my attention. When I look at him, I can't keep the tears in my eyes from spilling out. I drop his hand and run away. I can hear Andrew apologizing behind me for our kissing scene and my sudden departure, saying, "She gets embarrassed easy. Her face is probably the color of a ripe tomato."

Everyone laughs again, but I don't stop to hear. I throw open the door to Andrew's house and run to the bedroom where I woke up to this nightmare life.

Chapter 9

Andrew

The flight from Hawaii is not as promising as the one to Hawaii. One thing is the same though—nerves. On the trip to Honolulu, I was full of nervous hope that the time away from my normal surroundings would give me the chance to clear my head and really consider my future.

But ever since I saw Eleanor in that alley, my options were cut in half, possibly more, because of the lie I chose to tell. The only nerves I felt on the flight home were ones that question my resolve to keep up the charade of now having a wife. I knew that Eleanor's life depended on my ability to not only keep her alive but to also keep our story alive as well. I remember looking at her unconscious body spread over two seats across the aisle from me and knowing one thing was true: I would never take back my decision to call this beautiful wreck of a woman my wife.

And I still wouldn't. Even after this disaster of a day. *So much for Eleanor's promise to not let me down.* Her hasty flight from lunch left me in an awkward and somewhat dangerous situation. I had to explain, at least a dozen of times, about Eleanor's attack in Honolulu as a way to justify her actions. However, talking about Honolulu brought me precariously close to a subject in which I did not want to discuss—how I met Eleanor and the details of our relationship. When I decided to take on the role of newlywed to a woman I had never even talked to, I knew it would mean lying to everyone. I just wasn't prepared to do so much lying to so many people in such a short amount of time.

After the meal, I was able to excuse myself in the disguise of checking on my wife. But I just couldn't imagine going back to the house. I got in my car and drove down to the local bar, hoping to find some solitude as well as some liquid courage. But when I reached the parking lot, Joshua was already there, leaning on his Firebird and picking something from underneath his fingernails.

"Can't a man get a drink by himself anymore?" I ask as I slam my car door.

"Evidently not, bro." Joshua shrugs as if to say, "Too bad for you", and follows me into the bar without another word. We sit in a booth near the back, and I nurse the beer in my hand. Joshua, always able to hold his alcohol better than me, has moved on to his third and belches as he sits the empty bottle loudly on the table.

"So are you going to tell me what's going on, or are you going to pout some more?" He fixes me with a glance I am overly familiar with, one that looks like he doesn't care, but in truth, I know he is dying for me to talk.

"Dude," I begin, "there is no way in the world that you would understand. Honestly, it's not even worth trying to explain."

He shrugs like he isn't bothered either way and calls the waitress over to order another beer. "Okay, man. That's fine. But no matter what you say to me, I saw the look on your face when Eleanor ran out of lunch today. I know that look because I have seen it before . . . in the mirror. That was the look of someone hurting but also the look of someone burning with desire. Now," he continues before I can say anything, "the desire I get. I mean, how long has it been since you've been with someone? Years, I'm guessing. Plus, you're a newlywed. I remember those days—every touch or flutter of an eyelash makes your blood boil. But what I don't understand is the hurting." He stops as the waitress returns with another drink and takes a pull from the bottle.

I sigh, trying to figure out a way I can talk to my brother without giving away any of Eleanor's secrets. "You're right. It was hurt and desire that you saw in my face." He nods and grins like an idiot, and I rush to continue before I can get the old "I told you so." "Having a woman in my house is strange in the extreme after so many years of being alone, especially my *wife*. But having an injured and abused woman is a totally different story."

Joshua rubs his chin absently, something I find myself doing from time to time and wonder if it makes me seem as old as it does him. "Well, I never thought about that. I just assumed you guys would be so glad to see each other after three weeks everything else would fall into place. You're the expert in these matters, of course. Is it not possible for you guys to . . . you know?"

"It's not about 'possibility' but about decency. I have to be very careful—Eleanor is in a delicate state right now. Even touching her hands or face causes her to shy away. And I don't blame her, not after all she has been through." I pause and take an encouraging breath. "Joshua, if you had seen her when I found her, in the hospital I mean, you would maybe understand. Maybe."

He nods slowly as I look back to him.

"But the desire is still there. You've seen her—you know how beautiful she is—her big brown eyes, her delicate features and soft hair." My voice drifts away as I imagine Eleanor's beautiful body draped across my bed right at this moment. Joshua laughs heartily, and I'm glad someone thinks it's amusing.

"Yes, your wife is certainly a good-looking woman. And now that you have explained the situation a little better, I can respect the predicament you are in. But answer me this, brother. Why the look of hurt? Is it because of what Eleanor went through, or is it something else?"

This is a tricky topic, one I was hoping to steer clear of. It seems, however, evasion is not in the cards tonight. I tip my beer back and finish its contents. Joshua catches the eye of the waitress and motions for another. I wipe my mouth with the back of my hand, torn about how much I should share. "Let's just say that Eleanor's attack is not the only thing keeping me from sharing her bed."

Joshua holds up his beer bottle as the waitress furnishes me with another. "At least that's one thing I can understand. Here's to complicated women," he says with a smile on his face and a bit of sadness in his voice. I tap his bottle with my own and ponder at the bad fortune of the Smith men: falling in love with complicated women.

Phone Conversation No. 2

9:50 p.m.

"Sorry I can't talk long, and I have to whisper, but I just wanted to inform you that she attended the family dinner today. She rushed out before it was over, but Dr. Smith was still introducing her as his wife, 'Eleanor Smith.'

"I learned nothing of a personal nature today, but I thought you might want to know she is up and about. Yes, sir, I understand. Anything I can learn is important."

Chapter 10

Eleanor

I'm not sure what time it is when my stomach starts to growl. I feel ashamed of my actions at lunch, so I have stayed in my room a long time. Listening for Andrew to return home was torture of the worst kind. I've sat still for so long, making sure to not miss his footsteps outside the door that my legs are asleep. I've been leaning against the floor-length mirror which has left a very painful impression on my back.

It's dark outside when I hear a car pull up the driveway, and I feel nervous butterflies in my stomach. How am I going to smooth things over with Andrew? What could I possibly say to make him forgive my actions? I promised that I would not let him down. But remembering his face as we broke apart from the kiss, I get the feeling that is exactly what I did.

I hear the front door opening up and voices talking softly. *It's now or never.* As I get up, feeling the pins and needles that accompany sleeping appendages, I am determined to make things right with Andrew.

I walk into the living room expecting to see only my husband, but he is not alone. His arm is wrapped lazily around the shoulders of a girl. He has an easy laugh, one that I don't know; and his body is relaxed, posture that I do not associate with him. I clear my throat, thinking that I am intruding on something and praying to God that I'm not. *Boy, he moves fast. I guess the fact that his pretend wife is in the other room has no effect on his dating game.* Andrew doesn't even acknowledge me, but the girl does; and as she turns, a wave of relief floods over me. Annie is staring at me with guarded eyes.

"I just came by to check on you. I know how hard it is to be around the family, that is why I was willing to sit with you at lunch, and then you just ran off." Her voice sounds sad, and I never thought about the fact that

I might have hurt her feelings. I walk the rest of the way around the couch and face them both. I notice that Andrew's eyes still do not meet mine. I sit on the coffee table in front of Annie and look at her. I don't need to *act* sincere for this apology.

"I am so sorry that I bailed on you. Andrew was right in telling everyone that I get embarrassed easy. One day you will understand how hard it is for newlyweds to keep their hands off each other, even in big crowds." She smiles, a little embarrassed herself, and looks to Andrew. He looks down into his younger sister's eyes, and his returning smile seems fake to me, but Annie doesn't seem to notice.

"I never should have run out," I continue, "especially since you were so nice to offer to help me. I promise that if we ever make plans again, you can count on me." Annie's smile widens, and so does the hole in my chest. *How will I ever be able to face this girl after lying to her like this?* I see Andrew looking at me, asking me the same question with his eyes. Annie spends the rest of the time telling me what happened after I left.

"Most people were really worried about you. Even after Andrew explained about your accident." She suddenly gets quiet.

"It's okay to talk about," I reassure her. "After all, not talking about it won't change the fact that it happened." This seems to put her at ease, and she continues with her story. I find myself laughing along when she describes Uncle Arthur's reaction to my hasty departure, saying that it was "proof of my instability and my unbalanced mental state." I even notice a small smile on Andrew's face.

When Annie leaves a little later with the promise to visit tomorrow, the distance between Andrew and I grows with each second she is gone.

"We need to talk," I say as he walks into the kitchen.

"Sure, okay," he answers and leans against the counter. I have rehearsed this speech several times in my room, but as I begin, it sounds flawed even to my own ears. But I know that once I start, I won't be able to stop until everything is out, so I let it fly.

"You will never know how appreciative I am of you saving my life. I would be dead in an alley right now if it were not for you. Not only your medical skill but also your quick wit has saved my life, and I will be forever grateful." *Take a breath, calm down.* I have to remind myself.

"Those things are just the beginning of your kindness. Offering me a future, *your* future, so that I will not be alone is probably what I am most thankful for. Not once have you thought about yourself in this entire situation."

He starts to interrupt me, and I throw my hand up to stop him. "I realize the extreme sacrifice of that. But the fact remains that even though

I feel safe and cared for with you, I have no clue who I am. It scares me to think that I may never know what my real name is or anything about my family. It also scares me to think that the person or people who did this to me might still be out there. I have to find out what happened to me."

I look into his eyes and almost plead with him. "You have to help me remember."

Chapter 11

Andrew

Today did not go like I hoped it would. When I woke up this morning, I felt hopeful. But after everything that has happened, all the ups and downs, the highs and lows, I feel . . . deflated. Like a balloon lying limp on the floor, the plans I had made for a life with Eleanor, although they were solely in my head, lay flat and discarded. Whatever made me think that the situation I now find myself in, the situation I chose voluntarily, would ever work out?

The house is quiet, a fact for which I am grateful. My head has already begun a dull throb caused by the alcohol I consumed earlier. I knew that trying to keep pace with Joshua was a mistake. The thought of a tall, cold glass of water appears in my mind. The body has a strange ability to fend for itself, and it amazes me. I slowly crawl out of bed, being extra careful to make no noise, not wanting to alert Eleanor to my awakened state. I don't think I can stand to see her right now. I know I will have to face her at some point . . . just not right now.

I pad toward the kitchen cabinet, resisting the urge to open Eleanor's door to check on her, a habit that is going to be hard to break now that she is conscious. The past few weeks have been beyond exhausting. I now know how new parents feel—sleepless nights, endless days, constant worrying. Although it was a lot harder to treat Eleanor in Honolulu, I didn't have so many other things to juggle. Keeping my family at bay was just as difficult as I thought it would be. Thank goodness my parents were out of town; otherwise my wife would have had a more sudden introduction to the family.

I shake my head as I remember Joshua, Nicole, and Annie's response to my sudden announcement. I recall the look of shock on Annie's face—I don't think her jaw could have gotten any closer to the floor without causing permanent damage. Joshua, on the other hand, smiled that stupid grin of his, and I thought, in that moment everything would work out, everything would be okay. How wrong I was.

The premonition I had that my sudden marriage would be more than a shock was my reasoning behind inviting only my brother, sister, and sister-in-law to the big house the night I brought Eleanor home. I could tell by the tone in their voices they thought I was either crazy or extremely drunk when I called and asked them to meet me. As they sat in their pajamas, rubbing the sleep out of their eyes and trying to hide their yawns, my resolve began to waver. I remember thinking that was one of the most important moments of my life simply because it represented the rest of my life.

The sound of Eleanor's moans coming from the bedroom brings me back to the present and causes my muscles to tense. The sounds of her whimpering are as familiar as my own voice. Every high-pitched shriek from the other room is like the scars on my chest—I know every detail. Her cries of pain seem to represent my own. I quietly open the door to see Eleanor's flailing body roll from side to side across the bed; her arms are pushing against an invisible force in the air, her legs are trying to run from whatever haunts her nightmares. She has had the same dream for the past three weeks. I know that in about a couple of minutes, the screaming will start.

I feel my head throb again and realize I can't handle hearing them tonight. With as much gentleness as I can muster, I grab each of Eleanor's wrists in my hands and pin them above her head. I then slowly and smoothly glide onto her prostrate body, holding her thrashing form against the bed with my weight. There is no doubt that our hostile embrace would more than alarm an innocent observer, and I take the time to thank my lucky stars that the only window in this bedroom faces away from my parents' house. This would not be a situation I would want to explain. "No, Mother, I wasn't raping my wife. I was just holding her down so she couldn't harm herself or me. Really, it's totally normal." I roll my eyes at the absurdity of such a conversation.

Eleanor's body is still twisting from side to side, so I begin the mantra I have said for three weeks.

"Just breathe, Eleanor. You are safe now." Her violent rolling remains steady, and her breathing does not decrease, so I raise my voice just a bit.

"You're okay, Eleanor. Calm down." I can tell that she has heard me this time because the crease between her eyebrows disappears. In truth, I'm not sure how much she does hear. All I know is that my voice has calmed her ever since that first night.

"Just breathe, Eleanor," I begin again. "You are safe now."

Her fists clench and unclench as she struggles for control—of what, I don't know. Her breathing is becoming less erratic, and her thrashing has been reduced to quick bursts of power. I feel like I am riding one of those mechanical bulls. There's no doubt she is registering my body on top of her, holding her down. This is my cue to slowly climb off.

As I am doing so, I continue to talk softly I keep a firm grasp on her wrists as I sit beside her on the bed, repeating, "Breathe, Eleanor. You're okay. Shhhhh . . ." I see tears running down her cheeks, and I know we have made it through another episode. I take my grip off her wrists and lean back quickly, trying to avoid any wild punches she may throw and wincing at the remembrance of a black eye I received for not being quick enough one night. After a few seconds, I glance back and see Eleanor's body finally relaxed, the shed tears still glistening on her flushed cheeks. I am reminded of a quote from Shakespeare, "To weep is to make less the depth of grief." I send up a silent prayer that with each tear she cries, Eleanor's grief lessens.

I find myself reaching out to touch this beautifully complicated woman. In the beginning, when all this started, I made a point to remain mentally distant from my patient. The distance allowed me to maintain a clear head, which was required for me to treat her. But as the days and nights grew longer and I became more familiar with her body, its needs and movements, I found it more difficult to keep a proper separation. However, as of yesterday morning, my resolve to keep my distance has been all but forgotten.

Seeing Eleanor standing in my kitchen wearing that silk nightgown was my undoing. Her gorgeous brown eyes, widened in fear and innocence, stopped my heart. When she asked me why I had kissed her that first time, I was only partly honest. Yes, I did believe that my family would have expected it. And yes, I was relieved to see her finally awake. But the truth of the matter was that I wanted to kiss her. I don't think I could have stopped my body from gravitating toward her, even if I wanted.

I feel that same pull now as I watch her ragged breathing trying to steady itself. I wait a few seconds, making sure my touch will not wake her. Then feeling like it's safe, I gently brush a curly strand of hair off her face. Eleanor scrunches up her nose as the offending locks tickle her flesh. *My god, she's beautiful.* I imagine what it would be like to touch this face every night. What would it be like to wrap my arms around her sleeping form whenever I wanted? I smile as I picture Eleanor's wonderful laugh, rare but infectious, making its appearance just for me. And for the first time in a long time, I weep. The idea of spending the rest of my life with this amazing stranger sits hauntingly out of reach. My body convulses as I allow the sorrow of my predicament to wash over me. It takes a few minutes for my nerves to calm back down. I feel more than a little foolish for not only crying but for also allowing myself to fall in love with this woman.

I dry my eyes with the back of my hand and allow myself one more caress of Eleanor's soft skin. I run my fingers through her thick, curly hair. I trail my fingertips lightly across her long eyelashes, noticing how she twitches at my touch. I move on to her cheeks and then her full lips. As I rub my thumb along her soft lower lip, I remember our earlier kiss on the lawn, and my head throbs, along with other parts of my anatomy. I quickly move on to her collarbones, still slightly bruised from her attack. From there, I trace the muscles in her shoulder, down her arm, and finally rest my hand in her palm. I intertwine our fingers for just a second before breaking the moment. Standing up, I look once more on the face I love and leave Eleanor's now-resting body.

There is no point in going back to my bedroom now. The evidence of a hangover is definitely showing signs, not to mention my worked-up mental and physical state will only hinder what little sleep I would be getting. The clock on the stove says 3:00 a.m. I sit at the kitchen table again and finish my glass of water, all the while trying to decide what my next course of action should be. It is clear from Eleanor's mood swings, continued nightmares, flashbacks, and rehearsed speech earlier that she is miserable here, and I cannot blame her. Her situation is so alien to me I cannot begin to understand the depth of her instability. Even though I see some evidence of it every night, hearing her plead with me to help her discover the truth just drove the point home.

But how? What can I do for her beyond what I have already done? Like I said to her earlier, brain injuries are not my specialty. Although I know a little, I am in no way an expert. But I do know someone. The doctor I mentioned before is a mutual friend of mine and Joshua's; he sometimes gets called into the hospital to consult on certain cases.

My mind begins to work slowly between the haze of alcohol and lingering stress. I make a plan as well as a vow to myself and Eleanor that I will do everything in my power to find the answers she seeks. No matter how bad it hurts.

Chapter 12

Eleanor

Going to bed last night was one of the hardest things I have ever had to do. Andrew and I resolved nothing, and I feel more apprehension this morning than the first day I woke up in this house. As I get dressed in some of Annie's clothes, I look at myself in the free-standing mirror. The bruises covering my torso are just as dark as they were yesterday, and they still far exceed the ones on my arms and legs, which seem a shade lighter; but maybe it's just my mind willing them to be. The scratches and bite marks still bother me the most. It's easier for me to walk this morning; my muscles aren't as sore. As I begin my new mantra, I start to hope that confronting my damaged body every day will have the effect Andrew told me it would. I am taking control of my situation.

I enter the kitchen, expecting to find a sullen and quiet Andrew, and I get the opposite. He has a phone book, notepad, and rolodex open in front of him, and he holds a phone up to his ear but is not saying anything. He smiles at me, not too friendly but definitely friendlier than last night, and motions me to the stove where I see he has made some scrambled eggs. I make some chocolate milk, grab a napkin, and sit across him trying to read the scribbles on the notepad. As I push my breakfast around my plate, I wonder where his change in mood came from. I hate to admit that I am probably the cause, but it's too late now to discourage his actions. There's no way I could have acted more erratic than I did yesterday at lunch. The family didn't seem to notice, but there is no doubt Andrew found my behavior more than a little unstable. Plus the fact remains that he kissed me too.

"Yes, thank you, we will be there." Andrew hangs up the phone, scribbles something that looks like a time and address on his notepad, and then looks at me. I can see determination in his eyes but not like before. This determination does not have heat behind it. Instead, I can tell he feels good to have something to do, a purpose, a mission of helping me discover the truth. I can imagine that same look in his eyes when he was nursing me back to health. I know this should give me encouragement, but all I feel is sadness. *Because I want to stay here with him.*

"I'm sorry I was a little harsh last night," he begins. "Not saying anything after you opened up like that was thoughtless. There is no excuse for the way I have been acting—all my actions lately have not had my usual restraint. I'm sure even though you don't know me, you know I'm telling the truth." He looks at me with those green eyes, and all I can do is nod.

"I realized I was being selfish, keeping you here to uphold the appearance of our marriage for my own sake. I should have taken charge of the search for your identity the second I saw you in that alley, but you know why I did not, and I stick by that decision. As for not helping you Saturday as soon as you woke up, I was so relieved to see you awake and walking around that I forgot again how important this is for you. Then my family was there and . . ." His voice trails off as I am listening only halfheartedly. Uncertainties start filing through my head. *If he doesn't want me here, where will I go? I have to find my identity. I have to leave this house behind and this man whom I owe my life. I have to leave because I cannot live a fake life with a fake husband. A fake life is not a life to me.*

He continues to talk while I stare at him with glassy eyes. He takes my hand in his and gives it a squeeze. "Yesterday was a mistake. Meeting my family like that had to be overwhelming, but I just couldn't think of a way to say no to my mother's offer of lunch without raising more questions. And then the kiss . . ." At this, he just shakes his head, and I almost lose it. He continues talking, and I look up to hear his last words. "So I have called a few friends, and I have developed a game plan." He is expecting me to say something, so I clear my throat.

"That's great. What's the plan?"

It is actually a good one. He has made me several doctors' appointments for the following days.

"I would like to get second opinions from some people who are specialists in their fields," he says. The first one scheduled for today is with a gynecologist. As I take a quick shower and get dressed, my nerves begin to build in the pit of my stomach. For some reason, I am expecting to hear the worst. The fact that a visit to the gynecologist is a necessity only reinforces the uncomfortable and awful truth that I was raped.

Andrew and I are silent on the drive to the doctor's office, and when I walk back to the exam room, he grabs my hand and gives it a squeeze. Usually, this comforts me, but all I can do is stare straight ahead. I look back toward Andrew for a smile of reassurance seconds before the door closes, but he looks just as worried as me. Unfortunately, my fears are confirmed. As a result of the massive amount of trauma I suffered, the doctor tells me I won't be able to have children. As we receive the news, Andrew looks pained; but surprisingly, I feel myself loosening up. I can't even begin to think about my future in that way: having children, being a mother. The prospect is so far from my mind all I can do is thank the doctor and prepare for my next appointment.

The rest of the day, Andrew and I spend shopping. I was excited to see downtown Carmel, and I was not disappointed. The town was picturesque. The spring sun warmed my skin and thawed my insides. We spent more than an hour in a small local grocery store walking up and down the tight aisles. Our time is split between picking out snack foods and frozen meals and talking to the other customers. I am surprised by the amount of people grocery shopping on an early Monday, and it seems like Andrew knows every single one of them. After the first few shocked looks when he introduces me as his wife, I get used to the questioning glances. I even notice a few of the women we meet look disappointed. Could they have wanted Andrew for themselves? He is a catch—handsome, rich, smart, doctor, the list goes on and on.

Exhausted from the physical and mental excursion, we make our way to the checkout counter with a full buggy. The cashier turns out to be the owner, and as he scans our groceries, he falls into easy conversation with Andrew. It seems their families go way back. As the two men chat away, I spend my time looking at the small shops lining the opposite side of the road. I see a couple of businesses anyone would expect to see occupying a downtown—a dentist, a lawyer's office, and dry cleaners. The rest of the retail space is full of art galleries and specialty shops.

One storefront in particular catches my eye. The clothing store's picture window is full of bright, matching outfits. Shoes and handbags are paired with an array of seasonal ware. I see bathing suits, business suits, and even a ball gown. I let my mind drift and find myself wondering what types of clothes would be in my own closet, wherever that may be. Did it consist of mostly work clothes, pant suits in blacks and grays, sturdy shoes, and basic black handbags? Or was I the sporty type with running pants, souvenir T-shirts from gyms and 5K races, twelve pairs of tennis shoes? Maybe I liked to dress nice with fashionable dresses and skirts with matching jewelry and shoes.

As I try to picture my unruly hair in a neat bun, Andrew's voice brings me back to the present. I help grab the paper grocery bags while he tells the owner good-bye. I smile my thanks, and we head outside. I glance once more at the clothing store and long for the day when I can fill up a closet of my own again.

We have a late lunch in downtown Carmel, and I have to admit that the town is idyllic. The small town lies within one square mile, and that mile is packed with more charm and beauty than one can imagine. The white sand on the beach is perfect, and while Andrew and I sit at a small café, I enjoy hearing the crashing waves in the distance. I marvel at how lucky I have been and start making a mental list: lucky that a doctor just happened to find me close to death in an alley; lucky that said doctor's family is rich enough to own a private jet, making our hasty retreat from Hawaii uncommonly easy; and lucky the same doctor is by far one of the most caring, beautiful people I have ever seen.

Thinking back to our time in the grocery store, there is no doubt everyone else knows what I am just piecing together: Dr. Andrew Smith is beautiful, both inside and out. With a gentle breeze seemingly blowing my cares away, if only for a moment, I am finally able to enjoy the town and the beautiful spring weather. Andrew sits across me sipping his drink and giving me a questioning look.

"What are you staring at?" I ask as his gaze becomes steadier.

"I wish your OB-GYN diagnosis had gone better." He begins to frown again I lean over, grab his hand, and give it a little squeeze. It's funny how our roles have reversed today, but I realize it's my turn to give him a little comfort. He continues in a shaky voice. "I knew your body was healing because of my exams, but to hear you will not ever be completely healed . . ." His voice cuts short. To hear him talk, you'd think I was damaged goods. But I know he doesn't mean it that way. *He is disappointed for me. He even feels like a failure—like he did not do enough to help me heal.* I've only known Andrew for two days, but I know my instincts in this matter are right on. I just smile.

He gets a little cloud over his features and looks at me seriously as he continues. "You know your next appointments could give you some real answers. You could find out when your memory should return." As he says this, I can tell he is restraining some sort of emotion—joy to be rid of me or sadness that I could be leaving.

"Yes, you're right. I could be finding out what I want to know, but don't think for a second it will be easy for me to learn the truth."

It's dark outside when we finally reach the house. I'm not sure how I feel, and I can tell Andrew's thoughts are also clouded. I fall onto the couch as the phone by the door rings. Andrew answers it, pausing only briefly to give me a pained look. "Sure, Mom, we'll be there in a minute." He hangs up as I hang my head.

"I'm nervous about seeing them again, Andrew. I know they think I am rude and maybe even a little unstable." *Which I am.*

He reaches for my hand. "I know you are worn out after today, and we still have a lot to talk about, but I promise this little meeting will go a long way with my parents."

I excuse myself to the restroom and stare into the mirror. My curly brown hair stands unchecked around my face. I try to smooth it down as I search the rest of my face. My brown eyes are lined with dark circles underneath, and I wonder if the stress of the last few days has given them prominence. I take my time brushing my teeth; I want to steal my nerves for the encounter with Andrew's parents. I realize how important this meeting is going to be. It's up to me to convince these strangers I am just the opposite, not a stranger to their son. Someone he has known and apparently loved for months now. Someone he feels so strongly for he would marry without their blessing. And the most important thing I have to convey to them is that I love Andrew just as much, if not more. If I cannot convince them, I will be out on the street, alone with nowhere to turn. This next hour might be the most important of my life. I give myself one more quick look and head out of the room, not wanting to see the apprehension in my eyes anymore.

Tonight, a maid answers the Smith's front door, and Andrew causally greets her. "Hello, Mary. I don't think you had the privilege of meeting my new bride yesterday. Eleanor, this is Mary, the head housekeeper." As I stick out my hand, Mary grabs it excitedly and chuckles as she shakes it.

"It is so nice to meet you, Eleanor. I heard about your hasty escape yesterday. But I can't blame you for not keeping your hands off this one."

I immediately feel my face turning a brilliant shade of red, but when I look at Andrew, he is trying hard to suppress a smile. Mary's laughter fills the entry way, and he joins along. In this moment, I can imagine the playful banter and shouts of joy from the four Smith children filling these halls. I find myself joining them when Andrew's dad leans his head over the banister and calls for us to join them upstairs.

"Mary, can you please get us some refreshments?"

"Of course, sir," Mary says as she gives me a wink and turns toward what I assume is the kitchen.

Andrew looks me in the eye. "I know you're nervous, but I will try to keep you out of the line of fire. Just trust me and go with the flow." I raise my eyebrows at his choice of words and then paint a smile on my stretched out face.

We start upstairs, and when we reach the top, he stops and kisses my forehead. The familiarity of his action causes me to start, but I shut my eyes, trying to let his calm seep into my bones and steady my beating heart. I tell myself the flush I feel creeping up my face is from the climb up the stairs and not the fact that Andrew hasn't touched me like that since yesterday's very public kissing scene. We walk into a small den where my in-laws sit facing a large TV screen. They are holding hands across a small table, and when Andrew's mom reaches for her drink, she spies us standing in the door.

"Come in, you two. We're all family here." I know she is trying to comfort me, but her words sound as strained as the smile on my face feels. As we sit across them on a love seat, I grip Andrew's hand tightly. His dad turns off the TV, and they both sit there, like they are expecting me to say something.

"I know yesterday I did not give you all the best of impressions, and I am truly sorry," I begin, "especially to you, Mr. Smith, because you went out of your way to make me feel welcome in a very . . . overwhelming situation." I give him a small smile, and he returns it willingly.

"Please call me Sean," he says, and I nod my agreement.

I then turn to Andrew's mom, and I know her opinion matters more than anyone. And I find that I want her to like me, not for my sake (and my immediate future) but for Andrew's sake as well.

"Mrs. Smith, I also want to apologize to you. I can only imagine what it must be like to come home from a trip to learn you have an unexpected family member waiting for you. Looking back, I wish there was a way we could have told you before, given you some indication of our relationship." When I look to Andrew, he is returning my gaze with his own. He smiles a sweet smile, and I know his emotions mirror my own—regret mixed with a sense of duty.

I direct my attention to Mrs. Smith and notice the apprehension slowly turning to happiness in her eyes. "I can promise you that from now on, I will do my best to be the kind of person who deserves your wonderful son." I can feel the tension in the room lift like a blanket.

"Please, call me Laura," she says. I'm not sure if this allowance means I am forgiven, but I see Andrew raise his eyebrows in his father's direction. Sean just shrugs his shoulders and turns the TV back on which I take as a good sign.

Before we leave, Andrew's mother places her hand on my arm, which takes me by surprise. I feel a quick sweep of heat and fear rise through my body, and I stop my procession out the front door and turn toward her. There must be alarm in my eyes because she immediately drops her hand and takes a step back.

"Eleanor, I was wondering if you would like to join me for lunch tomorrow. I'm sure that you and Andrew are eager for some time to yourselves, but I would like to get to know you better. I've had my other daughter-in-law, Nicole, around for so long. She is more like a daughter to me. I would love to have the opportunity to spend some time with you as well."

I turn, searching for Andrew, and see him in conversation with his father, so I am left to answer the request on my own. "I think Andrew has scheduled a doctor's appointment for me tomorrow. I'll have to check with him first and then let you know."

Laura looks genuinely disappointed, so I hastily add, "I'll see if I can't reschedule it or something."

"Now, don't go to any trouble or anything," she adds, already looking happier. I get the feeling I'm going to have to do just that if I want to stay on her good side. I remember Aunt Tilly's words from yesterday at lunch about keeping Laura happy.

As we head back to Andrew's house, I turn to see Sean and Laura standing at the threshold of their enormous mansion, with arms around each other, and wonder what kind of family I have stumbled upon.

I could tell it was a last-minute decision on Laura's part to invite me to lunch today. I think she realized the only way she could get any real answers from me was to separate Andrew and me. It was unclear how Andrew felt about me accepting his mother's invitation to lunch. Honestly, I think he was glad to have some time away from me. The realization didn't affect me like I thought it would. If I wasn't afraid our secret would be found out, then I would probably enjoy a ladies lunch date. I can tell all the tension between me and Andrew is starting to wear on us, so I called and rescheduled my ear, nose, and throat doctor's appointment for one day next week and confirmed my attendance at the big house for noon.

I've spent a good hour getting ready—taking a long shower, shaving my legs and underarms, completely drying my hair, which I found out to be a bad idea. In its dry state, I look like I have on a large frizzy football helmet. I'm wearing yet another one of Annie's outfits and remind myself to say something to Andrew about getting my own clothes. I'm not one to stick up my nose at handouts, but it's going to come to a point when the weight I lost during the last three weeks is going to catch up to me, and Annie's already tight clothing is not going to cut it anymore.

Andrew has been home most of the morning, drinking coffee, reading the paper, and surfing the Internet. I don't want to pry, but I couldn't help but ask what he was searching for so intently.

"Nothing important," he said casually, his answer giving nothing away. I was hoping he would confess to extensive brain injury and amnesia research, but I was sadly mistaken. I checked the mirror in my room one more time before heading out the door. The cotton short-sleeve dress seems extra tight; however, I know it is just my nerves setting in.

"What will you do while I'm gone?" I call to Andrew.

"Probably stuff around here. I have to run into town for a few errands, and then I might visit Joshua at work while I'm there." I feel sad suddenly and realize it is because I don't want to be away from Andrew, even for a little bit. It's obvious we need some space, but I can't shake the feeling of nausea in the pit of my stomach. I walk out of the bedroom determined to say something about cancelling on his mother, but when I see his face, I don't have the heart. He looks excited—for me to spend time with his mother or to have some time to himself, I'm not sure. I just can't be the one to wipe that expression off his face.

"You look great, as always," he says.

"Ha! Now I know you are lying. You've seen me beaten and bruised, so I have a serious problem believing you when you say that I *always* look great." Andrew just smiles.

"Believe what you will, but I *always* think that you *always* look great." I cannot hide the blush creeping into my cheeks when the fact hits me that he is completely serious.

"I should probably go," I add quickly, embarrassment drawing my gaze to the floor. "I wouldn't want to be late."

"That's probably a good idea." Andrew gently takes my chin in his hand and lifts my face until I am looking into his beautiful green eyes. The tension between us has suddenly changed from a dull throb of stress and pressure to a steady pulse of something I dare to label desire. "I'm only a phone call away if you need saving," he whispers.

"And you are the perfect man for the job." Andrew lets go of my chin, and I make my way to the door. As I turn around, trying to lighten the mood, I say, "Wish me luck!" "Good luck," he says as I head out into the sunlight. I cannot be 100 percent sure, but I think he followed up with "You're going to need it."

As I ring the doorbell to the big house, I take the last second to check my reflection in the glass windowpanes that outline the front door. I can hear voices inside and a clicking of heels on the polished marble floor. The door is thrown open, and I am greeted, not by Mary, the housekeeper, or Laura, Andrew's mother, but by Annie. The surprise must have shown on my face because her smile quickly fades into one of hurt.

"Mother said you were coming over for lunch today, and I just had to be here. I hope that is okay," she says.

"That's great," I add hastily. "I just wasn't expecting to see you, but it is a very pleasant surprise." Annie hears the honesty in my voice and perks back up. The fact of the matter is, I could not be happier about Annie's presence. I hope it will take some of the pressure off of me.

Annie loops my arm through hers, ignoring my sudden flinch at her touch, and marches me straight toward the large living room. A small round table has been set up on the left-hand side of the room, and Laura is standing behind one of the three chairs.

"Eleanor, it is so good to see you, dear. Thank you for taking time out of your busy schedule to have lunch with us." Laura's voice is sweet, and I dare not say anything about feeling pressured to do so.

"Thank you for having me. And thank you, Annie, for loaning me the clothes. I plan on doing some shopping soon, so I promise to have them back to you shortly."

"Don't worry about it," Annie says with a flick of her hand. "I have a closet full." I laugh at her bluntness and wonder about her childhood— privileged, pampered, and spoilt, I'm sure. I nod my acceptance, and we all sit down. Mary, the housekeeper, brings out a pitcher full of some delicious-looking juice and informs us that our first course will be a soup, of which I have never heard of.

"That sounds wonderful, Mary," Laura says. With a quick and small bow, Mary returns to the kitchen. "Do you drink, my dear?" Laura asks. I am slightly confused by her question, and when she sees it, she adds, "Alcohol. I wasn't sure if you should be having any because of your . . . incident." She looks apologetic for bringing up my attack, and I give her a smile. "There is not much alcohol in this drink, but I wanted to make sure. If you would rather have something else . . ."

"Andrew has not said anything about me not drinking, so I guess it's okay." Laura returns my smile and pours me a glass of the juice.

After we all have our glasses full and I take a sip of the wonderful drink, Annie dives right into the nitty-gritty of it all. "I for one am so excited to be doing this. Your and Andrew's relationship has been so shrouded in mystery I cannot wait to hear all the details."

Laura's cough on the other side of the table is proof that Annie's blunt statement was just as unexpected to her as it was to me. "You will have to excuse my daughter's lack of tack." She throws Annie a quelling look. "You must understand that it is difficult for us to accept this sudden addition of a family member. However, we love Andrew and trust him, and if he loves you, then I am sure we all will. We realize you have been through a horrible ordeal, and you still have a lot of recovering to do, and we, as your family, will do everything in our power to help you. That includes being sensitive to your feelings and situation." Laura looks directly at Annie when she says this, and I think Annie gets the hint.

I address Laura, "Thank you for your support and your willingness to accept me. And thank you, Annie, for your eagerness to get to know me. It just proves to me that you love your brother, and it makes me feel welcome."

Annie smiles at me as Mary brings the soup to the table. It looks just as delicious as the juice drink did, and I am not disappointed when I take my first bite.

The lunch has gone well so far. Between Annie's constant chatter and the singular answers I have been giving to questions, I have managed to keep from spilling mine and Andrew's secret. But I have a feeling that is all about to change as Annie asks me a question I was hoping to avoid.

"So, Eleanor, how did you and Andrew meet?"

I put my fork down and paste a pleasant smile on my face. "We met at the hospital."

"Yes, yes, we all know that. What I want to know is how you went from being Andrew's patient to being his 'partner'." Annie's eye light up mischievously.

Laura jumps in. "Annie, that is neither appropriate nor any of your business." She must have noticed my flushed face because she adds, "Eleanor, you do not have to answer any of Annie's intrusive questions.

"But, Mother . . .," Annie starts, sounding like a whiny teenager. Laura shoots her a look Annie clearly understands as "Keep your mouth shut." The two women turn back toward me, looking slightly embarrassed, and it takes all my strength not to laugh.

"You'll have to excuse us, Eleanor. We are all curious. I am not sure how long you have actually known Andrew, but for those of us who have known him all his life, we are genuinely surprised at his sudden relationship with you. He is not usually so . . . secretive."

I can tell Laura is choosing her words carefully in the attempt to not offend me.

"Please do not apologize. As I said last night, Andrew and I are the guilty party here. Plus, Andrew said as much to me before, and I got the idea he has never done something like this before. Trust me. This is a new experience to me as well." I smile at my own private joke.

"Does that mean you have never been married before?" Annie asks quickly.

"Angelica Jean Smith," Laura spits out, truly embarrassed by her daughter's rudeness. Annie looks at her mother and shrugs her shoulders as if she does not understand her fury. I feel the need to interject on Annie's behalf.

"It's okay, really," I assure them. "I knew what I was getting myself into when I accepted the invitation to lunch. To answer your question, Annie, no, I have not been married before. At least, not that I know of." I cannot help myself from truly laughing, and Annie joins along. Laura seems to settle more comfortably into her seat, and it is only then I realize just how nervous, not just me, but everyone is.

I start again. "I promise I am not trying to be cryptic, but you must understand that my attack has really taken its toll on me." I cannot keep the tremor out of my voice or the tears from forming in my eyes. Annie reaches over and grabs my hand in a gesture so sweet it makes the tears fall even faster. I fill my next words with the conviction I feel. "Annie, all I can tell you is this: the first time I ever saw Andrew, I trusted him. And I also thought he was the most gorgeous man I had ever seen." I give Annie a quick wink, and we both begin laughing. The admission of my last statement only drives her to want to know more.

"Tell me something else. Something about your first date or . . . Oh, about your wedding, tell us what it was like."

The blush sweeping up my cheeks is hot as I try to think of an answer. "Well," I begin slowly, "it was . . . um . . ."

"Beautiful," a voice says from behind us.

I turn around and see Andrew standing in the doorway dressed in khaki shorts and a T-shirt. I am afraid Laura and Annie see the look of pure relief on my face, but I cannot hide it. Andrew walks purposefully toward me, and I stretch out my hand for him to take. I did not realize how much I missed him until this second. The sad part is we have only been away from each other about an hour or two, but what a stressful time it has been. He takes my hand and gently kisses my palm in a gesture so tender I see his mother and sister looking away from us, trying to give us some privacy. Once again, I feel the heat in my cheeks, along with other parts of my anatomy. Andrew clears his throat as he stands behind me with his hands possessively on my shoulders.

"Oh, sister of mine," he says. "Have you been badgering my new wife?"

"Of course we have," Annie replies, her wicked grin matching his. "One minute you're a carefree, fun-loving bachelor, and the next you're a married old fart. It's only natural for us to be curious."

"I resent that. I think my carefree, fun-loving days are still ahead of me. What do you think, Elle?" I physically start when Andrew calls me by a nickname and wonder if his family noticed my surprise.

I recover quickly, saying, "That remains to be seen."

Andrew directs his attention back to his sister. "Well, I was coming to rescue Eleanor from your probing investigation, but you seem to be taking it easy on her. Do you mind if I go see my father while you finish up?" I don't want to tell him I would happily leave this moment to avoid having to answer any more questions in fear that I will screw up. Instead, I settle with "No, go ahead. I'm fine."

Andrew leans down and places a soft kiss below my left earlobe and whispers into my ear. "Just remember, when you get to the end of your rope, tie a knot and hang on." I am both confused by his phrase and turned on by his intimacy, so I barely notice as he addresses his family.

"Ladies," he says as he gracefully glides out of the room. I wonder if he knows the effect he has on the three of us. He is obviously aware of my heightened state that his brazen closeness toward me has caused. I look at Annie who is squirming in her seat and laughing with glee at her brother's cheek. Laura, on the other hand, is beyond embarrassed and even looks slightly confused; almost like she is trying to figure out the change in her son.

As the three of us return to our lunch, Annie starts questioning me again. However, this time, she focuses on the future, a topic which is just as tricky but involves a lot less lying.

"Do you have a job, Eleanor?" she begins.

"No, not at the moment." One question down, zero lies told.

"But you said you were in sales," she states, confused.

"Yes, I've worked in sales before." Okay, that might not be a complete lie.

"Do you plan on continuing in that line of work?" Laura asks.

"I'm not sure, really. I guess that is something Andrew and I need to discuss." Well done, three questions and only a half of a lie. So far, so good.

Laura nods her head in agreement. "Yes, you are probably right. Occupations can be a problem for couples. When I first met Sean, he was less than pleased that I planned to work outside the home, but I was adamant. It worked out, however, when I began working in his family business. I don't know if Andrew has told you, but we are in overseas shipping." I nod and she continues. "Well, it just so happened that my major in college was finance, so I found a job within Smith Shipping, and I have been there ever since. In fact," she says, pausing to think, "I believe we may have an opening in our sales department. One of our employees, Rebekah, just went on maternity leave. She will be gone for a few months, and we were going to have to hire someone on a temporary basis. But if you would like, we can arrange for you to take her place. With your experience in sales, it would actually be ideal."

Uh-oh. I've gotten myself in a pickle. I do not want to turn down the offer of a job from my "mother-in-law", but the fact that I know nothing about sales would end up being a huge problem for both me and Smith Shipping. I have to figure out a way to politely decline. Or do I?

"That would be ideal for us both," I say. "However, I still need to discuss it with Andrew."

"Of course, of course, dear. You two can let me know in a couple of days." Laura seems satisfied, so I believe I've dodged a bullet for now.

Annie jumps in. "Well, if you don't work, what will you do?"

I sit there for a second and wonder the same thing. "I have no idea," I answer honestly. Annie chuckles.

"I'd say these first few weeks at home you'll stay pretty busy," Laura interjects. Annie nods her agreement, and I can't help but look confused. Laura explains. "Of course, you will want to make some changes to the house. And you said something about doctor's appointments. Then you both will need to make lists of people you would like to attend your showers."

"Yes, and don't forget registering for gifts," Annie interrupts excitedly. Now I am truly confused.

"Wait, I am afraid I don't understand. Why would we change the house? And 'showers', what do you mean by that?"

"Well, your bridal showers, of course," Annie says. "I expect you will have three or four—a family shower, a friends' couple shower, your personal shower." At this, she gives me a wink. "And I assume someone at the hospital where Andrew works will want to throw you one." I just sit there, in shock I think, and shake my head. Laura must feel the need to explain.

"Bridal showers, as you know, are expected and usually appreciated." I understand her meaning. She is trying to say "You are going to have a shower whether you like I or not" without actually having to say it. I nod my understanding. "Now, since your and Andrew's courtship, engagement, and marriage was so out of the ordinary, people will be even more enthusiastic about celebrating it."

I take a sip of my drink before answering, "Um, okay. What do I need to do?"

Laura waves me off. "Annie, Nicole, and I will take care of everything. Just talk to Andrew about the couple's shower guest list and let me know by Friday. Also, you need to register. You need to pick out things for people to buy you. Most couples register for kitchen gadgets, towels, china, etc." I screw up my face at the thought of spending hours picking out things I don't really care about.

Annie laughs. "Haven't you ever bought anything for a friend's shower off a registry?"

I just shrug and answer as honestly as I can. "I've never been to a wedding shower."

"What?" Annie practically yells. "Boy, are you in for a surprise?" I can't keep the shiver from running through my body at Annie's tone. This all sounds so . . . intimidating.

"I'll tell you what," Laura begins slowly, "because your marriage has been unconventional, we can be unconventional when it comes to your showers. What if, instead of the traditional wedding shower, we have a big cookout on the beach? That way, there is not as much pressure on you, dear." I give Laura an honest-to-goodness look of relief.

"That's a great idea, Mom," Annie says. "We can even have Andrew invite people from work." I can see the wheels turning in her head as she begins to make plans. I look toward Laura and mouth a silent "thank you."

"I do have one question, though. Well, two actually," I begin, loud enough for Annie to hear. "Andrew and I already have everything we need—plenty of towels and utensils. What on earth are we supposed to register for?"

"That's a good question," Annie says. "Maybe we can tell people to just bring money." I notice the small sound of disgust coming from Laura. She quickly catches herself and looks slightly embarrassed. "I was just trying to think of something they would and could use," Annie says defensively.

"Actually, that might be a good point, Annie," Laura says, recovered from her agitation. She sits there for a second in deep thought before continuing. "It's true we do not usually stray from tradition in this family. However, if we can find a tactful way of presenting the request, I think money would be the most beneficial gift for the couple." She turns her attention back to me.

"Yes," Annie chimes in. "Maybe you will get enough to pay for a proper honeymoon." At this, my face turns the color of a ripe tomato. Annie is looking at me so intently I clear my throat.

"That would be nice" is all I can manage to say.

"It's all settled then. I'll make the arrangements. All you will have to do, my dear, is show up," Laura says.

"That sounds good to me," I sigh.

"What sounds good to you?" Andrew asks as he walks back into the room. I stand to help clear the plates as Annie explains to her brother all that we have discussed.

As we say our good-byes, Laura reminds me to ask Andrew about the job position. I catch a strange look in his eyes as he overhears our hurried conversation and make a point to ask him about it later. He opens the front door for me, and I remember another question I had for him.

"What is a personal shower?" I ask innocently. Now it is his turn to look embarrassed, and I wonder what exactly I have done to make him blush so.

"Who said something about a personal shower?" he asks quietly.

"Well, your sister was listing off all the showers that we were supposed to have, and that was one of them. Why?"

Andrew looks like he really doesn't want to answer, which makes me even more curious. "A personal shower is basically where all your girlfriends buy you lingerie to wear on your honeymoon." I don't think it is possible for him to look more mortified, so I try to ease his embarrassment.

"Seeing as how I don't have any girlfriends . . ." My voice drifts off as a face floats through my vision—a beautiful blond girl with blue eyes smiles at me from across a table. I stop walking, and Andrew does as well. I take a second and try to pin down the recollection of the face, but nothing else appears, the idea of a personal shower no longer important.

Chapter 13

Andrew

"Well, that was certainly interesting," Eleanor says as she flops down on the couch, her eyelids becoming heavy. I'm not sure if she is talking about the lunch or the flashback, but I stay quiet, hoping she will say more. After several seconds pass by, I can't hold my tongue any longer. I choose lunch, in case she is still shaken up from whatever she saw in her mind.

"It seems to me you held your own at lunch today." I hope the pride in my voice is easily detected by her. Eleanor rolls her eyes.

"I'm just lucky they didn't ask me anything too difficult. And I have to give you a little credit for saving my behind on the wedding question." I keep my back to her and make it look like I am busy with something in the kitchen. I am actually thinking about what I heard before I made my presence known, and the truth is I feel a little cocky. Eleanor's voice starts again from the couch.

"By the way, how long had you been standing in the doorway before you walked in?" Her question sounds innocent, but I know what she is really asking. I decide to string her along.

"Why," I throw over my shoulder.

"Oh, nothing really. I was just wondering what all you heard." I can tell she is nervous I heard what she said.

"You mean, did I hear you tell Annie you thought I was the most gorgeous man you had ever seen? No, I didn't hear that." I quickly look at her flaming red face which she is trying unsuccessfully to hide behind the couch. I throw her a wink, and she sinks further into the cushions.

"I just can't seem to keep my foot out of my mouth today or my eyes open," Eleanor says behind a yawn. I walk around the couch to face her.

"I'll tell you something if you promise not to hold it against me." She nods slowly, so I sit on the opposite end of the couch, lifting her feet out of the way, and place them on my lap. "You need to realize that before I even say this out loud, I know how ridiculous it is going to sound, but here it goes. When I was a little boy, I used to dream about a brown-haired angel every night. It started when I was pretty young and lasted for quite some time. Every night, without fail, the angel would appear in my dreams. At first, I thought she was there to hurt me, but I soon realized what she did . . . nothing. In my good dreams and my nightmares, the angel simply observed. She said nothing, did nothing, just watched. It was actually even creepier to think of her as a silent bystander than a force for evil. At least that way, I could assign some sort of label to her. You know, angel equals bad instead of angel equals—?" I pause and take a ragged breath. Eleanor is watching me with curious eyes.

"After a few months, I had learned how to ignore the angel. Her penetrating gaze became normal, even familiar, and I didn't think of her with any importance again. The dreams continued, but as I grew older, they became less frequent. Instead of dreaming about her every night, my dreams became less frequent; eventually they began to fade away. Even now, I rarely dream; but if I do, the brown-haired angel is present, watching me."

I look into Eleanor's eyes. "Can you guess who the brown-haired angel reminds me of?" I watch her eyes widen, and she raises her hand and runs her fingers through her own chestnut-colored hair. "The first time I saw you in Honolulu, it was like my dreams had become reality. There was the brown-haired angel of my dreams, sent to Earth in a bruised and battered body. I decided right then that I would not be like the angel of my dreams. I would not be a bystander to your hurt and pain. I decided then I wanted to give you the chance to do something I never got to—put a label on your fears."

Eleanor's response takes a few agonizing seconds. "Being called an angel is a little daunting."

"Yeah, well, I did warn you of our immediate departure into crazy town," I say with a weak laugh.

"I actually feel sorry for you," she admits. "I cannot imagine your disappointment when you found out your angel is even more bruised and battered than you thought. I may be mysterious, Andrew, but unfortunately, not in the way you had hoped, huh?" The emotions crossing Eleanor's face are difficult to read: anger, disgust, sadness. I feel the need to salvage the remaining pieces of sanity the two of us have.

"You're right. You are not what I expected my angel incarnate to be. But I have a feeling you will continue to defy labels."

When Eleanor wakes up from her nap, I am on the phone checking on the status of my patients. She heads to the kitchen table and grabs an apple from the bowl of fruit. I watch her take a bite and then fall to the floor instantly, her unconscious head barely missing the countertop.

****

Eleanor

The breeze on my bare legs feels good as I swing my feet back and forth. Mom said it was too hot to be outside today, but it feels like heaven in the shade. I feel the rough bark of the tree under my fingers and look up into the branches. If I climb to the top, I could see the creek. I look back down at my dangling feet and the ground below. I've always liked climbing trees, but getting back down is a different story.

"Sweetie," I hear my mother calling, "time for lunch." My stomach growls on cue, so I bite the bullet and jump straight to the ground. Pain wracks my body as my ankle hits the grass at the wrong angle. I cry out, praying my mom hears me.

****

Andrew

The scream coming out of Eleanor's mouth is unlike any I have heard from her before. It is high-pitched, and where her night-terror screams are full of fear, this one is full of pain. Her eyes are closed tight, and sweat glistens on her upper lip.

"Eleanor, Eleanor!" I repeatedly yell her name. Shaking her slightly causes her to focus her now-wide eyes on my face. Her scream cuts off, and she whispers, "Oh, Andrew." Her arms clamp around my waist, and I rub my hands up and down her back soothingly. After a couple of minutes, she pulls away from me, and I help her to her feet.

"Are you okay?" I ask.

She nods slowly. "I think so. I had another flashback when I bit into the apple." Eleanor tells me all about it, stopping occasionally to wipe her tears from her eyes.

"That's twice now you have remembered something about your mother." She nods her agreement.

"It feels so real. I could smell the leaves, the bark. I could hear the birds chirping. I heard my mother call me. I heard her voice." Silent tears fall down her cheeks. She puffs out an irritated breath. "I hate this! Will it always be like this? I hate feeling so weak and vulnerable. When am I going to remember?" Eleanor looks desperately at me, waiting for answers I cannot give her.

"You have had a busy couple of days, both mentally and physically. You should probably rest tomorrow. I can reschedule your doctor's appointment."

She sighs before responding. "I'm glad you brought that up because there are a few things I would like to talk to you about." I must have a worried look on my face as I help her walk to the couch because she quickly continues. "Don't look so nervous. They are more like discussion topics, if that makes you feel any better." It doesn't, not really, but I do not want her to know I cannot focus on anything but her epic mood swings. It worries me that she can be so calm and sane one minute, and the next, she is screaming in terror; and still the next minute, she is back to her old self. But I do not want to bring up my concerns right now.

"Sure, okay. What do you want to discuss?" Eleanor sits up straighter, which gives me the feeling I might have been misled when she told me not to worry.

"I hesitate to even bring up the first topic because I don't want you to think I am ungrateful." She quiets and starts twirling her thumbs, a habit I have never seen her do.

"Eleanor, look, you are really starting to freak me out. Just say what is on your mind because I guarantee it's not as bad as I am imagining right now." *Especially after that last episode.*

She looks up quickly. "I'm sorry. I don't mean to worry you. It's just that, well, um . . . I would like to go shopping."

What? "That's what this is all about . . . shopping?" I laugh out loud, feeling myself relax immediately. I had imagined all sorts of horrible scenarios in the past thirty seconds and not a single one of them had anything to do with shopping. As my laughter dies down, I notice the look on Eleanor's face. She evidently didn't think it was that funny.

"Yes, shopping," she says seriously.

"I'm sorry. It's just that I was . . . oh, never mind." The look on her face is not one open to explanations from me, the laughing lunatic.

"It's not so much that I want to go shopping as it is a have-to kind of thing," she says.

"What's wrong with the clothes Annie let you borrow?" I ask.

"Nothing is wrong with them. They are beautiful, and I am more than grateful to her for letting me borrow them. It's just that they are a little snug." My eyes take in her relaxed form. She quickly covers her midsection with her arms.

"I think you look fine," I say honestly.

Eleanor blows out a huff. "Well, I don't feel fine. I can already tell the clothes are tighter today than they were Sunday. There is no doubt I'm going to gain back some of the weight I lost while I was unconscious."

"You're right about that. Okay, we can go shopping tomorrow if you want. Would you like me to go with you, or would you rather take Annie or maybe even Nicole?" She thinks about it quickly and then answers.

"It would be nice to have a woman's opinion, but I just don't feel comfortable enough to ask your sister or sister-in-law. You don't care to go with me, do you?"

"Not at all. I grew up with two sisters, practically three if you count Nicole, which I do. I have done my fair share of sitting in dressing rooms." Eleanor gives me an apologetic look. "I can take a book or something." I receive raised eyebrows with my last comment.

"Do you read often?" Eleanor asks.

"No, never, but I might have to start." My joke hit the mark, and she lightly punches my shoulder. "Why were you so nervous about asking me to take you shopping?"

"I guess it was because I knew I didn't have any money, and if we went shopping, you would have to buy everything. I am already in your debt so much . . ." I stop her with a raised hand.

"Eleanor, I am not usually a boastful man, but I feel like we need to get this conversation out of the way now before things progress in any manner. Because of several factors, my age, my occupation, and my lack of costly hobbies, I have quite a bit of money put back. I feel ashamed to even have this conversation, but I want you to understand that although I am not wealthy by any means, I have enough money to take you shopping along with anything else you might want or need." It's official—I feel like a scumbag. I've never had to explain my financial situation to anyone, and it was just as unpleasant as I thought it would be. I look at Eleanor and shrug my shoulders.

"Oh, okay." Her lack of response makes me feel just as uncomfortable as she looks. "So what you're saying is that you're filthy, stinking rich?"

"No, god, not at all. I just meant—" I am interrupted by her laughter, and for once, I feel my own face heating up. "Ha, ha, I'm so glad you think this is funny," I say to her. "I was really worried about having this conversation with you." Eleanor is actually slapping her knee with hysterics.

"You should have seen your face," she says between snorts. I roll my eyes, not thinking it was that funny. Now I know how she felt earlier. "I'm sorry. I guess it's just nice to realize you struggle talking to me about things too." We both smile at each other for a few seconds, letting the tension fizzle away.

"What else did you want to discuss?" I ask, less apprehensive than the last time.

"I'm sure you heard your mother say something about me working at Smith Shipping." The smile quickly fades from my face. Eleanor notices but continues. "I know the whole story about me being in sales is a total load of bull, but it got me thinking about what I could do, you know, while we figure things out." I am entirely unprepared to have this conversation with Eleanor right now, but I guess it's as good as a time as any.

"Eleanor, I don't think that is a good idea," I say plainly.

"What's not a good idea? Me working at Smith Shipping or me doing anything at all?"

"Both for now. Have you given this some serious thought?" I know I sound like an adult scolding a child, but I cannot help it. "How did you think you would perform the job when you know nothing about it?"

"Well," she says defensively, "I figured I would just wing it." She is so completely serious in her answer that I start laughing again. "What?" she demands. "I could do it, you know. Like you said earlier, I've been doing a pretty good job of holding my own with your family these past three days. The longer I am there, the more I could learn."

"Please," I say through sobs, "you cannot possible be thinking of doing this. What happens when you get an assignment you don't know anything about or you have to make a sales call?"

She shrugs. "I'll just Google it." This revelation sends me into complete hysterics. "Would you please stop laughing," Eleanor screams. I am taken aback by her forcefulness and realize I have hit some sort of nerve with her. "You have no idea what I am capable of—I can do anything I want to, anything I put my mind to. How dare you think you can tell me what not to do? You're not my boss. You don't even know who I am!" She jumps up off the couch and runs into her room, slamming the door behind her.

The hours tick by. I feel like an epic asshole. Every time Eleanor opens up to me, I completely screw it up. First, not listening to her plea for help Sunday night and then today, laughing like an idiot. I have been concerned with getting through each day, one at a time, whereas she has been looking toward the future since day one. No matter how bad I feel, though, I will never be comfortable with the idea of her working for my family, for several reasons. And today's little chat with my father only secured that opinion.

While the women were eating lunch, I joined my father in his office, a place he has spent more time in than any other. I was just a little guy when he moved his work office to our house only after my mother insisted that if he was going to work all the time, he might as well be in the same vicinity as his children; that way, we could at least see him as we were running through the house. The office used to fill me with a sense of amazement, seeing the numerous files piled on top of each other and all the shiny recognition plaques hanging on the walls from various city and state authorities for things like: Most Environmentally Friendly, Highest Quality of Safety, and Beautification Award. Now I just feel cramped. Honestly, I don't know how my father and brother get any work done in the mess.

When I reached the door, I noticed my father was on the phone, but he motioned me inside, and I plopped onto the same old leather chair that has been there as long as I can remember. The warm brown leather is comforting, and I relished the feeling.

As I listened to his voice, I thought back to the feeling of the soft skin of Eleanor's neck on my lips just moments before. Not an entirely safe topic to have on your mind when your father is sitting just a few feet away. I could feel my khaki shorts getting uncomfortable, so I quickly hopped up and paced around the room, my father giving me a questioning look the entire time. By the time he reached the end of his phone call with a "yes, sir, I look forward to meeting you as well, and I hope we will be able to do business together", I had calmed my boiling blood. My father hung up the phone and looked at me.

"Son, are you having trouble keeping that beautiful wife of yours off your mind?" His grin is mischievous, and I had the sudden desire to punch it off his face. I really need to get my head straightened out.

"I don't even want to know how you do that—read people's minds and stuff, but I really wish you would stop," I said, a little more forceful than I meant to.

"Son, I have been married for more years than you have been alive. If you think I don't know when a woman is possessing a man's mind, then you are sorely mistaken. How is the lunch going in there?" he asked as he shuffled some papers on his desk.

I shrugged my shoulders. "Fine, I guess. When I dropped in, they were talking about wedding stuff, which I hastily removed myself from." He smiled.

"Good man. I'm sure they are having a pleasant time without us interfering." I could tell he was distracted with trying to find something on his desk, so I offered my assistance.

"What exactly are you looking for, Dad?" I made my way around the desk so I could have a better view of the chaos.

"Your brother wrote down a name of a new client while we were out of town, and now I can't seem to find it anywhere. I just got off the phone with the man, and I need to write down the date and time of our meeting." As we both picked up stacks of papers of every size and moved things around, I caught a small Post-it note out of the corner of my eye scribbled in my brother's chicken-scratch handwriting with a name I have only recently become familiar with.

My blood ran cold as I held up the piece of paper. "Is this the one you were looking for?" I asked in a shaky voice.

"By golly, you found it." My father's voice seemed so far away. It took all my strength to hand over the note with Joshua's handwriting: Dan Childs, CEO of MicroCorp.

Thinking back now, I realize it wouldn't have mattered if I crumpled the paper and threw it into the wastebasket. The damage was already done. My father had talked to the man himself on the phone, made plans to meet with him, and nothing I could have done would have made a difference. That is one of the reasons I have for keeping Eleanor away from Smith Shipping—not the only reason but definitely one of the biggest. I'm not sure if the appearance of Dan Childs on my father's to-do list is just a coincidence or if there is any connection at all with Eleanor and her attack. But because I don't know those things, I will do everything I can to keep the two separate.

There is no question whatsoever that I handled the whole conversation wrong earlier. I was in shock. Eleanor has *always* surprised me, since the moment I laid eyes on her. Why did I think once she was conscious, it would be any different? I knew she was strong willed that first night in my hotel room, but her strength keeps surprising me. She has handled this whole situation better than I have, really, and I admire her for it. She has taken every obstacle and overcome it like it has been nothing. And the fact that she is already making plans for the future both amazes me and scares me to death. What if her plans don't include me? I'm not sure I could handle that.

I tried knocking on her door and apologizing for the first forty-five minutes. That's when I realized how badly I screwed up. I got in my car and drove to town, stopping at the first florist shop I came to and bought a dozen of roses. Even making the decision on what color of roses to get was more difficult than I thought it would be. Red roses ooze romance, which is something Eleanor and I do not have. Yellow roses symbolize friendship, something I hope the two of us share or at least will share in the future. But I wanted something more, something to express my true feelings. The sales clerk was more than helpful with explaining different flowers and their meanings, and in the end, I think I made the right choice.

As I drive home, I say a silent prayer that my offer of truce will be accepted. What if I get home and she is gone? What will I do then? The thought sickens me, and I know exactly what I would do. I would get back into my car and drive until I found her. I am not only worried about her physical and mental stability, which are at the top of my priorities list. But I am also worried about myself—what I would do without her, and how I would move on.

My fears are put to rest as I open the front door and see Eleanor sitting on the couch watching television. When she looks up and sees the bouquet of white roses in my hand, her mouth drops open, giving me a wonderful feeling in the pit of my stomach.

"Are those for me?" she asks quietly.

I nod. "Yes, they are. I wanted to apologize for being such a huge idiot earlier."

"They are beautiful," she says as she stands up and makes her way toward me. I hand the flowers to her and watch as she delicately sniffs each of the twelve roses, her eyes closed in pleasure of the aroma. At last, she looks back to me. "Thank you so much." I see her eyes beginning to water. I don't think I can stand to see her cry.

"I picked white roses for a certain reason," I explain hastily.

"Oh, really," she says. "I didn't know they had a specific meaning."

"Oh, yes. I am an expert now in case you ever need rose color-picking advice."

"I'll be sure to remember that," she says with a tight laugh. I continue, hoping to keep the conversation flowing.

"The white rose represents humility, purity, and innocence." Eleanor looks a bit confused, but I continue. "It also symbolizes truth and reverence. It sends a message of loyalty, basically saying, 'I am worthy of you.'" Still unsure if Eleanor grasps my meaning, I explain. "Eleanor, since you have come into my life, I have been a fool in so many ways. And in truth, these roses are more for me than they are for you. They remind me to *always* be truthful to you, but even more, they remind me to *always* keep striving to be worthy of you. Because you, my dear, are worth being worthy of." Her answering smile is breathtaking, and I cannot keep my hand from cradling her face.

"Well, I feel like a total loser," she says after a minute. "I just wrote you an 'I'm sorry' note." She laughs, and I join her.

"I promise to be on my best behavior from now on. I promise to listen to your opinions and your feelings when we discuss anything. I want you to trust me with your thoughts, and I give you permission to punch me in the face if I ever act like a horse's ass again."

"Agreed," she says with a smile. "Do you have a vase somewhere for the flowers?"

"Um, I don't guess I thought of everything," I admit.

"That's okay. I'm sure I can find something that will work."

In the end, we use a plastic pitcher that usually houses grape Kool-Aid when my nieces and nephews come over. It doesn't seem to bother Eleanor. She continues to look at them sitting on the kitchen table and smile, her reaction being worth every penny I spent. As we eat supper, we talk about our day, both of us avoiding the topic of her working at Smith Shipping.

"How was your father today?" she asks before taking a sip of Diet Dr. Pepper. I'm not prepared to discuss the whole Dan Childs thing yet, so I go back on my word from before to always be honest and simply omit some information.

"He was fine. Busy, you know. When he and my mother are out of town, Joshua looks over things, and my father always has a hard time figuring out what my brother has screwed up while he was gone."

"I'm sure it's difficult to be in business with your family. Is that why you chose a different profession altogether?" Her question is not a hard one or a really invasive one, but it is not something I want to get into at the moment.

"That, among other reasons," I say simply. She seems to sense that I do not want to talk about it and continues on eating her cheese lasagna.

"What about you?" I ask. "How was lunch with my mother and sister, really?"

"It was fine, good even. Your mother is very accommodating and friendly. She made me feel special and valued. Your sister is a trip to be around, very funny and honest, which I admire. She was not afraid to ask me anything. There were a few times I was afraid I would get tripped up, one of them being the wedding question." She puts her fork down. "That reminds me," she continues, "I meant to ask you something."

"Shoot," I say around a big bite.

"That quote you whispered in my ear at lunch. What did you mean?"

"Oh, that. I know how overbearing my family can be, so I thought you might need a little encouragement to hang in there. I believe it came from one of our past presidents, FDR maybe." Eleanor considers this for a second and seems satisfied.

"Okay, one more thing," she says anxiously. I nod my head for her to continue. "I like my nickname." I look up from my food to see her face starting to pink.

"I hope you didn't mind it. It just slipped out, seemed to fit, so I went with it." For some reason, I feel embarrassed, like I have been caught doing something I'm not supposed to do.

"No, really," she says. "I like it." Her genuine smile relieves my nerves.

"Well, then, if you like it, Elle you shall be." She smiles again, a big bright smile that could light up a dark room, not to mention the blood in my veins.

The rest of the night is peaceful. After dinner, we clear the dishes and decide to take a stroll outside. The air is the perfect crisp of spring, and I feel the suffocating closeness of the house fall off like a lead jacket. As we walk around my parents' property, we talk more about our day, my family, and the possibility of her returned memories. I feel myself tensing whenever she explains her desire to discover the truth about her attackers and her past, but I stay silent, not wanting my opinions or feelings to muddy up the already cloudy waters of our situation.

Before she closes her bedroom door, I cannot help but ask, "Do you want to talk about the flashback you had earlier?"

She simply answers, "Not tonight." So I let it slide.

Chapter 14

Eleanor

As Wednesday dawns bright and sunny, I feel a sense of anticipation unlike anything I have felt since waking up Saturday morning. Gone are the fears of uncertainty and insecurity. They are replaced by nervous excitement and, dare I say it, hope. Today is going to be a good day, I tell myself as I shower. Today, I get to go shopping.

Unfortunately, our first stop is not the closest clothing store but a doctor's appointment. I dread this one, especially because of the pain I know will accompany my visit. Andrew insisted that I see a phlebotomist because of the nature of my attack. I insisted he stay with me the entire time.

After the first prick of the needle, I'm not sure how I ever got enough guts to get a tattoo. I did finally realize the anticipation was worse than the actual needle, and once the torture was complete, I felt like a new woman.

On our drive to the mall, Andrew explained again it would take a week or so to receive all the test results. I did not want to mention to him the depth of my fear of having some sort of rare, deadly, blood-borne disease. Not just for my sake but for his as well—I could tell he was worried too.

As we pull into the parking lot, I feel a sense of trepidation. I guess all women feel this way before trying on clothing, the chance of nothing fitting or not finding anything that looks good, or when you do find something you like, it being out of your price range, etc. I'm glad, at least, the last scenario does not apply to me. When Andrew broached the subject of money last night, I was certain I had never seen him look so uncomfortable, which is why I tried to play it off as smoothly as I could. However, I have to admit I felt relieved in a way. I know these doctor's appointments and tests he has been making for me are not cheap, and when I explained my hesitation for asking to go shopping, I didn't lie. In the back of my mind, the amount of not only money but also time, energy, and investment has been weighing heavy. I make a vow to repay Andrew somehow when all this is over, but I know I will never be able to offer him the value of saving my life.

I open the car door with sweaty palms and watch as Andrew grabs an umbrella from the backseat of his Outback. The sky has turned heavy and gray and looks like it's about to burst. A crack of thunder catches me off guard, and I jump an inch off the ground. The hairs on my arm stand at attention, and I feel a cold sweat break out on my forehead. I try to shake off the effect of the weather before Andrew notices the change in my demeanor.

"We better make a run for it," he calls over another boom from the sky. My frozen limbs are rooted to the spot, and it's only when Andrew walks around the car and grabs my hand that I am able to follow along after his sprinting form. By the time we make it to the doors, the rain has begun, and we slide through the revolving door, sharing one of the cubbies. I trip over his feet, falling into the foyer of the department floor, and Andrew catches me at the last minute. As we both laugh at our entanglement, he pulls me close for a second to help steady my clumsy feet, and I once again note the strength in his touch.

"Are you okay?" he asks in a shaky voice, either from the laughter or our closeness, I'm not sure. Before I can answer, another crack of thunder pierces the air, and I am back to feeling frozen again. Unlike last time, I am unable to hide my reaction to the noise. With his hands on my upper arms, Andrew feels my tension.

"Hey," he says, "what's up?" I cannot bring myself to answer him but allow my eyes to search his for added strength. His grip on my arms lightens as he begins slowly rubbing up and down my biceps.

"It's okay," he says softly, out of the earshot of the other patrons. "We're safe now. It's just a thunderstorm. We are not in danger now that we are inside." I give him a tight smile and step away from him tender touch. "Now, let's go spend a lot of my money," he jokes. Andrew grabs my hand again and pulls me toward the women's section. As we make our way around the jewelry and perfume counters, I can't help but notice once again how the thunder outside sounds just like the shot of a gun.

"Well, what do you think?" We have been in a total of five stores in the last two hours, and I am beginning to get a little tired. Andrew, on the other hand, has been a trooper. Not once has he complained or whined about the amount of time and money we have spent in this mall. Not even when he had to take a load of shopping bags to the car in the pouring rain because we couldn't possibly carry any more.

I step out of the dressing room in what seems like my one hundredth outfit to see his attentive face taking me in. At first, it was a little awkward, having Andrew appraise me like a piece of cattle at auction, but I quickly dismissed the feminist thought and began appreciating his opinions. It made it a lot easier to do so when I realized his opinions were the same as mine. This store specializes in dresses, and it was a last-minute decision on my part to even come in here.

I remembered the wedding shower/party that Andrew's mother and sister are throwing us and decided a dress would probably be more appropriate than the mostly casual clothes I had bought so far. This dress is my favorite—not too formal, form fitting, and a little flirty with white lace over a printed sheath of pink roses. Andrew's eyes light up immediately, and his posture changes from "I'm getting over this quick" to "Hello!" I feel a shallow sense of pride and decide that no matter what his voice says, his body is saying, "Hell, yes."

"Well," I ask with a satisfied smile, "what you think?"

"It looks to me like you know what I think." He smiles crookedly. "You're absolutely stunning, Elle."

"I really like it too."

"Then it's a done deal. Hang it back up, and I'll go pay for it." I sashay back toward the dressing room and throw a quick wink over my shoulder at him.

"You wicked thing." He laughs.

I shut the door, rather pleased with myself for having such cheek when the lights suddenly go out. It is pitch-black in the small dressing room, and I instantly feel a fear rising from my belly. My feet are stuck, frozen once again in panic. I hear the storm crashing outside, and my mind is thrown back to a dark room, a cold floor, and I feel a pressure on my wrists. Something small and cold is being held against my head, and I can't take it anymore.

My scream pierces the dress shop. I fall to my knees, placing my hands over my ears to keep out the sound of the pounding noise and my own panic. I hear Andrew's muffled voice but cannot find the strength to do anything about it.

"Elle, it's okay. The power just went out. Elle, let me in."

He must be banging on my door because the noise is still there. Who is banging? I'm trying to picture the face of my savior, but I'm having a hard time seeing anything. I don't have to close my eyes in the darkness to allow this flashback to haunt me. The pitch-black dressing room is theater enough for my nightmares. Shadows slink across a brown concrete wall. Moisture in the air is making my nose run, and I cannot stop coughing.

I struggle to sit up, to free my bound hands. I feel someone grab at my feet, and I kick them off. My body is being dragged across the floor, and I scream for help. With my eyes now shut tight, I feel hands on my waist holding me down. I fling my body from side to side, trying to wrestle away from the force that is restraining me.

Through the sounds of my screams and the pounding of fists, I hear a voice calling my name. I reach out with what small piece of my sanity I still have left and grab a hold of that sound. It's like being thrown a lifejacket in stormy seas. Just out of my reach, I kick and flail about, doing my best to hold on to the voice. I pray to God that it's not just in my head, and I am rewarded with a bright light.

"Eleanor, it's me. You are okay. You're safe. Just breathe." I feel strong hands combing through my hair and realize this is not an action of aggression but one of love. I open my eyes to a partially lit dress shop and break into heavy sobs. I can hear a woman's voice in the background, asking, "Sir, is everything all right? Do I need to call the police?" Andrew's voice is tight but calm.

"No, everything is okay. She is fine now." He is rocking me like I am a small child, my body gathered onto his lap in a tight ball. I try to stifle the sobs and raise my face to his.

"Oh, Andrew. I'm so sorry. I don't know what happened . . ."

He interrupts me. "Hush, now. Everything's fine. You don't need to apologize." He continues to rock me, and I let him. Our bodies being this close feels so good, so comforting I do not have the heart to pull away.

"When the lights went out, I just freaked. It was awful, totally awful. I don't want to ever feel like that again—helpless and scared and out of control. I don't ever want to feel like that again."

"Shush. I know, Elle, I understand. But it's over now. You're okay."

I look at him questioningly. "What do you mean you understand?"

"It's a long story, but you'll just have to trust me on this, okay?" It's his turn to sound fierce. With conviction dripping off of every word, I decide to do just that. Andrew continues to rock me back and forth while I steal a glance at the dressing room. The door is still shut, and I'm guessing Andrew had to pull me out from the bottom because he could not get through the locked door. That must have been the dragging sensation and the feeling of grasping hands that terrified me so much. *Geez, I am really messed up.*

During the past few days, I have been so preoccupied with keeping up the impression I am Andrew's new bride; it has been somewhat easy to forget why I am in this mess to begin with. However, when my flashbacks occur, I lose my grip with reality. The scary thing is not knowing if I will ever regain it.

I gently pull myself off Andrew's lap, standing with weak knees. I turn around and see the sales clerk giving me a worried look. I smile at her, hoping I haven't scared her too much. She looks away quickly and begins to replace clothes on one of the circular racks. I start to feel self-conscious and ask Andrew if we can leave.

"You need to get that dress out of the changing room," he says.

"Don't worry about it," I tell him. "Let's just leave."

"Are you sure?" I nod my head and walk out of the store, not able to bear the strange stares of the girl behind the counter any longer.

Chapter 15

Andrew

When I opened the front door of my house in the dead of night over three weeks ago, I realized it would be the last time, at least for a while, I could call it my bachelor pad. So far in my adult life, I had enjoyed being a bachelor. My hours at the hospital are so erratic and sometimes long I had often felt glad there was no one home waiting for me—I would pity them for the lack of attention and affection I could give. I enjoy doing what I want when I want, and being a bachelor is the ultimate lifestyle. I turned to look toward the waiting car that held my fake, unconscious wife and decided to take one more stroll around the house to enjoy the solitude.

The furniture is old and sparse but nice and clean. For a couple of minutes, I walked into each room tidying up and rearranging. Eleanor was clearly going to need the master bedroom, even though she had no clothes or personal belongings, so I hastily changed the sheets and empty out the drawers, throwing all my clothes and other items into the spare room/office. I quickly wiped down the bathroom sink and mirror, clean the toilet and tub, and take out what little garbage I had.

The weird thing is I felt like I was having a girl over for the first time. That wouldn't be happening for quite some time. In truth, I was not that disappointed. I haven't been much of a dater—in the past year, I had only been out with one girl, and I could tell within the first five minutes there would not be a second date. Like some kids in high school, I had a serious girlfriend who stuck with me a little while after graduation. But when I told her I was thinking of going into the military after I graduated, she split faster than I could say "Wait for me."

Looking back, I can't blame her. The military was at a very scary time then, right after the 9/11 attack, and she couldn't see herself waiting up each night for the news to scroll my name across the bottom of the screen. As heartbroken as I was, I entered boot camp and never looked back. The last I heard, she was married with two children and moved to another county.

I wonder what Eleanor would think of me going into the military.

As I had been doing of late, I considered Eleanor, or who she was before the attack. I have a pretty good picture in my mind of what she would be like. There are only a few characteristics I had added or taken away, but most of them had remained the same since I found her:

- Tough – she had to be to survive the extent of her injuries
- Beautiful – no question, without a doubt
- Athletic – her muscles and lean body are testament to that
- Kind – her brown eyes have wrinkles in the corners from laughing
- Brave – the bruises on her knuckles and skin underneath her fingernails paint the picture of someone who fought back

As I headed back out to the car to carry Eleanor in, I glanced over my shoulder one last time at my bachelor pad and realized this is just one of the many ways my life would change for a woman I now call my bride.

I glance at Eleanor in the passenger's seat and notice a strange look on her face. It's a mixture of pain, anger, confusion, and disgust. I want to reach over and grab her hand in a gesture of sympathy, but I'm pretty sure the touch would be unwelcome and unwanted. I turn my eyes back to the road as I struggle to find words to comfort her instead.

"I hate your day ended on such a low note. I could tell you were enjoying yourself. At least, I thought you were." I see her turn her head quickly in my direction and then back to the road.

"I had a great time, Andrew. Thank you for taking me." Her voice is pleasant but reserved, so I decide to let the conversation end there. I pull into a fast-food restaurant and order from the drive-thru for both of us, not even asking Eleanor what she would like. I realize it will be a miracle if she eats anything tonight.

Her latest flashback has been the worst so far, and I wonder how many more she can handle mentally, not to mention physically. I shudder to think about what would have happened tonight if I had not been in the store with her when the power went out. What if it had taken longer to come back on? I remember the sound of her terrifying scream from the dressing room, and thank God that I brought in my cell phone from the car. I used its light to stumble my way through the maze of doors, finding hers locked and reaching past her prone, flailing form to grab her waist and drag her out.

When we reach the house, Eleanor tells me she is going to bed. I bid her a goodnight and watch as she shuts the door behind her. I sit on the couch to eat my supper, wondering if her neurology appointment on Friday will give us any indication about Eleanor's diagnosis, her symptoms, anything really that will shed some light on what we can expect. The thought of what will happen when and if her memory returns creeps into my head, and I push it back out. I don't have the guts to explore that train of thought tonight.

I finish with my burger and fries and surf through the channels with the volume low. After about thirty minutes, I hear Eleanor's door open. She is standing just outside her room, dressed in some of the pajamas we bought earlier in the day—flannel pants and a pink tank top. She looks beautiful.

"Do I need to get you anything, Elle?"

She seems to hesitate before answering. "I can't seem to get to sleep. I'm so tired, but I . . . I was wondering if you would mind lying with me for a while. You know, just to help calm my nerves. You don't have to if you don't want to, of course."

I'm on my feet before she even stops talking, and I curse myself for appearing too eager. Thankfully, Eleanor doesn't seem to notice. She turns back to the bedroom and waits for me to enter the room. As I do, she closes the door behind me and then makes her way to the bed, climbing in slowly and somewhat timidly. I hesitate shedding my blue jeans but decide to stay above the covers for propriety's sake. I unbutton my Oxford and drop it on the floor, leaving on my undershirt, and slide onto the bed next to Eleanor. I can tell that she is nervous because of the way she is lying—flat on her back with the covers pulled up to her chin. I mirror her stiff position but choose to fold my hands behind my head. Her breathing is slow and steady. I want to ease her worries about our situation; however, I struggle finding the right words.

"Elle, you don't have to worry about anything. Just try to get some sleep, okay? If it makes you feel any better, this is not the first time we have shared a bed." I am met with silence, and I wonder if I was wrong about her being asleep. After an agonizing minute, she answers.

"Honestly, I'm not sure if that makes me feel any better or not because I'm pretty sure I was unconscious when that happened." I look over to her quickly and find that she is smiling at me.

"Well, after sleeping on a hotel floor for nine days, my back couldn't take it any longer. To put your mind at ease, I kept most of my clothes on then too." I was expecting a small chuckle from Elle's side of the bed,

Instead, I hear sobs and turn to face her. She is on her left side, looking at me with tears running down her face. Her sudden mood swing is yet another reminder of the trauma she has endured. I reach up to wipe the tears away with my fingertips.

"Please tell me what's wrong, Elle. I want so badly to help you."

She shakes her head slowly and answers. "I'm just scared, Andrew."

I gather her into my arms like I did in the dress store. "You don't need to be scared tonight, Elle. I'll make sure you're safe."

As her sobs subside, I hear her whisper, "Once again, my savior." And I find myself smiling as we drift off to sleep.

Phone Conversation No. 3

Thursday, 8:30 p.m.

"Yes, sir. She has been to several doctor's appointments this week, and each has given her a clean bill of health. She goes to the neurologist tomorrow. Yes, I will be sure to call you when I hear the results of the tests."

"She has been civil enough to me."

"No, sir. As far as I know, she has had no memories of what happened to her."

"Sir, what did happen?"

"I know, I know. Yes, sir. I'm sorry, sir. I know it's none of my business. I was just wondering. Yes, sir. I will stick to my job."

"No, sir. I have not had a change of heart. Absolutely, I will call you with any news."

Chapter 16

Eleanor

After my last flashback on Wednesday, Andrew and I decided to rest on Thursday. We did a few things around the house, and I hanged all my new clothes up in the bedroom closet. Looking back, I regret not buying the white dress from the last store, but I could not bear to go back into the dressing room.

For lunch, we packed a basket full of snacks and drove down to the beach. The air was still a little cool, but it was a bright, sunny day. We spent most of our time walking up and down the sand. I found the water extremely comforting. The steady back and forth of the waves felt like a constant to me—something that has been there for millions of years, something that will be there for millions more. Something dependable, reliable. But at the same time, ever-changing; knowing this beach will never be the same as it was that moment; those grains of sand will move on from there and deposit somewhere else. It's a perfect metaphor for my life—I am ever changing, learning more about myself each day, each minute, really. But in the end, I will always be myself—strong, in mind, body, and spirit.

It is now Friday night, and after this morning's diagnosis, I'm not sure if I can handle any more stress. My mind drifts in and out as Andrew talks to his parents.

"Mom, I know you are excited about planning our reception," Andrew says. "But I hate to admit that Eleanor and I will be going out of town soon." This is news to me, but something tells me he has been planning this trip all day. "Since we never really got a honeymoon, I thought I should take some more time off work and take advantage of my newlywed status." At this, he wiggles his eyebrows for the sake of his parents. I feel the redness in my cheeks again.

"Look at that," Sean says, "she really does embarrass easy."

"I think that is a great idea, Andrew, since your short marriage has been plagued with such tragedy." With this, Laura takes my hand in hers, and I realize this is the first time I have felt any sort of motherly affection, and I relish it.

Yes, that sounds like a good idea," comments Sean. "Where are you planning on going? Fiji, Barbados?" I look at Andrew, eager to hear the answer to his question.

"I thought we would go to Atlanta." I can tell by the looks on his parents' faces they think he is joking; however, I know he is not. All I can hear, as they try to discover his reasoning behind such a strange honeymoon destination, are the doctor's words in my mind: "Don't stick to a routine. Go different places, do different things, try different foods. The more experiences you have, the more likely you will hit on something that is familiar." Andrew is trying to give me answers to my questions. Even though he knows he might get hurt, he *will* get hurt when we discover the truth.

After my doctor's appointment today and hours of going through machines, being asked question after question about things I cannot possibly remember, my head is hurting, and I just want to lie down. Andrew sits down next to me with a sandwich in one hand and the remote control to the TV in the other. He turns on the power, and the screen lights up.

When the doctor explained my condition to me, I felt like I was falling. "You have hysterical (fugue) amnesia. It is a very rare phenomenon in which patients forget not only their past but also their very identity. A person, like you, could wake up and suddenly not have any sense at all of who he is. This type of amnesia is usually triggered by an event that the person's mind is unable to cope with properly. In most cases, the memory either slowly or suddenly comes back within a few days. The bad news is that there is no guaranteeing when your memory will return. As you have been able to figure out on your own, your short-term memory has not been affected, that is why you can remember what you had for lunch today and even remember the first thing that happened when you woke up on Saturday."

He gives Andrew a look, like he is searching for confirmation. When I see Andrew close his eyes and nod his head, I prepare for the worst, which is what I get. "The very bad news is that the memory of the shocking event itself may never come back completely. However, knowing what happened to you that might be a good thing. I feel it is important for you to know all the facts."

The ride home was unbearable until Andrew grabbed my hand. That is when the thought crossed my mind: *This might be all I will ever have. This half-in and half-out feeling of being between lives might be the only life I will know.* I take some comfort in knowing I could be okay with that prospect, especially if I have Andrew there with me.

As I sit on the couch, not really watching TV, I remember something the doctor told me. "I know you must be discouraged, but there are a few things you can do to try and jog your memory. First, keep a notebook of all you remember. Even if you think is it inconsequential, write it down."

At that moment, Andrew comes into the room and hands me a notebook. Written across the front in magic marker are the words "Memory Journal." I was so lost in my own thoughts I didn't even realize he had left.

Phone Conversation No. 4

Saturday, 8:30 a.m.

"Sir, there's been a recent development, and I'm not sure how it's going to affect things. At her neurology appointment yesterday, they informed her that her memory loss seems to be caused by trauma."

"Yes, I know that's what you were thinking, but now your suspicions have been confirmed."

"What does that mean for me?"

"No, sir. I told you, I have not had a change of heart. I'm just wondering how long they intend to keep this up."

"I'm not sure what their plan is, but knowing Dr. Smith, he'll be on top of things."

"Yes, I will talk to you soon."

Chapter 17

Eleanor

As the departure day of our trip gets closer, I find myself getting excited. I might get some answers about who I am. Even though I know this "Trip around the World", as we are now calling it, might turn out to be a gigantic waste of time, I have high hopes that something we encounter will spark a buried memory. I've let Andrew make all the arrangements because I can sense that is right up his alley. I just sit and listen to his detailed plans: where we are going to stay, what we are going to do, departure times, and arrival times. As I understand it, we will be doing all the touristy things, which sounds great to me since it will be like my first time going on a vacation. I can't help but think: At least there's a positive side to memory loss!

I am also excited that Andrew and I will get to be alone together. I am curious to see how he acts away from his family. Not that they aren't growing on me, but I am beginning to see what he meant by the "compound" comment. Since last Monday night and my reconciling with Sean and Laura, every member of the family has stopped by to meet me individually. With around seventy-five people living on the compound, Andrew and I have barely been alone, and I am eager to see his true personality.

Besides our constant stream of visitors and Andrew's obsessive planning, he has given me a job of sorts. Every morning, my alarm clock is set, and I find a list of daily activities taped to my door. At first, I was mad that his treatment of me was childlike. But as the days went by, I understood his reasoning. The doctor's words again ran through my mind: "Don't stick to a routine. Go different places, do different things, try different foods. The more experiences you have, the more likely you will hit on something that is familiar."

The only consistent task I have is running, which I hate, but Andrew says it's the best thing for me now. "Builds up your endurance," he says. Other than that, my "activities list", which I choose to call it, is filled with all sorts of things to do.

Tuesday, Annie came over to help me with the laundry and show me around the main house. That night, Andrew insisted that I cook dinner. It was a total disaster but a lot of fun. I never knew spaghetti could burn!

Wednesday, Laura took me to meet with the catering company who is in charge of mine and Andrew's reception. I was especially nervous about being alone with her for such a long time, but to my relief, she invited Annie to accompany us, so I didn't have to talk all that much. I am overwhelmed with gratitude when she informs me that she and Sean are going to pay for the entire party (and more than a little bit of guilt), so I just nod my head.

I stay busy the rest of the week with the activities that Andrew has set for me. I don't see him that much during the day because he is at work, and the nights are full of family. However, Andrew and I make time to talk about our days, watch movies, play games, even go out to eat. Our first week together, we were both giant bundles of nerves. Besides the doctor's appointments, the fact that we were basically strangers really weighed heavily on us. But Andrew and I have an easy relationship now that we have a common goal.

We joke around and act how I think a brother and sister would. He calls me Elle almost all the time now. But there are times when I notice him staring a little too long, or he catches me looking at his scars or smiling at his funny habits. We always brush these awkward moments aside like they mean nothing, but I know there is more to our relationship than we care to admit. Every night, I am plagued with nightmares. Sometimes I remember details—shadows and bursts of color, red mostly. I hear screams and gasps. Most of the time, I don't remember a thing, only pain. Every morning, I make a note in my memory journal; and every morning, I find Andrew lying on my floor. He hasn't joined me in bed since the last time I asked him. However, I see his exhaustion, and I'm hoping that the change of scenery will be good for both of us.

The signs of my injuries have almost faded, and my time in front of the mirror every morning has dwindled. However, in addition to the nightmares every night, I sometimes lose my bearing; my heart races, and I can't breathe. Just like my first day here, and the episode in the dressing room, my body starts shaking, and my fingers go numb. When this happens, I go to my room and close the door. If we have company, Andrew excuses me and then joins me when they leave. He counts the seconds out loud. I found that counting comforts me. Andrew assures me my panic attacks are normal and will one day go away. "Probably the same time your memories return," he says.

As my second week of consciousness draws to a close, I notice how easy it is for me to call this place my home. After finishing my chores at home, I spent the rest of the day with Andrew's family, helping to decorate for the reception. The large tent in which the reception is to be held overwhelms me.

I hitched a ride on one of the workers delivering supplies and was awed by the expanse of land laid out in front of me. I have been up and down the driveway a dozen of times, but never have I paid attention to the land around me. Vineyards stretched as far as the eye can see, their vines just beginning to green and bud with the promise of new life. I know nothing of wine or vineyards, of growing anything actually, but I love the idea of a fresh start, a new beginning. It's just a little comical my own fresh start could be right around the corner—our "Trip around the World" is just a couple of weeks away. When the van reaches the tent, I see Andrew's mother, Laura, standing with a clipboard in her hands and a stern expression on her face.

"No, no, that's the wrong place. The drink table is supposed to go on the other side. You there, Andres, bring those tables and chairs from the van and place them where I have designated—see, I have marked on X in the sand. Yes, Olivia, that's the material I was looking for. Just bring it over here . . ."

I see Nicole, Annie, Lily, and even Andrew's father, Sean, carrying boxes and straightening tablecloths. I'm afraid to interrupt Laura's instructions, but when she sees me, she immediately calls out.

"Eleanor, dear. I am so glad to see you. Would you like to help me pick out some of the things for the reception?"

"Oh no, ma'am. By the looks of things, you have been doing a great job. I'm sorry Andrew and I have not been here helping you, but I am here now. Just tell me what I can do."

"Nonsense, you are not required to do anything for a reception that we are giving you. Just make yourself useful."

I joined Andres in unloading the tables, which took a considerable amount of time. After losing count of the number of chairs after two hundred, I decided it was probably a good thing I didn't ask how many guests had RSVP'd to the hastily sent-out invitations.

And this is how I spend the rest of the day. It is after dark when I return home to an empty house. I call take-out Chinese for Andrew and I eat on the couch, watching reruns for the rest of the night.

This morning, my spirits are pretty low. I am extremely nervous about tonight. Seeing such a huge effort being put forth by most of Andrew's family to give us this reception has weighed heavy on my heart. I hate the fact we are deceiving them all, and I hate to think of the repercussions of our actions. I haven't seen Andrew this morning—he was gone by the time I woke up. However, before my downward spiral could get too consuming there is a loud and forceful knock on the door. I slowly make my way out of my bedroom, and before I reach the door, I hear several excited female voices and cringe at the optimism waiting on the other side.

Nicole is the ringleader of the group of family members surrounding my kitchen table. Covering the countertops and standing on every available surface in the living room are makeup bags, hair products, dryers, curling irons, and even some things I have never seen.

"We know this is unexpected, but we thought that you could use some help getting ready today. The reception starts at five, so that means we have seven hours to make you over."

Annie sighs and rolls her eyes while Nicole hastily adds, "Not that we think you need a makeover. In all honesty, we wanted to do this for you. We all know the rough start your marriage has had, and we thought you deserved a little pampering."

I am so overwhelmed all I can do is nod my head while the tears fall down my face. I am quickly fed a wonderful breakfast that one of Andrew's aunts fixes: biscuits, gravy, eggs, pancakes, fresh fruit, sausage, and bacon. We are all sitting around the kitchen table, and I am enveloped in cheery chatter and laughter. It feels nice having everyone fuss over me, and I start looking forward to the day.

****

Andrew

My mother told me the girls' plans for getting Eleanor ready for the reception, and I decided I could stand a little pampering myself. However, my idea of a relaxing day is blaringly different than a female's. While at the bar last night after work, Joshua and I decided on a day of bachelor fun, even though neither one of us is technically a bachelor. Our day is starting out at a local diner with the best pancakes in town. After stuffing ourselves silly, we head to a Putt-Putt course on the outskirts of town. When we were young, the game was the way we settled our differences. Our parents would get tired of hearing our bickering and load us in the car and head straight to Sir Gooney's Golf. I'm pretty sure our family was the business's best customers, at least during our adolescent years. I am surprised to see Joshua pull out our old record book from his back pocket.

"I can't believe you've kept that thing all this time!"

"Are you kidding? I didn't. But Mom did. I knew she has a stash of keepsakes somewhere in the attic, so I dug it out early this morning." The thoughtfulness of my brother once again hits me, and it's all I can do to not throw my arms around him in gratitude.

"You have no idea how much that means to me. Not just that you found the book, but that you thought enough about me to take time to do so." I can tell Joshua is stunned by my declaration; usually he is the emotional one. He simply clears his throat.

"You're welcome, bro. Now let's play!"

After our game, in which I suspect Joshua let me win, we head back toward town to the barbershop. Bob the barber greets us with handshakes and congratulations.

"Andrew, I hear you got yourself a real firecracker. Ha, that's good, son. She'll keep you on your toes." He must see my questioning look because he adds, "Your father and Jeremiah were in here earlier."

Because it's my big day, Joshua and I go for the full treatment: haircuts, facial trimmings, and hot shaves. I have to admit I can see why women are so crazy about going to the spa. I promise myself that whatever happens after tonight, I will make time to treat both myself and Elle. I thank Joshua one last time and think to myself, *This was the best way to say good-bye to bachelorhood.*

By the time we head home, I only have an hour to grab a bite to eat and get into my tuxedo. Thankfully, Elle's bedroom door is closed, so I have one last chance to calm my thoughts and my nerves and figure out how I'm going to ask her. But most importantly, I have to figure out a way to say good-bye to what I know.

Chapter 18

Eleanor

As I stand in front of the mirror in my bedroom, the familiar routine of the past few weeks calms my nerves. My arms and legs look so smooth that it's hard to remember the first time I saw the deep purple and blue bruises, the bite marks, and the cuts. I almost don't recognize the rest of me; my hair has been straightened and then curled on the ends; I have on makeup, which is a new thing for me; even my fingernails have been painted. I've been plucked and waxed and lotioned to death, but it was worth it. My dress is lying on my bed, the one I was trying on in the dress shop the night the power went out. Andrew must have gone back and bought it sometime during the last week without my knowledge.

As I look at the clock on my bedside table that reads four thirty, there is a knock on my bedroom door. I call out, "Who is it?" and Andrew answers back.

"It's me. Can we talk for a few minutes before we have to leave?" I answer yes and take one last look at myself in the mirror before slipping the dress over my head and putting on my shoes. When I walk out of the bedroom, I freeze midstep. Andrew is standing outside my door wearing a black tuxedo, and my breath catches in my throat. He is so beautiful it hurts.

****

Andrew

If I die this second, I will die a happy man because one last look at the beautiful woman in front of me is all I would need for eternity. I cannot take my eyes off Elle the whole way to the reception. Before she walked out of the bedroom, I had an entire speech prepared; but the second I saw her, every coherent thought I had went out the window.

Knowing my parents and their tendency to take everything to the extreme, I am not a bit surprised at the sight before me. I do hear Elle's intake of breath, and I squeeze her hand. The pavilion is lit by thousands of Christmas lights which keep the night at bay. The hundreds of people in attendance cannot seem to keep their eyes off us, and their voices are raised in congratulations.

"This is all for us. Don't worry about anything. Just enjoy the night."

She nods and gives me a small smile. The gleam in her eyes makes my hands burn with the desire to take her into my arms, but the cheers erupting from the reception crowd startles me out of my thoughts. I notice a slight blush in Elle's cheeks, and I wonder if she is thinking the same as me.

There are at least ten tables covered with different types of food— Mexican tortillas and burritos, Chinese soups and eggrolls, Italian meatballs and spaghetti, American hot dogs and hamburgers. My mother said she got the idea from our "Trip around the World." "I liked the idea of mixing it up. Now there is something for everyone." She lowers her voice and continues speaking only to me. "Also, I don't know a lot about Eleanor. Where she's from or what she likes. This way, she does not feel left out."

"I know that the suddenness of my marriage is not what you expected, and I understand how hard it must be to give me away to someone you know nothing about, but I promise you I am happier than I have ever been. In the coming months and years, you will grow to love her just like I do." I catch myself and realize this is the first time I have said the words out loud. I hate Eleanor didn't get to hear them. I add hastily, "Plus, this reception is great, Mom. Thank you so much for doing this."

Her eyes wet with tears, she says, "Now isn't it nice to get a surprise every now and then?"

I look at Elle and smile. "You're right. It is nice."

The rest of our night goes by in a blur. I'm not sure if it is the number of people who form a wall around us all night giving their well wishes or the amount of food I consume or my beautiful wife's glances which stop my breath and my heart. Only a few faces stick out in the crowd. I see Bob the barber and his wife sitting at a table with my elementary school principal. When we finally reach the table of my friends and their wives, I am more proud to have Elle on my arm than ever before. At eleven, the party is still going strong.

****

Eleanor

I have met so many people tonight; my head is swimming with names and faces, of which about 5 percent I'm going to remember. Nicole has pulled me off to the side to ask about our upcoming trip.

"Now, do you guys have a detailed itinerary? I'm sure the family would like to know where you are going and what you plan on doing while you're away."

"Nicole, I have to be honest. Andrew is in charge of making the plans. I'm just along for the ride. But I will talk to him and see if he can get you a copy. That way, you can pass it out to everyone who is interested." When I spot Andrew making his way through the crowd, an audible sigh escapes my lips.

"I hate to steal the bride away, but I think we are required to dance to one song before we retire for the night," he says to his sister-in-law.

"I had no idea we were going to dance," I say, my voice sounding strained.

"Just one, I promise."

I excuse myself from Nicole as Andrew takes my hand and leads me to a spot on the crowded floor that has somehow been vacated. The music starts playing over the sound system, and he places his right hand on my waist and places my left hand on his shoulder. He joins our other hands and begins to move his feet.

"I have never danced before," I quickly tell him.

"It doesn't matter—I have. Just follow along and keep your eyes on me."

That is exactly what I do, and the rest of the world disappears. I end up lying my head against his chest while he moves us across the floor. Before I know it, the song is over, and we have stopped swaying. Our guests cheer and clap once more, and Andrew holds up his hand for silence.

"Thank you all for coming and showing your support for both myself and Eleanor. We are so blessed to have such loving friends and family. I know that my marriage seems sudden to a lot of you. It does to even me sometimes, but the moment I saw Eleanor, I knew that I had to make her mine. Her loving, giving, and brave spirit is so special I was afraid someone else would snatch her up! It's true the beginning of our marriage has been plagued with hardships. But I wouldn't want to spend one second of bliss with anyone else." Andrew turns to address me.

"Elle, you have given me my life back in more ways than one. You make me a better man, a stronger man, but most of all, you make me a happy man. Not only do I give you my name and my family, but also my body should you ever need protecting. I will spend the rest of my life trying to make you smile."

There are a few sniffles in the crowd when Andrew stops talking. I am so moved by his words I just stand here for what seems like an eternity looking into his eyes. Anything I could say would sound inadequate, but I have to say something, so I look away from Andrew and start slowly.

"First of all, I want to thank my new family, the Smiths, for all they have done to welcome me into their lives." I take this moment to search each one out of the crowd—Sean, Laura, Nicole, Joshua, Annie. "Thank you for sharing your wonderful son and brother with me and trusting me to care for him. I only hope my support of him can match yours, but I promise that I will spend the rest of my life trying. I have been overwhelmed by the rest of you and your willingness to accept me. You have no idea how blessed I feel to know each and every one of you." I turn back to Andrew and address only him.

"Andrew, you talk of me giving you your life back, but we both know it was the other way around. From day one, you have been my savior and my biggest advocate. I am so undeserving of your kindness, and I will spend forever trying to show you how grateful I am for the second chance you have given me."

Andrew looks at me and smiles, shaking his head slightly as if to say, "You don't know what you're talking about." The guests begin clapping and cheering again, and the family make their way toward us. There are hugs all round, and Andrew's father gives us a little nod of his head. We take that as our cue to leave.

As we make our way to the car, our guests flank us on each side and blow bubbles as we race between them. I find myself squealing with delight as Andrew and I reach the car decorated with shaving cream and balloons, even soda cans tied to the bumper. As we pull away from the pavilion, I look to Andrew's face, which is covered is a goofy grin, and say, "Tonight has been the best night of my life."

He reaches for my hand and gives it a squeeze. "The night is not over yet." He wiggles his eyebrows, and I try to keep from giggling too loud.

Something happened tonight which I cannot explain. I'm not sure if it was the dancing or the heartfelt speeches, but a huge shift has occurred in mine and Andrew's relationship. I guess I always knew the feelings were there between us. I knew we cared for each other, even loved each other in our own ways, but hearing the words spoken aloud seems to have broken the spell of civility we were under.

Andrew and I barely make it into the house before his jacket and my shoes are off and lying on the floor. The pressure and tension of the past two weeks is causing my hands to shake while I try to undo Andrew's bowtie.

He starts laughing and says, "Let me help you with that."

I refuse to allow any distance between us, so my mouth never leaves his. Our kisses are urgent and even forceful driven by our longing to be with each other. There are no gentle caresses or uncertain touches. We are purposeful in our passion, even possessive. He is mine. This gorgeous man is all mine. We stumble to my bedroom, barely making it into the room before we collapse on the bed. Andrew's sharp intake of breath is the only thing that could make me stop. When I focus on his face, he is wincing with pain.

"Oh my gosh, I am so sorry." I fuss over him for a minute, but he waves me off.

"Don't worry about it, love. I just got the wind knocked out of me for a second. I wasn't watching where I was going. You have the tendency to do that—take my mind off of everything else." He smiles, so I know he must not be in too much pain. I notice he is trying to prop himself up. I take the moment gravity has given us to stop and think about what I'm doing.

"Andrew, you must know how I feel about you," I say quietly.

He nods his head. "Yes, I do. And can I say for the record I consider myself to be the luckiest man on the planet?"

I chuckle but continue. "And you must know that right now, I want nothing more than to be with you . . . in that way. But I can't," I say as I look down. "I just can't."

I feel Andrew's fingers on my chin and force my eyes back to his. "Do you want to know what I have to say about the matter? I understand completely. What happened to you is inexcusable. And in no way, fashion or form, am I going to force myself on you, but if you ask me to stop touching you, I think I'll explode." I lean forward, allowing our lips to touch once more and then pull him down to the bed. I wrap my arms around his waist and hear his heavy sigh. He does not protest, but I can tell he is unhappy.

Chapter 19

Andrew

I have to agree with Elle's statement: Last night was the best of my life. The food, the music, the atmosphere was only the tip of the iceberg. Seeing all my friends and family welcome Elle, a stranger to them, into their arms was more special to me than anything. I lie here and try to remember every detail: the sounds of shouts and cheers; the feel of Elle's soft hand in mine as we slow dance; my mother's tear-filled eyes; Joshua's booming laugh from across the pavilion; Dr. Adams quiet declaration, "You are indeed a lucky man. I can see why your heart is with her. She is a beautiful woman"; the brightness of the Christmas lights; the smell and taste of the different foods. Elle's light snores beside me have a calming effect. I look toward the clock—five fifteen. I wanted to sleep longer, but the sunlight won't allow it.

Another Sunday means another family lunch at the big house. I used to dread going to eat with my family, seeing everyone's happy faces and hearing the same stories being told over and over again. However, now that I have Eleanor, my sense of apprehension is replaced with one of excitement. The next week will either make or break our relationship, and I send up a silent prayer that we leave on our "Trip around the World" closer than ever and ready to face what may come.

I look at Eleanor's sleeping face and marvel at what I have been given—a loving family, a wonderful job, the opportunity to help people and serve my country, plenty of friends, a fulfilling life, and now a beautiful woman to share it with. I can't resist kissing her cheeks before heading to the bathroom for a shower. I spend the rest of my early morning going over last-minute changes in itinerary and remind myself to make a copy for Nicole.

Phone Conversation No. 5

Wednesday, 3:45 p.m.

"Yes, sir. I know it has been a while since my last phone call, but I have been doing a little digging of my own."

"Well, I thought it would help. It, at least, couldn't hurt, sir."

"No, sir. I understand you have people who are capable of such things."

"Yes, sir. They are still planning to leave for their trip this Saturday."

"I don't understand, sir. No, sir. I will continue to stay silent when it comes to our agreement."

"Yes, sir. I will call you with any further developments."

Chapter 20

Eleanor

"As you can see, dear, we have a large operation based right here in Carmel." Laura is doing her best to show me around the Smith Shipping office complex but keeps getting interrupted by phone calls or people asking questions.

"You seem to be an important component yourself," I add.

"Well, most of these people have grown up in this business, so they consider me somewhat of a mother figure in the office. Most of my time anymore is spent solving problems, putting out emotional fires, and dealing with any drama that might arise." She leans a little closer. "And let me tell you, when you're dealing with family, there is always drama."

I give her a nod of my head in acknowledgment. "Oh, I don't want to scare you away, my dear. We have a wonderful time and get a lot accomplished too. I personally think you would make an excellent member of our team here, with your skills and background in sales. The job was practically made for you." She gives me a wink and continues down the hallway of the three-story complex.

I feel more than a little ashamed about lying to her and to Andrew. Although I technically didn't lie to him when he asked this morning what my plans were for the day. When I said "I'm not sure", that's exactly what I meant. I just happened to leave out the rest of my statement—"when I'm going to the Smith Shipping office." We never continued the discussion, which led to our first fight about me working for his family. I assumed he was simply worried about my mental health, but after almost a week with no flashbacks, I cleared myself for active duty, so to speak. I figured I could take the tour and introduction of the business from his mother and talk it over with him while we were on our trip. I had no intention, however, of telling him while we were still sharing the same bed at night.

After our intense make-out session after the reception, mine and Andrew's physical relationship has increased. And when I say "increased", I mean holding hands and cheek-kisses increased. Basically, we act like we are in middle school and ignore our raging hormones as best we can. I hated to be the firm one on the subject, but I made it perfectly clear that any more physical contact was virtually impossible for me at this point. I wouldn't dare tell Andrew, however, that I would bet my own money his libido was not suffering as much as mine.

As Laura and I round the corner, we meet Joshua hurriedly talking with another man. "Well, if it isn't my firstborn. How are you today, Joshua?" Joshua stoops down to place a kiss on his mother's cheek.

"I can't talk now, Mother. We have a very important client coming in five minutes, and I have to prepare the conference room."

"Oh well, don't let us stop you," she says. "Good luck."

Joshua continues down the hall. "Hi, Eleanor. Bye, Eleanor. What are you even doing here?"

I flush at the questioning look on his face but try to play it off. "Your mother was kind enough to give me a tour."

Joshua shrugs. "Okay, have fun."

"Good luck." Laura shouts before we head into a large office. My father-in-law, for all intents and purposes, is sitting behind a large cherry desk with his feet propped up, reading the newspaper. He doesn't look one bit worried about the very important client, and I say something.

"I'm just the face of the business these days, Eleanor. Joshua runs things, and all I have to do is show up. After working so hard for so many years, I believe it's my right to take it easy."

"I couldn't agree more." I say. However, I feel his wife has a different view of things.

"Well, while you're taking it easy, your son is having a stroke trying to get everything together to keep our retirement thriving."

Sean waves off Laura's concern. "It's his own fault. He's known about this meeting for over two weeks now, and he just completed the presentation this morning. Serves him right, the lazy bugger." He continues. "Tell me, Eleanor. How do you find our little operation?"

"I have to admit it is a little daunting."

"Nonsense. What I love about our company is the feeling of teamwork. Every person has their specific job to do, but if someone gets in a pinch, everyone chips in to help." He gives me a big grin and then winks at Laura who rolls her eyes in response. I can't help but notice Andrew's parents' attempts to showcase the wonderful aspects of Smith Shipping. They either want to make a really good impression, or they are genuinely this passionate about overseas shipping. I flash Sean a quick smile and wonder what Andrew would say if he knew where I was. Joshua pokes his head in the door.

"Pop, do you know what I did with the laser pointer?"

"Of course not," Sean answers. "Why don't you check up your—" Thankfully, Laura cuts her husband off before he can finish his train of thought.

"Why don't I help you look for it, dear?" she says as they hurry back out the door. I stifle a laugh when I see Sean's eyes light up with mischief.

"Can I ask who the 'very important client' is?"

"Absolutely. After all, if you plan on working here, you should begin to get acquainted with all our customers. Have you ever heard of MicroCorp?"

"Eleanor, my dear. Did you hear what I said?" Sean's voice sounds far away, even though I know he is standing right beside me. I feel his warm and steady grip on my arm, leading me toward a winged-back chair. "You don't look so good. Are you all right?"

I regain enough composure to answer him. "Yes, I'm not feeling very well all of a sudden. Can you point me to the nearest restroom?"

"Of course. It's down the hallway on the left. Do you need help getting there?" He seems genuinely worried, so I try to put his mind at ease.

"It's probably nothing, just a little tired, I guess." Thankfully, Sean doesn't question my self-diagnosis as he helps me stand and points the way.

"Let me know if I can get you something." I nod my acknowledgment and hurry as fast as my shaky legs can take me toward the closest ladies room.

What am I doing here? I never should have gone behind Andrew's back. Now I am stuck in the same building as the man I suspect was behind my attack. I have to get out of here and quick. I stop my hurried rambling and realize I have missed an important factor. I don't need to be asking what I am doing here but what is MicroCorp doing here. Have they always been customer of Smith Shipping? Have they had a long-standing relationship with the Smith family? Do Sean and Joshua know that the president and CEO of MicroCorp might be responsible for my situation?

And then it hits me: Does Andrew know about this? Is that why he was so against me getting involved with the family business because there was a chance I would find out the connection between his family and the MicroCorp family? Was this entire thing an act on his part? Was he supposed to gain my trust only to deliver me to the waiting hands of Dan Childs? My head is swimming with all sorts of scenarios as I fill the sink with cold water and dunk my whole face underneath. When I emerge a few seconds later, I feel calmer but no less confused.

Maybe I am looking at this the wrong way, I try telling myself. Maybe this is simply a coincidence. After all, I am the one who chose which day I wanted to visit the office, and I didn't make the decision until this morning. Surely there is no way Dan Childs could drop everything and turn up at Smith Shipping, Incorporated headquarters at the drop of a hat. Sadly, I realize there is no way I am going to receive any answers stuck in this bathroom with a sopping wet face.

However, no matter how brave I like to pretend to be, that fearlessness does not apply to anything involving MicroCorp. I peek out of the ladies room door and scan the hallway. Empty, good. If I can make it to the stairwell, I can slip outside and hide in Laura's car, claiming I needed some fresh air after my episode in Sean's office. I turn left and head the opposite way from which I came and stop in my tracks. A familiar voice sounds behind me, sending shivers up my spine. I creep back toward the corner and look around carefully to see a very unpleasant sight.

****

Andrew

"It's nice to meet you, Andrew," Dan Childs, CEO of MicroCorp, says as he shakes my hand. "I've heard all about you."

"Is that so?" I ask with distaste in my voice.

"Why, yes. When I talked to your brother a few weeks ago, he informed me that you were out of town at a medical convention. Honolulu, was it?"

"That's right," I say stiffly. "Can I ask how you and my brother got on the subject of my vacationing habits?"

"It's quite simple really. When I called the office and asked to speak with your father"—he nods toward my dad who is giving me a very serious stare at this point—"I was told he was out of town and directed to Joshua. We got onto the subject of parent's vacation, your vacation, and how the poor chap was stuck all alone having to run the business by himself. I have to admit, though, I didn't feel sorry for the man. He seemed to be handling things fine."

Dan Childs's smile sends chills down to my bones, and it takes all the strength I can muster to not punch his teeth down his throat. Even though I have no proof whatsoever that Eleanor's attack was prompted by the man standing in front of me, the mere thought of her flashbacks and fainting spells are enough cause in my mind to end the guy right here, right now.

What in the world is he doing here? Is this coincidence—that he chooses to visit Smith Shipping, Incorporated the day Eleanor shows up for a visit? I have to find her and get her out of here quickly, preferably without Mr. CEO even laying eyes on her.

When I don't say anything, Mr. Childs speaks up. "By the way, I believe congratulations are in order." He notices my questioning look and smiles deviously. "I hear you have been recently married. That is definitely something to celebrate." I shift my focus to my father who simply shrugs his shoulders.

"My goodness, it's nothing to be ashamed of, son. Eleanor is a beautiful, bright woman. Speaking of which, you should probably check on her, Andrew. She wasn't feeling well and excused herself to the restroom." I groan inwardly at my father's unknowing disclosure of Eleanor's whereabouts.

Dan Childs gets a hungry, greedy look on his face, and I have to clinch my fists to keep from striking out at him. "Your wife is here? How wonderful! I would so like to meet her."

"Yes, I'm sure you would," I say through clinched teeth.

"Excuse me?"

"Nothing," I say hurriedly. "Dad, where did you say Eleanor was?"

"I pointed her toward the bathroom down that way." I nod to them both and hurry off in that direction, praying to God Eleanor is still inside. As I round the corner, Eleanor is just walking out of the ladies room. I can tell she has had an episode because of the strained look on her face.

"Hi," she says sweetly. "What are you doing here?"

"I could ask you the same question." The strain of the last few minutes oozes out of my voice.

Eleanor innocently shrugs. "Your mother wanted to show me around, and I didn't have anything else to do today. What's your story?"

"Well, you weren't answering the phone at home, so I called the big house, and Annie said you weren't there. I finally got in touch with Nicole who told me you had come with my mother to the office."

"Since you knew where I was, why come all the way down here?" Her eyes take in my doctor's coat. "You must have been in a hurry you didn't even change clothes." I suddenly remember Dan Childs's closeness and pull Eleanor into the closest stairwell.

"I just had to see you," I say and pull her into my arms. And that is no lie. When I couldn't get a hold of Elle and finally contacted Nicole, I remembered today was the meeting between my father and Dan Childs. I drove like a bat out of hell, blowing my horn so many times I believe I broke it.

Elle seems content to be in my embrace. She looks up to me with wide, misty eyes. "I'm glad you had to," she says as she reaches onto her tiptoes and kisses me gently. Placing her hands on either side of my face, she speaks softly. "Promise me you will never lie to me, okay? No matter what, promise you will always tell the truth. I don't know what I would do if I found out you were untruthful."

Confused by her statement and feeling a little unease at the fact she called me out, I answer quickly, hoping to avoid looking suspicious. "Of course, Elle. *Always.*"

I hear a discreet clearing of someone's throat coming from the doorway, and the two of us jump apart like school kids being caught doing something we are not supposed to be doing. I place Eleanor's body behind mine, up against the wall, and turn to see Joshua's floppy black hair on the other side of the open door.

"I hate to break up the party, but I was sent to find you guys," he says, his eyes looking anywhere but at us. "Mom wants to know if you want to grab some lunch."

I glance over my shoulder. "I have to get back to the hospital, but I'll be taking Eleanor home first."

I can hear Joshua's snide comment of "Oh, I bet you will" and kick the door into his face. "What?" he asks innocently.

"Just let Mom know we have left, okay?"

"Sure thing, Stud." I roll my eyes at my childish big brother and follow Eleanor down the stairs.

Chapter 21

Eleanor

On Friday night, our bags are packed, and we are sitting on the couch. Andrew is going over our plans for the one hundredth time, and I am staring at my memory journal for the one hundredth time. I scan the lines I've written: I hate to work out; I like grilled cheese sandwiches and chocolate milk; my mother used to make them for me; I like to count, it comforts me; MicroCorp = bad.

As I read the last entry, I shudder at the memory of the news report. I still don't know what happened to me, but I can't shake the feeling that MicroCorp is at the root of all my problems, and seeing Dan Childs in the hallway of my father-in-law's office building only confirms it. I have brought this up a couple of times to Andrew, not the fact I saw Dan Childs at Smith Shipping or the fact I saw them interact with one another but the creepy feeling I get. He seems hesitant to embrace the idea, and I am beginning to wonder if it is because I am grasping at straws, trying to find a connection or because I have already found it.

There is a knock on the door which we are not expecting. Andrew goes to open it, and when Nicole and Joshua walk in the door, I look forward to a pleasant visit with two people I have come to enjoy. Instead, I sense a dark cloud hanging in the air. Andrew asks them to sit while I offer them something to drink, and when they refuse, I place myself on the arm of the couch next to Andrew while he rests his hand on my back.

This has become one of our poses, starting out of the necessity to look like newlyweds but staying out of comfort. As I rub my hand through his hair, I catch Nicole and Joshua giving each other a pointed look. All of a sudden, I feel self-conscious about touching their brother, and I pull my hand away. If Andrew notices the difference in their usually joyful demeanor, he does not say. Instead, he asks them, "What's up guys? It's nice to see you, and we are always happy for a visit, but we've got a lot to do before we leave in the morning."

Joshua looks at Nicole and sighs, and I swear I can feel it in my bones. He takes a raged breath and blurts out the words that could topple my comfortable new world.

"We know everything, Andy. We know about Hawaii. We know about Eleanor's injuries, her memory loss, and we know about your fake marriage. We know everything." He just sits there and stares at us, like he hasn't delivered the biggest blow of our lives. I expect Andrew to ask him what he is talking about, but instead he shakes his head.

"I'm surprised it took you guys so long to figure out." All I can think is, my comfort is gone. I have nothing. He squeezes my hand, pulls me close, and whispers, "Don't worry, you are safe here." And I believe him just like I have believed him since the first time he said it. He kisses me gently, our first kiss since the stairwell, and then turns to his family.

His voice is stern when he addresses them. "I want to know how you figured it out. Every single detail that went into making your minds up this is fake." As he gestures toward our linked hands, he must sense he has hurt my feelings because he looks at me and gives me an apologetic smile. "I have to know because I have to make sure we don't make another mistake. I have to know because I have to keep Elle safe."

Joshua, Nicole, and Andrew have been talking for thirty minutes, piecing together the story of our failure. I got the gist of what they are saying in the first five minutes. The "nail in the coffin", so to speak, was a call from their mutual friend, the doctor who did my brain scans, just checking in on me.

"So much for patient, doctor confidentiality," a very tired Andrew says. I was hoping our trip would give us some much needed rest, but now we have more responsibilities to juggle.

As I think about what Joshua said: "We know everything, Andy. We know about Hawaii. We know about Eleanor's injuries, her memory loss, and we know about your fake marriage. We know everything", I feel like I should say something to these people who so willingly welcomed me into their family, but my mouth is dry, and I come up blank.

Andrew asks, "Do you think Mom and Dad know?"

Joshua shakes his head at the same time Nicole speaks. "No, definitely not. They have been too wrapped up your reception plans to notice anything funny. But we will do our best to keep the waters calm." She looks at me, and I see a familiar look in her eyes, *pity*.

"Thanks," replies Andrew, and I find myself nodding in agreement. As they get up to leave, Andrew grabs my hand and steps in front of Joshua and Nicole. "Now that you guys know the whole story, I need to tell you some recent developments." He looks to me with timid eyes. "Even though our marriage is a fake, mine and Elle's relationship is not. I feel confident in saying that we care deeply for each other, and we are in this journey together. I don't know about Elle, but no matter what we find out about her past, I'm going to be there every step of the way."

I wish I could bask in Andrew's words. The reassurance he will be there for me only causes more confusion. I don't see the worried expression passed between Joshua and Nicole, and I don't notice their hushed good-byes and wishes for a safe trip. What I do notice is the way Andrew lingers by my side, afraid to break the force holding us together, and I'm unsure if that force is a good thing or a bad thing.

When I walk toward my room, I stop the doorway, and Andrew wraps his arms around my waist and buries his head in my hair. I try to still the butterflies in my stomach and the rapid beating of my heart. Every time we touch, there is no denying our desire; however, I wish I understood what was going on. I felt so sure of Andrew and our relationship just two days ago. Everything had been perfect, too perfect, I guess because now I am plagued with doubts. I think about all Andrew has done for me: saving my life, risking his future and his relationships to keep me safe, welcoming me into his home, into his world with no clue about my true identity, and the possibility he is working with Dan Childs makes my skin crawl. The truth is, I don't know what to believe.

He gives me a smile as he says, "I'm going to do a few more things, so we'll be ready to go in the morning." And I walk to my bed. I'm not sure when I fall asleep, but I know from the softness of my bones when I wake up, the nightmares were only in my mind. I kept seeing Andrew with his arms reached toward me. However, when I finally got to him, he would turn his back on me, leaving me feeling dejected and alone. It was the same thing over and over again. I try to push the uneasiness of the dream and the uncertainties of our trip out of my mind, what we will find and what truths we will be faced with. Who knows what obstacles tomorrow hold? Regardless of Andrew, his family, and their possible connection with Dan Childs, I know I will not be alone when I face them.

PART 2

Trip around the World

Chapter 22

Eleanor

I wake up early to get a little bit of quiet time before our hectic day begins. I creep toward the bathroom for a shower but pause when I notice that the door of Andrew's room is cracked open. I cannot believe that I have been here for weeks, and not once have I seen inside. I push the door open further to reveal what is obviously a guest bedroom. There is a small computer desk on one wall with a spare TV perched on top and a futon on another wall.

In that moment, I feel I am getting a quick look into the real life of Andrew. There is stuff all over the floor—clothes, his doctor bag, magazines covering various topics, even a basketball. That is when the thought strikes me: I really don't know anything about this man. I have no clue about his likes and dislikes, his hobbies, even his past.

As I turn to leave, a little uneasy with the facts staring me in the face, I notice a set of dog tags hanging on the closet doorknob. I cross the room and gently pick them up to find Andrew's name pressed into the metal. Why has he never mentioned his military service before? Probably because I never cared to ask. I've never asked him anything about his past. Are his scars a result of a battle? Leaving the room with more questions than I entered with, I head for the bathroom.

After a shower and a bowl of cereal, I go to wake Andrew up. It is not like him to sleep so late, but it was obvious he needed it. He hears me enter the bedroom and sits up sleepily. He rubs his eyes, yawns, and stretches his arms.

"Good morning," I say, a little shy.

"Good morning to you," he replies and pats the spot next to him on the bed. I head over there, and he wraps me into a warm hug. "Today is the big day—the first leg of our trip around the world. Are you excited?" He looks a little worried about hearing the truth, but I decided after last night I will hold nothing back from him. We need to be a team, a united front to face the future.

"Yes," I say clearly, "I am excited but of course a little nervous too." He smiles and squeezes my hand. I sit there, wanting to say more before the moment is broken, and I think he knows that.

"Last night was incredible," I say quietly. "I never thought I would feel safe again, but I was wrong. I was so worried when Joshua and Nicole confronted us, but hearing you say 'no matter what we find out, you will be by my side' probably means more to me than anything you have said, or done, up to this point. You have no idea how scary it is to wake up one morning knowing nothing about yourself and your surroundings. I have known since the first time I saw you, I could trust you. But to hear you say you will continue on this journey with me was just the reassurance I needed. It gives me courage to take the risk of finding out my identity. But like I told you before my brain scans, I might be finding out what I want to know, but don't think for a second it will be easy for me to learn the truth."

He nods and smiles, but it doesn't reach his eyes.

"You do realize that we might not find out anything," he says. "But I have to admit I am okay with that prospect."

I smile and hug him again, knowing I said those words to myself just a few days ago. When we pull away from the house, most of the Smith family is there to send their love. As I feel their warm hugs and see their enthusiastic smiles and waves of love, it is the first time I feel okay with whatever my future holds.

****

Andrew

This is the third time in a little over a month that I have been on a plane. However, each time is different than the one before. However, there is a common denominator in all three flights, which is nerves. This flight is possibly more nerve-wracking than the first two for a couple of reasons: I have a companion on this trip, a conscious companion. I look at Elle who is sitting next to me with an excited expression on her face. Walking up to the airplane, she practically squealed with joy at the memory flash of riding on an airplane before. I try to be just as excited as she is every time she remembers something, but I cannot lie and say, with each remembrance,

I am not cringing on the inside, just waiting for the moment she recovers from her amnesia, and my world is shattered.

The meeting with Joshua and Nicole last night, although a shock, was a much needed thrust into reality for me, and I suspect for Eleanor as well. For the past two weeks, since she woke up, we have been living a life of easy truce, neither one of us caring to rock the boat by saying how we really feel about the other. There are moments I know she catches me staring at her or times that her laugh is only for me. In these moments, it is all I can do not to grab her into my arms and shout, "Can you not see that this is all for you? It has been since the moment I laid eyes on you!" Of course, besides scaring her to death, I am also afraid a declaration like that might not be returned. And disappointed as I may be, if she said that is all she wanted from me, then I am happy to have only that much.

I have been second-guessing her feelings for me since Wednesday. She seems more distant in a way. I was hoping it was simply the upcoming trip, but something in my gut tells me she knew Dan Childs was in my father's office building. Was it my imagination, or did I actually catch a glimpse of curly brown hair around the corner from where Mr. Childs and I stood? I was afraid Eleanor might have seen the two of us talking and shaking hands and somehow come to the conclusion the exchange was more personal and pleasant than it actually was.

Phone Conversation No. 6

Saturday, 2:00 p.m.

"Yes, sir, their flight just left."

"I cannot talk long. No, sir, I don't know every stop they are going to make. I was able to get only a partial itinerary. However, I do know they are headed to Atlanta first."

"I'll inform you as soon as I know something."

"Yes, sir?"

"Yes, sir. I'll keep up the good work. I know it's for the best."

Chapter 23

Eleanor

I can hardly wait for the plane to come out of its climb before I jump to get my carry-on and drag out my memory journal. My last entry reads: I remember flying on an airplane before. Slow progress is better than no progress at all. My spirits soar as the plane does, and I am enjoying looking out the window when a man in a uniform approaches. Andrew unfastens his seat belt and shakes the man's hand.

"Tom, we really appreciate your willingness to take us on this trip. We know you were looking forward to some time off since our last flight." At this, Tom, the pilot of our plane, looks at me with sadness in his eyes.

"It's my pleasure, sir. I am just glad that I get to meet Mrs. Smith on better terms this time."

As he speaks, I understand why his look is so sad. He must have flown us home from Honolulu. That means he saw me beaten, broken, and unconscious. Immediately I feel the need to hug this man and impress upon him my deepest thanks. I can't get my seat belt unhooked fast enough and practically throw myself into his arms. He seems shocked at first but gives my shoulders a tight squeeze in return.

As I pull away, Andrew smiles and says, "Tom, may I have the pleasure of introducing you to my wife, Eleanor Smith." Then he turns to me. "Eleanor, may I have the pleasure of introducing you to the man responsible for helping me save your life." Tom stands a little straighter and a little taller.

"It is so nice to finally meet you, Tom. I will never be able to repay your kindness to me, but if you ever need anything, I am in your debt."

"It was my pleasure, ma'am."

The feeling of flight seems comfortable to me, and I wonder if I flew a lot before the accident. I don't get sick, and I feel at ease with the views from the window. There is calm between Andrew and me during the flight as he reads a newspaper, and I draw doodles in my memory journal.

Our first stop is Atlanta, and from there, we are renting a car and heading North, through Tennessee, North Carolina, and up to Washington DC. Andrew suggested we not go any further north because my accent is so distinctly Southern. "I'm afraid it will be a waste of valuable time, but I thought you would enjoy seeing our nation's capital." I agree with his explanation, but I sense there is something he is keeping from me, and I pray it's not the news I have been dreading to hear.

I decided to play it cool while Andrew and I are on our trip. I'm not going to mention the scene from the Smith Shipping hallway or the sudden questions I have about Andrew's seemingly perfect timing in finding me in Honolulu. I plan on getting through this trip, discovering answers about my past while trying to ignore the feelings for Andrew that continue to build in my ever-confused heart. I don't want to seem in a hurry to get away from him, and I'm not going to turn down the opportunity for free room and board on my quest to find the truth.

As planned, we do all the touristy things in Atlanta, which turned out to be not only fun but also enlightening as well. The Atlanta Aquarium was a real interest to me. As I watched the workers in their wet suits feeding the different fish, I realized I had done something similar before and immediately wrote it down.

The rest of our trip to the northern portion of the United States continues in much of the same fashion. My memory journal starts filling up with each stop at a new place. It's not necessarily the locations that trigger my memories, but each place brings with it a bombardment of experiences; some are new and exciting, but every once in a while, a memory is revealed.

- I have ridden on an airplane before.
- I love fish and might have been scuba diving.
- Hotdogs remind me of Saturdays (?)
- I remember riding through the mountains.
- My mom's eyes were (are) brown.
- Seashells remind me of family.

To anyone on the outside, the journal would just seem like random scribbles. But to me, and even Andrew, these scribbles are the patchwork of my lost identity. It was Andrew's idea to add as much as I can to each memory flash. So under each entry is a specific description of what I see, feel, and on a couple of occasions, smell each time I have a memory flash, i.e.:

- I remember riding through the mountains: I see out the car window; the leaves are orange and yellow; it must be fall; I look out the front window, and the road winds in front of me.

As I stare out at the rolling tide, I am once again pleased to see the image of my mother and father walking hand in hand down the beach. I close my eyes, and it's like I am watching a movie reel play on my eyelids. I can see them plain as day: their arms swinging back and forth, the gentle waves lapping over their feet. My brother, with his unruly brown hair almost identical to mine, runs back and forth between the surf and the soft sand, picking up seashells and handing them to my father who comments and then puts them in his pocket. My brother, Robert (I now remember), runs back to me, holding something very sharp, a shiny black color.

"It's a shark's tooth," he tells me with great enthusiasm.

"But I thought shark's teeth were white." Robert rolls his eyes and dashes once more into the water.

The memory flash caused me so much joy and pain I actually sank to my knees in the sand and wept like a child. Andrew didn't say anything, simply dropped next to me, and gathered me into an embrace. The remembrance of my family is almost more than I can bear, and it's a long time before I am willing to turn my back on the beautiful ocean.

I am reading through each journal entry during our flight to DC, editing the descriptions and sometimes adding to them. Andrew nudges my knee and nods toward the window. I shield my eyes from the setting sun and look out at the U.S. Capitol building. I'm not too interested in its architecture, but I marvel at its grandeur. I feel a little prickle of recognition and make a quick note of it in my journal:

- Capitol building?

There are a few more entries similar to this one, and unfortunately, they bring more questions than answers.

****

Andrew

I still haven't told Elle the truth behind my reasoning for coming to Washington DC. I don't know if I am scared how she will react or if I'm scared what memories it might bring back to her.

Chapter 24

Eleanor

Our hotel in DC has a comforting feeling. It might be because I know in five minutes, Andrew and I will finally be in our room, alone. This trip has been so rushed; with a new city every two days, our nights have been a sanctuary of sorts. We share the same bed, and I have to admit it still gives me the feeling of safety. Andrew closes the door to our room and makes a beeline to the balcony where I am staring out at the hotel garden. He wraps his hands around my waist. "Are you sleepy tonight?" he asks in a quiet voice.

"Not really," I answer, "just more physically worn out than anything. Do you know what I mean?"

He kind of chuckles and agrees. "I know exactly what you mean. That's why I have been thinking about taking tomorrow off. We have been going nonstop since Carmel. Even though you seem strong, your body is still trying to heal. Even I forget the trauma you have recently gone through. But tomorrow, I propose a day of rest and relaxation. It would be good for both of us."

I raise my eyebrows and laugh. "So what you're saying is that *you* are the one who really needs a break." I keep forgetting he has just as much invested in this trip as I do, in what way, I'm not sure.

Andrew's laugh joins mine. "Okay, you caught me. I do need some rest, plus I need to check in with the hospital. I need to have a conference call with them. I have to check on the progress of my patients as well as let them know when I plan to return." He looks worried, and his forehead creases.

"Andrew, we can fly home tonight if we need to. You don't need to take any more time off from your job."

He seems thoughtful for a second and then asks, "Elle, what are you going to do when I have to work twenty-four-hour shifts? Sit around the house for days on end? I've been on a shortened schedule at the hospital these past few weeks. You can't get a job because you don't have the necessary information to fill out an application."

I hate to admit my decision to work at Smith Shipping was only strengthened when I saw Dan Childs there. But since I haven't told him anything about that, he thinks that his revelation has stumped me, so I hastily reply, "I can pick up a hobby or something. Don't worry about me, please."

He gives me a pointed looks and says, "That is exactly what I am going to do. I know you think you are fully recovered, but you are not—mentally more so than physically." He must know he hurt my feelings because he reaches for my hand. I snatch it away, making the space between us feel insurmountable. He tries to catch my gaze instead, but I cannot bring myself to look at him. What is he playing at? When he says stuff like this, I feel like there is a hidden meaning behind his words, and I'm just not smart enough to decipher it.

Andrew continues. "Eleanor, please understand you are still my patient. Your health and well-being are my first priorities. Now, I organized this trip hoping something we encounter will boost your memory, and thankfully, it has proven to be a good move. But I will not leave you alone for hours at a time when I don't know if you will have another panic attack or fainting episode. You could knock your head on a counter and bleed out before I get home." He doesn't see me flinch at this and continues uninterrupted. "Not to mention you are still having horrible nightmares, which keep you from getting enough sleep at night." He uses his thumb to rub the dark circles under my eyes. "I am not saying you are a weak person, Elle, but the fact remains you *are* weak."

I sit on the bed quietly while I try to process everything he has said.

He's right. I have just been busy lately. Busy does not mean better. "Andrew, I hate to admit you are right." I smile at him, and he smiles back. "However, I hate even more the thought that one day, when this is all over, you could resent me for causing you to lose your job."

He sighs and sits beside me. "I knew I was right about the degree of your healing, but don't think for a second being right about this makes me feel good." He squeezes my hand. "I promise to never lie to you to protect your feelings or because I don't think you can handle the truth. Therefore, I am going to tell you something I have been keeping to myself since last Wednesday." I hold my breath when I notice the seriousness in his eyes, scared of what he is about to disclose, but sure I know what it is going to be—he is working with the help of his family to return me to the hands of Dan Childs. Fear overwhelms the anger building up inside of me, and I nod for him to continue.

As we sit in front of the fire in our hotel room and eat the food Andrew ordered from room service, he proceeds to tell me that since my fainting incident at the MicroCorp commercial, he has been researching the company and its history. "At first, I shrugged it off as trauma—you had to process so much information that first day. But something in my gut told me I needed to learn all I could about MicroCorp. Every night after you went to bed, I would get on the Internet and read every article I could find about the company and its origins." *Now I know why he has been so tired.*

"The company started in 2000 doing technical work for banking institutions. I have been in foreign territory since I started my research, so I'll try to explain it as best I can. When banking institutions first open, they would hire MicroCorp then a small company with about twenty employees to set up their computer systems. These systems were basic—payroll, e-mail systems, and general company information such as the names of CEOs, board members, and company policies. The company grew when the banks they had done work for referred them to other opening banks. MicroCorp must have benefitted from word of mouth because now, 75 percent of opening businesses use MicroCorp for all their technology needs. They are also one of the top employers in the United States."

This all sounds pretty normal to me—that's how businesses grow, through the referral of past customers to possible new ones. Andrew must recognize the questioning look in my eyes because he impatiently says, "Think about it, Elle. MicroCorp has handled thousands of people's personal information. Not to mention their clients' company financial records. They have even done some work for the government."

Andrew's last words cause a memory flash unlike any I have had before. It's like someone presses a button attached to my brain and a video tape begins to play.

Chapter 25

Eleanor

I can see a set of tall glass doors with silver handles. I reach to push them open and check over my shoulder. I see no one on the rainy streets who pose a threat, just a homeless woman asleep on a bench. I turn back to the massive doors before I lose my nerve. *Just walk in. One step at a time.* It takes all my body weight to shove open the doors, and immediately I feel the air-conditioning. Drops of sweat slide down the back of my shirt, and I'm not sure if they are products of the humidity or my nerves. I know where I need to go as I walk to the closest bank of elevators and pull my ID badge from my back pocket. I swipe the card and then step in as soon as the doors open. I push the floor I need, 30, and count as the elevator climbs.

One, two, three. *Breathe.*
Four, five, six. *I'm doing the right thing.*
Twelve, thirteen, fourteen. *I can do this.*
Twenty-one, twenty-two, twenty-three. *Stay focused.*
Twenty-seven, twenty-eight, twenty-nine, thirty. *People's lives depend on this.*

The elevator dings, the doors open, and I step into the hallway.
Get what I came for, and then I'll be safe. My feet fall into their normal routine, so I don't even have to think about how to get to my cubicle, which is a good thing because my brain is going over the next details of my plan. *Download the file, exit through the back, walk 137 paces to Waterton Street, catch a cab to the apartment, ask it to wait, pick up the bag next to the door, get into the waiting cab and ride to the airport, take the ticket to the*

check-in desk, and board the plane. Be there in enough time to turn on the laptop and send the e-mail before takeoff.

It sounds easy enough, but I purposefully omit the possibility of being caught, stopped in traffic, or even spraining my ankle because I know any lost time means the loss of lives and possibly the loss of my life. Thankfully, I don't sprain my ankle, not yet anyway, and I reach my desk at nine fifty-three. My flight takes off at eleven, so I have just barely enough time to complete everything I have to.

As I turn on my computer, I look to the desks around me that will be filled tomorrow by my fellow employees, some of them friends, others just acquaintances, but none of them enemies. What will they think when they find out it was me who destroyed the company and caused them to lose their jobs? *This is what I was sent here to do. Don't forget.*

I see a flash of the Capitol building as my screen blinks to life, pulling my thoughts back to the task at hand. I navigate my way around the screen and find the correct file, marked "October", and download it to the flash drive I brought with me. I don't worry about deleting my personal information from the computer because I know the team will do that as soon as they receive my e-mail from the airplane. As soon as the download is complete, I don't even take the time to turn off my computer before I am on my feet.

When I walk past a wall clock, I notice the time, nine fifty-eight. I can't believe it took me five minutes. *Not good. That means I only have one hour to reach the plane. Fingers crossed for that unsprained ankle.*

As I swipe my ID badge to access the elevator, I know the danger is very real. The doors open on the ground floor to reveal an empty lobby. I pick up the pace as I head toward the back exit when I hear an unmistakable voice. "Ms. Greene, I've been expecting you."

****

I wake to see Andrew's closed eyes only a few inches from mine. His thick eyebrows are relaxed during sleep, and I lie there enjoying the privilege of getting to stare at him without scrutiny. Finally, I roll over to see the sky is still dark. The clock on the bedside table reads one forty, and I am immediately transported back to the wall clock in the office: nine fifty-three. *Who Am I?*

I know I should try to sleep, but all I see when I close my eyes is the word "October", and all I hear is the sound of Dan Childs's voice saying my name. I creep out of bed and make my way onto the patio. Just past the hotel's gardens, I can see the dome of the Capitol building. The sight which brought me such curiosity earlier now brings only fear. I hear Andrew coming up behind me, and I lean into his warm embrace.

"Please come back to bed, Eleanor. It's cold out here." Hearing him say my name, my fake name, causes me to freeze. Anger rises up from my toes. I can feel it creeping up my legs, burning in my belly, and reaching its peak in my chest.

I swing around to face Andrew and scream at the top of my lungs, "That's not my name! Don't call me that. Don't you dare call me that." He tries to reach out to me, but I slap his arm away. "Stay away from me," I continue screaming. "You don't know who I am. I could hurt you. I might hurt you. Just stay away from me!"

My voice is becoming more hysterical, the anger fading away being replaced with fear. Andrew does not back away from me but keeps advancing forward with his arms outstretched. "Please," I whisper. "Stay away from me. I don't want to hurt you."

My body is racked with sobs, and I finally collapse into his waiting arms. He holds me tight and whispers back, "You could never hurt me."

Andrew leads me back into the room and deposits me in front of the fireplace. As he tries to get the fire going again, he begins talking, so quietly at first I have to strain my ears to make out his words. "You're wrong, you know. I do know who you are, Elle." He turns with a fierce look on his face. "I'll admit I don't know your real name or your birthday or where you were born. I don't know your parents' names or what you do for a living. But I do know who you are. I see your true self radiating in all you do. You are beautiful and brave. You are smart and adventurous and trusting. You are gracious and giving, and you love completely. Those are the things that matter about a person—their character. But more importantly, those are the things that matter to me. All that other stuff may seem important, but it does not define you. Your actions are what define you, Elle. The person you choose each day to be in spite of what you have been through—that is who you really are."

I sit there in silence as his words sink in. *What have I done to deserve this man?*

I stand up and close the distance between us in two strides. Instead of Andrew reaching out to me, I am the one who folds him into an embrace. "You were right about one thing," I say into his chest.

"Just one thing?" he chuckles.

"Well, maybe more than one thing, but you were right about the most important thing: I do love completely—I love you completely." The sudden realization and admission take my breath away. After two weeks of not knowing anything about myself and two days of being in complete agony about the man I love possibly being the one in charge of hurting me again, I'm not sure if I can stand on my own anymore.

I take Andrew's hand and lead him toward the bed. I put my hands on his chest and feel a hint of his scars under his shirt. I look up, wanting to ask how he got them, but he shakes his head. Not now, he seems to say. We lie quietly in bed holding on to each other as the minutes turn into hours, and we drift to sleep.

Chapter 25

Andrew

I knew that bringing Eleanor to this city was a risky move, but I never dreamed it would have the effect it did. As I lay here, looking at her slow breaths and watching her eyelids fluttering at some unknown dream, I am filled with emotion so strong it takes my breath away. After Elle's fainting incident in Carmel, I knew that MicroCorp was deeply tied to what happened to her in Honolulu. Seeing Dan Childs standing in the hallway at my father's office only confirmed my suspicions. What I didn't know was the extent of that connection. I guess after all this time, I never registered the fear that was buried in Elle's subconscious.

After her most recent memory flash, all she could do was rock back and forth, making no noise and not answering my questions. I felt more helpless in that moment than I did when I first found her. This type of trauma is not easily fixed like a broken bone or a cut on the cheek. All I could think to do was hold her until she surrendered to a fitful sleep.

Her outburst on the balcony was even more frightening simply because I had no way of reaching her—it's like she shut me out. I was determined to let her know the truth of how I felt, and I poured my heart out unlike I ever had before. All the things I have wanted to say to her finally felt appropriate and wanted, even needed, and so that is what I did. I laid it all on the line, and it's like I could see the mask of insecurity fall off her like a blanket, and she was my brave girl again. I knew more than ever there was no going back—I am completely and totally hers.

****

Eleanor

Sometime around noon, Andrew and I emerge from the honeymoon suite. We have no plans for the day, and when we exit the hotel lobby, my spirit soars with the clouds. We walk hand in hand along the street.

"My conference call is at four, so we have a few hours to kill. What do you want to do?"

I shrug my shoulders. "The weather is so nice today I hate to think of us wasting it by staying inside."

"I could have slept all day," he says seriously. "I think I'm becoming lazy."

I smile as I say, "You might not ever return to work full time." He gives me a pointed look. "I know you miss it, Andrew, and we'll have plenty of time to devise a long-term plan."

It wasn't the deal Andrew wanted, but we both agreed we needed to find a degree of normalcy once we returned home. I know I will have to continue Andrew's research into MicroCorp if I have any hope of finding out the truth. However, the more I think about it, the less certain I am discovering my past is what I really want.

We are pleasantly surprised to find a book fair taking place on one of the streets downtown. I have discovered in the last two weeks a love for reading, and I lose myself in the rows and rows of tables piled high with books of all kinds. I notice Andrew looking at the books too. But mostly, he is looking at me. Each time I tear my gaze away from the tables, I find him staring at me with a light in his eyes, which has nothing to do with the Steven King novel in his hand. Finally, he cannot stand the distance between us and gathers me into his arms and kisses me fiercely. I am lost in the feeling of his lips on mine. I regretfully pull away from him, my lips red and swollen. Andrew runs his hand through his blond hair and chuckles a bit. He turns to walk away, and I find myself truly smitten.

The two of us walk away from the book fair with a plastic bag full of used books, most of them mine, but a few of Andrew's choosing. One book we both agreed to get was a book of love poems. I was really surprised to find Andrew pouring over the words on the pages. Even though I know he is romantic in his actions and deeds, the idea of him showing his feeling through words is a little strange to me. However, I realize there are many things I do not know about my husband.

"I should be back before five," Andrew tells me as he walks out of the bathroom. "Do you plan on staying in the room?" I look up from the weather channel.

"Actually, the rain is supposed to hold off, so I thought about going to that coffee shop across the street. You know, try to do something normal. I've been out of the loop for too long, and when you go back to work next week, I have to be comfortable on my own."

Andrew sighs, "If it was up to me, I would keep you locked up where I know you'd be safe. But I understand your desire for independence." He leans over to place a kiss on my forehead. "Why don't you take my cell phone and call Nicole and Joshua? I'm sure they would love to hear about your progress. Plus, she can give my parents a satisfactory update. I know they're chomping at the bit for a piece of news." He reaches into his pocket and pulls out his phone, an extra room key, and some money.

"Thanks," I say as I place them in my small purse. "If I'm not here when you get done with the conference call, I'll be across the street." I stand from the bed, and we walk toward the door together.

As Andrew puts his hand on the doorknob, he stops and turns to face me. "I'll be just a short distance away, and I promise I'll come find you right after I get finished." I can tell he is hesitant to leave me after my episode last night, so I put on a brave face.

"I'll be fine, Andrew." I pull him into a lingering kiss before he can sense my nervousness. The kiss lasts longer and has more heat than I had planned. He breaks away first.

"On second thought, I hate my job. I don't care about my patients, and I don't ever want to go back." We both laugh as he walks down the hall and throws me a kiss before stepping into the elevator.

When I walk into the bathroom to comb my hair, it is still full of steam from Andrew's shower. On the fogged-up mirror, he has left me a message. I guess he figured if I didn't see it now, I would see it the next time I took a shower of my own. The words are beautiful, and I wonder at their origin but for only a second. I am so filled with awe my mind reads the words over and over again.

> "Even so we met and after long pursuit,
> Even so we joined, we both became entire;
> No need for either to renew a suit,
> For I was flax, and She was flames of fire:
> Our firm-united souls did more than twine;
> So I my Best-beloved's am; so She is mine."

Chapter 26

Eleanor

Capital Cups Coffee Shop is a cozy small place with no more than ten tables. Beside me and the barista, only two more people are in the shop. I noticed them when I first walked in because the table between them is piled high with thick books. The pair appears to be college age, one male and one female. In their laps lay notebooks similar to my memory journal but filled in every square inch with messy script. I assume they are studying and turn my eyes to the menu.

I order a regular coffee and sit as far from the students as I can. I choose a seat facing the street and pull Andrew's phone from my bag. I press the correct speed dial button and wait for Nicole to answer. She sounds relieved to hear from me, and our conversation starts with the news of the week with me telling her about our trip and my flashback.

"We are truly having a great time. However, my memory flash last night was a bit of a shock. I haven't had one so traumatic since the dressing room incident. Needless to say, Andrew was so sure everything was going well with my recovery. He did not like the surprising turn of events."

"Andy never has liked surprises. Hates them, in fact. Christmas and his birthday are always torture for both him and us because he cringes when he thinks we've done something for him. A few years ago, he finally asked us to stop getting him gifts. To be honest, we were all relieved. It's no fun giving to someone who hates receiving."

I laugh a little myself and say, "He has said from the beginning finding me in that alley was the biggest surprise of his life. I'm sure he hated it."

Nicole stays quiet for a few seconds and then answers, "Yeah, you're probably right about that."

"Nicole, since we are on the subject of Andrew, I have a couple more questions for you."

"Shoot," she replies.

"Why are you the only person who calls Andrew 'Andy'? I've noticed that everyone, even his parents, call him Andrew."

She really laughs now. "I've always called him that. Joshua and I met when we were in eighth grade, so that put Andy in third grade. The first time I came to the compound to study, this nerdy little kid came up and shook my hand. 'I'm Steven Andrew Smith, and it's nice to meet you,' he said. I thought his proper introduction was hilarious. I mean, he was only eight years old. I returned his handshake and said, 'Nice to meet you, Andy.' I saw him wince when I called him that, but he smiled great big, so I knew it didn't bother him too much. From then on, I called him Andy. And I am the only one who is allowed to call him that. He puts his foot down if anyone else tries."

"Whoa, I guess I'll keep calling him Andrew then."

Nicole sighs, "I think you could call him anything you want, and he would come running."

I'm not really sure how to respond to that, so I continue with my line of questioning. "When is Andrew's birthday?"

"August," she says, and I can hear her smiling on the other end. "It's August 6, 1978. He'll be thirty-five this year." I feel a twinge of sadness when I think about how little I know about him.

Nicole must sense my hesitation because she quietly adds, "Eleanor, I know you feel disappointed and a little scared by your recent episode, but I can promise you Andrew is probably the most capable person to help you through this."

"Why do you say that? How could anyone—"

She interrupts me before I can finish. "I can't tell you that. Andrew will share his past when he is good and ready. Honestly, I am surprised he hasn't mentioned it yet. My guess is it hasn't even crossed his mind. But when he does tell you, then you'll understand why he is so equipped to deal with trauma."

I can't handle any more evidence of my lack of knowledge about the man who is supposed to be my husband. We hang up with the promise of another phone call closer to our arrival date in Carmel. Nicole says she will call my neurologist with the information about my episode. "Maybe he can tell us if this is a good sign."

I feel encouraged as we end our conversation because since my "episode", as I am choosing to call it, I have been so busy questioning its meaning I never stopped to analyze its importance to getting my memory back. It was, by far, the longest and most vivid memory flash. I pull my memory journal out of my bag and begin the daunting task of writing it down in as much detail as possible. Andrew's phone says that it is four forty-seven. He should be done soon. Good, I miss him more than I thought I would. I start writing quickly, wanting to be done with the task and back in my hotel room when I hear approaching footsteps. I expect them to be the barista's, but when I look up, a different familiar face is looking back.

****

Andrew

I felt strangely buoyant as I rode the elevator down to the hotel's main floor. When we checked in yesterday, I made sure they had a way I could conduct a conference call. Luckily, they have a small computer room I was allowed to rent out for forty-five minutes. Elle was certain when I walked out of the hotel room, I was going to simply check on my patients at the hospital. And I was okay with letting her think that was my plan. But as the doors open onto the main lobby, I continued to have doubts of my own about the call that is going to change everything.

Unfortunately, the man behind the front desk informed me they are having problems with the Internet connection, and my resolve began to dwindle. The clerk told me they will have the problem fixed as soon as possible, and if I would like to find a place in the hotel bar, they will notify me immediately when it is working. For a split second, I thought of going back up to my room and surprising Elle, but I'm pretty sure she could use some alone time, just like me. I made my way to the bar in view of a flat-screen TV and watched with little interest.

As I sat there nursing a rum and Coke, I was amazed at the amount of anxiety I had over the possible events in next several hours. My plan was to thank the hospital board of directors for all their patience in the last couple of months and their willingness to take me onto their staff with such short notice three years ago. My hasty employment was not of my own doing but ended up being a godsend.

After returning from Afghanistan, I was having a hard time finding a place for my particular skills. Because I went directly into the military after high school and attended Uniformed Services University, then served as a field doctor, I had no practice with the art of compassion—the type of compassion needed to deal with an eighty-nine-year-old woman who is increasingly forgetful and has broken her hip simply walking to the car or the type of compassion required to deal with a mentally ill patient who refuses to take their medications or heed any sort of doctor's advice or the type of compassion needed to deal with a young child sick because of lack of nourishment.

My hands-on experience was with bleeding and busted soldiers in the middle of a battlefield with bombs exploding all around and bullets whizzing by. Needless to say, it took me quite some time to find any compassion to deal with my new normal, everyday patients.

There were times in the first few months I would have to excuse myself to go scream in the staff bathroom because I was so tired of dealing with people who were not interested in fighting for their own lives. The final straw was when a junkie father and mother of three small children came into the hospital claiming their five-year-old was sick, only to obtain pain medication for themselves. After I grabbed the father by the front of his shirt and pushed him into a wall, I had to take serious stock in why I was doing this job. Not to mention the disciplinary action taken by the hospital for my violence.

As I take a sip of my drink and watch the news report change to local weather, I can distinctly remember the knock on my door at home, which changed everything. From that conversation to this day, I have never again lost my temper while treating a patient. There are still times I leave the room to take a few calming breaths, but my compassion grew with each new person I treated; and for the next two years, I had a handle on the purpose of my life and where I wanted it to go.

Ever since I found Elle in Hawaii, I have felt that same sense of purpose in my life. I like having the ability to solely focus on her—treating her wounds, helping her face reality, and even now, finding out who she really is. And that is one of the things that went into my decision to leave the hospital. The one-on-one care I was able to give Eleanor seemed to make such a difference in her healing process, there is no other explanation for her rapid recovery. I have no doubt the constant supervision she was under is the main reason we are in Washington DC today. I believe my past will allow me to help patients, not only physically but mentally as well. The scars on my chest and back are not the only ones I carry, and I think that gives me a unique ability.

I was pulled out of my reverie by the young man who works as the hotel bellboy hovering by my right side. "Sir, I was sent to inform you our Internet is now working. Unfortunately, you have probably missed your conference call, so you have been given a free night in our hotel."

Looking at the clock behind me, I had no idea thirty-five minutes had already passed since I left Elle in the hotel room. More than likely, she is now at the small coffee shop across the street, and my heart aches with the sudden realization that she is farther away from me now than she has been all week. I thanked the bell hop and headed in the direction of the computer room to try to contact the hospital in Carmel via the hotel telephone.

As I exited the bar, I noticed a man sitting in one of the club chairs lining the walls of the room. With a newspaper in front of his face, I couldn't see him; but the moment I approached his chair, his cell phone rang, and he answered with an authoritative yes. I stopped midstep, right in front of him, and strained my ears to hear him say something else. I know I have heard that voice.

• •

Before the man behind the newspaper could say anything else, though, the bell hop cleared his throat and said, "Dr. Smith, the computer room is this way."

There was no way I could stand there another second and not seem like a crazy person, so I reluctantly followed the young man out of the bar. As I walked away, I can't help but have a bad feeling at the pit of my stomach, and it took all my strength not to run out of the lobby in search of Elle.

****

Eleanor

"Hello, Ms. Greene. May I sit down?" All I can do is nod my head as Dan Childs, CEO of MicroCorp, pulls a chair out and positions it across the table from me. "I was not expecting to ever see you again, so you'll excuse me if I don't seem enthusiastic you are apparently back from the dead. I don't want to waste any time," he continues, "so I'm going to get straight to the point. I want my file. You know which one I am referring to, of course, the one labeled 'October.' My body is so frozen with fear and confusion all I can do is clear my throat. "Come, come, Ms. Greene. My patience is wearing thin."

I continue to stay silent and try to keep the shaking in my hands from traveling to the rest of my body. "I'm sorry, sir. I have no idea what you are talking about. I believe you have me confused with someone else." I deliver the line, and it sounds weak even to my ears.

Dan Childs stares into my eyes with a look of pure hatred. At an unspoken signal, the two students, along with the barista, get up and walk out of the coffee shop at the same time two men in black suits approach my table and position themselves around me. My mind launches into finding an escape route, but it seems hopeless; I am surrounded with no way out.

"Don't even think about it, my dear. There is no way out. I have taken away all your options. There isn't anyone to aid in your rescue like in Hawaii." How did he get rid of everyone? Mr. Childs must see the question on my face because he answers as if I asked it out loud. "You see, when you are me, anything is possible. And you wouldn't believe how far a little cash will go. It just so happens that Dr. Smith's conference call was delayed when the hotel's Internet suddenly stopped working." When he says these words, I have to grip the table for support.

As he leans toward me, I can see the hint of a scar above his left eyebrow. "Ms. Greene, consider yourself lucky to be sitting here today. In my opinion, the cost of a file verses the cost of your life should not be a hard decision. But yet, here you sit, pretending not to know who I am." He gives me a questioning look. "You could simply give me what I want, and I will walk out of here and leave you and the good doctor to your happily ever after. Yes, Ms. Greene. I know all about your new marital status, and I can promise you there will be repercussions, not only to you but to Dr. Smith as well if I do not receive my file."

This is when I finally realize Andrew's innocence and wonder how I could ever have doubted him. Mr. Childs's threat breaks something loose inside me, and my fear is replaced with a hatred of my own. I start to see black spots on the edges of my vision, and I lean the rest of the way across the table, making our eyes level.

"Okay, Mr. Childs, I'll admit I know who you are." He looks slightly pleased at this. "However, you're not going to like what I have to admit next. I don't have a clue where your file is. You see, when your thugs beat me within an inch of my life, raped me, and left me for dead in that alley, they damaged more than my body." A fleeting look of surprise crosses his face, but I continue. "I can't remember anything. I have trauma-induced amnesia. There is no telling when my memory will return, if it returns at all, so you are out of luck. But I have to admit, if you are willing to kill me and threaten not only my life but also the life of my husband for this information, it must be pretty important. I can promise you I will never give you what you want, even if I did have it." I sit back in my chair slowly, never dropping my eyes from his.

Mr. Childs lets out a small laugh. "Don't think for a second your 'marriage' fooled me. I know it was nothing more than a ploy to get you out of Honolulu. I was hoping, however, you would cooperate, but you seem determined not to." He sighs, "Your memory loss is a shame. But no matter, it will only cause a short delay."

He's too calm. What does he mean by "short delay"? He flicks his wrist as if to dismiss there is even a problem.

"Mr. Childs, I am getting tired of trying to guess what you have planned for me, so can we just get it over with?" His answering smile almost sends my courage plummeting to the floor.

"Very well, Ms. Greene. I suppose you're right. I told you I did not want to waste any time, and here I am doing it myself." He sighs, stands up, and motions for me to do the same. I reach for my bag, but he shakes his head, so I leave it there and walk to the door, flanked by the two bodyguards. I stop before we reach the door.

"Promise me you will leave Dr. Smith alone. He has nothing to do with this. To him, I am only a patient. Promise me he won't get hurt." He nods, but I don't believe him. We walk outside toward a black car parked on the curb. One of the guards opens the rear passenger door and motions for me to get inside. I prepare a gaze that could melt flesh, but when I look at him, he gives me a small but distinct wink. I stop, momentarily confused, and then hear someone yelling my name. I turn to see Andrew racing across the street with a look of panic on his face and questions in his eyes. At the same time, I see the other bodyguard stop and reach for his revolver.

I have to keep Andrew safe.

I look back to Andrew, catch his eyes, and shake my head. I hope he understands what I am trying to say: *Stop, Andrew. Stay back. It's my turn to save your life.* Before I can lose my nerve, I dive into the backseat, and the last thing I hear are Andrew's screams: "Stop! Wait! Eleanor, please!"

Chapter 27

Eleanor

As we wind through the streets of Washington DC, I don't try to keep track of our movements. Even if I felt like counting the number of left and right turns, my mind is too full of agony. *What must Andrew think? I just left him standing there after all he's done for me.* I try to get a handle on my current situation. Mr. Childs's bodyguards have left my hands and feet untied, so I have the freedom to move around. They must not think of me as a threat. I can't fathom the fate that awaits me, so instead I close my eyes and think about my past. I conjure up the image of Andrew's face the first time I saw him. I focus on the joy that was radiating from his eyes, and I let it penetrate my bones.

A series of pictures flow through my mind, like a slideshow being played: sunlight streaming in a window; hills of vineyards; Joshua's wide smile; my mother's brown eyes; my ravaged reflection in the mirror; grilled cheese sandwiches and chocolate milk; Sean's deep laugh; Andrew's lips; the feel of his body against mine; an aquarium full of fish; a clock on a wall—nine fifty-three; the hotel's garden; Tom, the pilot's warm smile. On and on the pictures flow, a mix of my past and present. I let the good memories wash over me, and I wince at the bad ones, allowing them to sharpen my emotions. I can hear Andrew's voice, saying, "Take control of your situation, and it will never control you." I open my eyes to see the bodyguard who winked, staring at me. I give him a questioning look, but he turns back to the window.

"Mr. Childs, where are you taking me?" He seems busy with his cell phone and doesn't turn around from the front passenger seat when he answers.

"We are headed for MicroCorp headquarters. Just a couple more minutes, and we will be there. I suggest you take those few minutes to try and relax." Of course, his words have the exact opposite effect. Instead of relaxing, my nerves stand at attention, and my palms begin to sweat. I have no doubt this reaction was Mr. Childs's intention.

True to his word, we shortly arrive at a large modern all-glass building. The large parking lot is full of cars, and there are people everywhere. Relief rushes over me. *He wouldn't hurt me with all these people around, especially when he was so concerned about witnesses in the coffee shop.* We park in the first space which has a sign, saying, "Reserved for Dan Childs, CEO." The bodyguard who was driving gets out to open Mr. Childs's door at the same time Winky (that's what I'm calling the other bodyguard) gets out and heads for my door. He is out of the car for two seconds, but that gives me enough time to steal my nerves.

I can do this. Stay calm. Just breathe. Winky opens my door, and I fall into step behind Mr. Childs. As we pass people, they smile and nod, some of them even call out to him, "Good afternoon, Mr. Childs. Hope you're having a good day." Apparently, none of them see me as a hostage because their smiles are just as friendly to me.

We stop at a reception desk inside, and a young woman with red hair hands Mr. Childs a stack of papers. "Good afternoon, Cindy," he says. "Do I have anything urgent that needs attention before I retire for the day?"

"No, Mr. Childs, just the usual—missed phone calls, awaiting e-mails, and your schedule for tomorrow. Will you be needing anything before I go?"

"Yes," Mr. Childs answers. "Please direct all my cell phone calls to my office phone. I will see you tomorrow, Cindy. Thank you."

Cindy returns to her work, never once glancing my way. My heart sinks as we make our way to the elevators. The last time I rode one in a MicroCorp office building, I was alone, in danger, and risking my life. Now here I am again, going to my possible death with no one to help me, not even Cindy, the receptionist.

Dan pushes the button labeled "B" for the basement, and my reassurance about there being so many witnesses drops along with the elevator. The doors open to reveal a long concrete hallway, and I follow Dan and his bodyguard out of the elevator and past three doorways, two on the right and one on the left. I find myself counting our steps:

One, two, three, four. Stay calm.
Five, six, seven, eight. You can do this.
Nine, ten, eleven, twelve. Be brave.
Thirteen, fourteen, fifteen, sixteen. Just keep walking.

We stop at the second door on the left, and Dan precedes me into the room; but before I step through the door, I promise myself I will walk out again. The concrete room is sparsely furnished with one metal table and two metal chairs. I would classify it as an interrogation room, except for the fact I am still not handcuffed, and there is no two-way mirror. There is, however, a video camera in one corner, close to the ceiling. On the metal table sits a file folder with the name, R. Greene, written across the top, and my fingers ache with the desire to grab the folder.

That's my name on the folder. That must be my folder. I have to get my hands on whatever is in there. Then I stop myself. Dozens of questions replace my determination to get a hold of the information lying on the table. Why does Dan Childs have a folder with my name on it? How did it get down here in the basement? I know no one carried it in just now. That must mean he believed I would return here with him. Well, he guessed that one right. Dan motions me to one chair, and I sit on the edge of the seat, trying to get as close to the table as possible. It's like there is a cord connecting my gut to the folder.

"Ms. Greene, I know you must be apprehensive about what I have planned for you. All I can say is hurting you is not my intention. After you told me about your memory loss, I contacted Cindy and had her place your file down here. I thought the easiest way to retrieve the information I want would be to let you look over your personal information which was collected when you began working for MicroCorp, and then after your, um, hasty resignation? I did my own digging into your life. However, I was not able to find out too much. That is probably because of your involvement with the government." I sit here in stunned silence as he openly discusses his knowledge of my infiltration into his company.

He continues, "I did realize, of course, not everything you put down on your MicroCorp application was true. Obviously, you couldn't put down your work for the government as a spy."

My eyes widen until I feel like they are going to pop out of my head. Dan's voice is full of a quiet rage, and I remind myself just how dangerous this man is. After my "episode", I figured my job was exactly like Dan just described. However, "government spy" is a little hard to wrap my head around. But in that moment, I am filled with snapshots of my previous life: I see my reflection looking back at me, only red hair hangs straight to my shoulders, instead of my usual curly brown hair; I push a cleaning cart down the stately hall of a large house; I wipe down a table, focusing on the men at the next table and not on the rag in my hand; I'm jogging on a treadmill surrounded by dozens of other masochists with a set of earbuds tuned into a private government conversation instead of my workout playlist.

In those two seconds, I get more memories of my past than the previous two weeks of globe-trotting. I feel excited I might actually gain some insight to the question that has been plaguing me since I woke up in Carmel.

Dan slides the folder into my outstretched hands as he says, "I'm sure you are just as eager to read what is in here as I am to retrieve my file. Take your time but know when you are finished, the hard work begins." As he stands up to leave, he says, "I will leave Jones outside of your door, if you need anything."

I look up only to see which bodyguard he indicates as Jones. *Damn, it's not Winky.* I nod and return my focus to the folder. I wait until I hear the door shut and then dive into my past.

I'm not sure how long I stare at my name. It feels like hours, but it must have only been a few minutes. Rebecca Elizabeth Greene is such a pretty name. I wonder if I am named after someone, maybe my mother. The idea gives me a warm feeling, but I'm so desperate for more information I don't dwell on the warm and fuzzy for long. The next line contains my birth date: May 13, 1984. That makes me twenty-eight years old, soon to be twenty-nine, very soon. All I can think is, gosh, I'm older than I thought. But I remember Andrew is thirty-four. *Andrew.* A sharp pain stabs through my heart, and I make myself continue reading.

Hometown: Knoxville, Tennessee. No wonder the mountains were so familiar.

If I stopped reading right now, I would be satisfied. However, one of my biggest questions is still unanswered. *What about my parents?* I search line by line trying to find a "Relations" section. When I do find the right spot, the line is left blank. Oh well, that would have been too good to be true. With the feeling of disappointment creeping into my stomach, my eyes light on the next line down. There are two lines for emergency contacts, and while the first was left blank, the second is filled in completely. My heart leaps in my chest as I read the name Lauren Price, and a face flashes in my vision—beautiful blue eyes and blond hair, a smile that is spread wide and friendly.

"Hello, I wanted to introduce myself. My name is Lauren Price, and I live next door. It is so nice to have a new face in the complex. Unfortunately, most of the other tenants are either old or unfriendly. I see you are definitely not old, so I am just praying you are not unfriendly." A smile spreads across my face as I remember my friend. I admit to myself I feel a wave of relief coursing through me. At least I was not completely alone in my old life. I have to contact her after I get all this straightened out.

My eyes jump back to the top of the page, and I start reading in detail the rest of my application. I'm pretty sure most of this information is false.

The "Education" portion is short, having just one school and degree listed: Vanderbilt University, bachelor of science degree in business. Under the "Previous Employment" section, I see that Dan was right—"government spy" is not listed. I chuckle at the completely ordinary answer I provided: office manager, at some place called Smart Financial.

I continue reading down the page when Jones walks in with a machine the shape of a box. I notice the wires and electrodes right away, and the only thing that can draw my attention away from the identity of my past is wheeled toward the table. I speak up, knowing I won't get the answer I seek but not being able to keep quiet. "What is that?"

Surprising me with both his answer and the softness of his voice, Jones responds, "It's a machine designed to retrieve information using electroshock therapy." I freeze in my seat and try to process this new piece of information. I'm not sure if what he said or the way he said it, with a cold sense of detachment, bothered me more. Electroshock therapy. Dan did warn me the hard work was about to begin. Did I really believe he would let me walk out of here unharmed? "Oh" is all I can say to Jones as he walks back toward the door and shuts it behind him.

• •

The promise I made to myself about walking back out of this room seems foolish now. There is no reason for me to devise an escape plan from a place that is inescapable. I let my barriers down, and the flood gates open for the second time in two days. Was it really only last night when I had my episode? It seems like so much has happened since I was in Andrew's arms. All the same fears come back.

Now that I allow myself to really think on it, every piece of information in this folder could be and, probably is, forgery. I was so desperate, too desperate for any clues I believed everything. If I really was (am) a spy for the government, there is no way they would allow my real information to get into the wrong hands, Dan Childs's hands, for example. My tears start pouring down my face, but I don't make a sound.

As I begin to count aloud, taking deep breaths to steady my nerves, I think I hear the muffled sound of shoes squeaking outside my door. I strain my ears but stay in place, afraid to leave the twisted comfort of my chair. I can hear Jones asking to see someone's ID, and then I hear a surprised grunt followed by more squeaking of shoes. I can tell there is a lot of movement by the grunts and heavy breathing.

It seems like the commotion goes on forever, and when I hear a heavy thud, I know the scuffle is over. Keys rattle in the door lock, and I spring from my seat, putting as much distance as I can between the door and me. I'm not sure what or who I expect to see when the door flies open, but when Andrew jogs into the room with a bruised and bloody face, I nearly faint. He runs to me, and I fall into his arms, the realization hitting me that I never expected to see him again. He kisses my hair and then pulls away to face me. I let out a small cry of shock when I see his face up close. His lip is cut and bleeding as well as his forehead. His left eye is swelling fast and almost completely closed over the shocking green I have come to love.

"Eleanor," he sighs. "Are you okay? Did they hurt you?" His eyes flash toward the electroshock machine and back to me with more panic than before. I can only shake my head. He must believe me because he gets that determined look in his eyes. He grabs my hand and heads toward the door, but I pull from his grasp. Before we take another step, I say to him, "Andrew, I'm sorry. I didn't mean to hurt you by leaving you there on the street. I was just trying to protect you. Getting into that car was the hardest thing I have ever had to do . . . I think." At this, he smiles and pulls me against him again.

"Elle, I appreciate you looking after me, but in the future, just know being away from you is the only thing that can hurt me." We start toward the door again, and as soon as we cross the threshold, I see Jones lying on the ground. Although he has less blood on his face than Andrew, he is knocked out cold. Andrew steps over his limp body and grabs his ID badge out of his front shirt pocket. Andrew's hand is so close to Jones's gun that I am surprised when he does not grab it. Instead, he looks up at me and says, "If you think there is anything he might have on him that belongs to you, hurry and get it because we have to get out of here, now."

I run back into the room, grab the folder, and run out again, not pausing to see Jones's body again. As we race down the hall, my mind becomes full of questions: How did Andrew find me? How did he get in here? Where is Dan Childs? How are we going to get out of here?

I feel a tad bit safer when Andrew swipes the ID badge, and the elevator doors open. He pushes the button for the lobby and turns to face me. His smile is the most beautiful thing I could ever have imagined, and I let it infect me. Over Andrew's shoulder, I see Jones pull himself up and take aim. I go to scream, but no sound comes out. In a split second, Andrew's smile turns into a mask of shock. When his body falls against mine, I know he has been shot.

The doors close a second later, cutting off the spray of bullets now coming from Jones's hand gun. "Andrew! Can you hear me?" I am screaming into his ear, and I can't seem to calm my voice. I try to support his weight instead of laying him down because I know I will ever be able to lift him up again.

He nods his head and grimaces. "I'm fine." His voice is barely a whisper and is laced with pain. I can tell he is trying not to pass out, so I ask him what I can do. "Look at the wound. Am I losing a lot of blood?" I gently turn him around, and he lets me guide his body to the railing which lines the elevator. I pull up his cotton shirt to see a small hole in his right shoulder. A small stream of blood is flowing in a line down his back and mingling with his scars, making his body look ravaged. The sight and smell of blood causes a wave of nausea to flow over me. I try to calmly explain what I see and tell him I do not consider it a lot of blood loss. He sighs with relief but continues to support his weight on the railing.

"Do you have something you can use to apply pressure to the wound?" he asks me. I pull off my sweater, leaving me in only a tank top and push his wound gingerly. "Eleanor, I promise you won't hurt me any more than I already am." He gives a strained laugh, and then his voice turns serious. "If you don't apply pressure, I could bleed out."

I'm not sure if he is trying to scare me, but he does, and I put all my weight on his right shoulder as the elevator doors open. I expect to see the busy lobby of before. Instead, we are met with emptiness. I throw Andrew's good arm over my shoulder and drag him toward the front door.

"There should be a cab waiting for us," Andrew grunts. "Tell him to take me to the closest hospital. It doesn't matter which one, just the closest." Sure enough, a taxi cab is waiting in a visitor parking spot.

• •

I carefully load Andrew into the backseat as the cab driver starts screaming about. "This was not part of the deal, a bleeding man in my taxi, what is going on?" I glace over at Dan Childs's parking spot. The black car I arrived in is still parked there. I wonder where he is now. Does he know he's lost his file again? I am certain of only one thing: if I ever encountered Dan Childs again, the third time would not be a charm.

As I sit in the surgical waiting room, I marvel at how my luck has continued and begin adding things to the "Lucky List" I started at the small café in Carmel: lucky that some of my memories seem to be returning; lucky that, once again, Andrew found me; and lucky that the nearest hospital just happened to be the best one in Washington DC. Of course, I should also count the fact our taxi driver was relatively cool with our situation. After he found out his reward for a closed mouth would be a large amount of money, he quickly stopped yelling, which gave me the chance to keep Andrew talking.

I had to make sure he stayed conscious until we reached the hospital for several reasons. The first reason was, ironically, the same reason why Andrew never took me to a hospital after I sustained my injuries in Hawaii—I didn't know any of his personal information. Thanks to my earlier phone call with Nicole; I now knew Andrew's birthdate. But other than that, his full name and current address, I know nothing else, which would be required in an emergency situation. For example, his social security number, any allergies he might have, his medical history, or his families medical history. I was once again reminded how strange our relationship was and also how few of the details of his life I was privileged to know.

The second reason I wanted to keep him awake was to learn how he had found me—what happened between when I last saw him on the street and when he burst into my holding room at MicroCorp headquarters. As I asked Andrew to explain what happened, I noticed how weak his voice was becoming. Through labored breaths and long pauses, he told me the story of my second rescue.

"After you got into that car, my first instinct was to hail a cab and chase you down. However, I had a strange urge to run into the coffee shop. Why, I could not tell you. But before I did, I made myself memorize the black car as it was driving away. Thankfully, its license plate was visible because the rest of the car was remarkably ordinary. I then ran into the coffee shop and saw your bag and journal on the back table. I grabbed it and ran out, thinking I might get stopped by the barista or manager, but I noticed there was no one else in the shop.

"As I ran back outside, I could barely make out the black car, turning right about three or four blocks down. I silently prayed it was the same car you were in—it was really too far away to tell. I hailed a cab, which seemed to be there instantaneously. I told the driver I was following a black car and where I thought it turned. As we started driving, I had a sense that your final destination would be MicroCorp headquarters. Once we spotted the car, three blocks down, it made a left turn, and I told the driver not to let it out of his sight."

At this, Andrew cut off, too tired to continue, and I looked toward the taxi driver's nodding head and realized that he was confirming Andrew's story. I wanted to push Andrew further into telling me what happened after they reached the headquarters, but at that moment, the driver spoke up.

"Lady, we are almost there. I don't know what happened, and I don't want to. I also don't want to be questioned by the police when I drop you off, so go ahead and get my money ready 'cause as soon as we reach the ER, I'm outta there."

I can't say I blamed him for wanting to make a hasty retreat, but in that second, I realized I didn't have a story for the police either about how my husband received a bullet wound to the shoulder. Andrew nodded his head toward his wallet, and I grabbed every piece of green paper in it and threw the cash into the front seat, a parking ticket along with it. I looked at Andrew, hoping to get his attention, and saw him grimace. I leaned my mouth toward his ear and asked, "What am I supposed to say when they ask me what happened?" He just shook his head like he had no more strength left. I decided right then, and there it was my turn to step up and take charge.

For too long, I had been the victim, and I was suddenly tired of it. I told Andrew not to worry, which is exactly what I meant. We reached the ER, and I helped get Andrew onto the sidewalk. I turned to tell our driver another "thank-you", but true to his word, he had already split.

I was surprised at how much strength Andrew had left in him when we had to walk a good twenty yards to reach the nurses' station. They immediately saw he had been shot and called for someone to bring a gurney.

The next hour was a blur of answering questions I either didn't know the answer to or made up the answer on the spot. I did refer to Andrew when they asked if he had any allergies—terrified he might have a reaction to some kind of medication. When the doctor finally got around to asking how this had happened, I broke down crying. He probably figured it was from the stress of the situation, and it was—but not the situation he thought.

The last two days, actually the last month, had severely shaken me, and I had already failed in my resolution to take charge. I dried my tears and explained we had been mugged while walking around the city. The robber had taken my wallet and my ID, which of course I did not have in the first place, but it seemed like a good way to explain its absence and also Andrew's money (which the cab driver was probably already using to buy lottery tickets). When the doctor asked where this took place, I once again lied and told him I was not sure.

"We are not from here, we're on vacation. I have no idea the name of the road we were on. We could see the Capitol building. That's all I remember." The doctor explained Andrew had to have surgery to remove the bullet which could take several hours. He also informed me the police would have to be called because of the nature of the injury, and I should expect a visit from them within the next couple of hours. When I finally got the courage to ask the most important question, I could feel the tears begin to fill up my eyes again.

"Please, doctor, is he going to be okay?"

The doctor put his hand on my shoulder and nodded his head. "He will be fine."

So I sit here waiting for word on my husband's surgery. Thank goodness Andrew had the good sense to go into the coffee shop and get my purse because we would have been without a phone. I find it inside my bag and reluctantly dial Josh and Nicole's number for the second time today. Unfortunately, this call will not be as happy as the first.

Nicole answers after the second ring. "Hey, Andy, what's up?"

"It's not Andy. It's Elle."

"Oh, hey girl. Two phone calls in one day, I feel honored." The happy sound in her voice hits a nerve, and I start crying again, wondering when I became such a baby.

"Eleanor, what's wrong?" is the next thing out of Nicole's mouth. "It's all my fault, Nicole, all of it."

"What's your fault, Eleanor? Where is Andy? Is he okay?"

"No, he's not okay. He's been shot. We are at a hospital in DC. He is in surgery right now, and I don't know what is going on." I explain to her the best I can about what happened without being too specific in case Dan Childs has Andrew's phone tapped, and she quickly tells me her and Joshua are going to be here as soon as they can. I realize, as I hang up the phone, it will probably take them a couple of days to make the trip since they are on the other side of the country, but I already feel better knowing they are on their way.

Besides compiling the "Lucky List" of my good fortune, I make another mental list of all the ways I have brought bad fortune to Andrew. His whole life has been corrupted by me. Ever since he found me, he has sacrificed his career, his honest relationship with his family, his future, and now, his physical body for me. How in the world do I expect him to forgive me—forgive me for taking away all his choices, all his options for a happy, normal life, and forgive me for thinking for a second he was in league with Dan Childs?

I didn't know Andrew before a month ago, but I have a feeling he was living a well-rounded existence. I know he had a great job which he loved and a wonderful, supportive family. He probably played basketball with a group of friends every Saturday morning, went to Sunday brunch on the compound every week. I can even see him volunteering at the local food pantry or homeless shelter on weeknights. But now, his every waking moment is filled with me and my hopeless cause. It must be just as exhausting for him to think about my situation as it is for me.

This train of thought is bringing me down even more, so I decide to put my pity party aside. My resolution to stay in charge and quit playing the victim is made anew, and I am more determined than ever to follow through.

I am surprised by the fact that the surgical waiting room is so full for a weeknight. I sit there and look around at all the worried and anxious faces of family members waiting to hear either good or bad news about their loved ones. The thought causes me to pull out the Rebecca Greene folder I took with me when we fled MicroCorp headquarters. Once again, I start at the top of the job application and read it thoroughly, only stopping once to focus on Lauren's name. I will find her and let her know I am okay but only after this mess is taken care of. I will not bring her onto Dan Childs's radar.

I turn to the second page, which I did not have the chance to read the first time. However, as I glance over the information held there, I notice the whole page is handwritten with cramped notes down each side with few phrases scribbled out. I am relieved and a little disappointed to see it only has my current information listed. Andrew's address in Carmel is at the top with his name and occupation directly underneath. His family is briefly mentioned along with information about Smith Shipping, Incorporated.

Next to Andrew's name is one of those cramped notes that says "Relationship?" and I know immediately it is referring to mine and Andrew's. Dan Childs was probably trying to figure out how we know each other. Below that are a few notes I find extremely disturbing, mainly because of their personal and sometimes intimate nature: living in the same house; being introduced as a married couple; gone to several doctors' appointments; runs every day; taking family jet to several destinations; Atlanta Aquarium; rented car to drive through mountains; stayed in Myrtle Beach, South Carolina; making way north; Washington DC—Four Seasons Hotel; staying in the "honeymoon suite"—intimate? (probably); conference call at four; coffee shop across the street from hotel.

· ·

As I sit here and go over the last of the handwritten notes, I feel extremely vulnerable. I don't know how long Dan Childs has been following us or even how he has managed to get this much information about our day-to-day lives without us knowing it. From the nature of the notes, I can tell there has been someone extremely close to the family giving this information to him. Who could possibly be spying on us, and why would they betray Andrew like this? Dan Childs must have some kind of leverage, some sort of blackmail. That is the only way he could have gotten this information.

I continue down the page and notice someone has walked up and stopped right in front of me. I look over the top of my paper and see a pair of very shiny black dress shoes. My heart stops beating for a split second and then starts back up again, going twenty times the normal rate. I instantly think of Dan Childs, but when the voice that belongs to the shoes addresses me as Mrs. Smith, I relax my posture and look into the face of, not the doctor like I had hoped, but Winky the bodyguard. Once again, I tense up, but either the man does not notice or chooses to ignore the terrified look on my face.

"May I have a seat?" he asks quietly.

I'm not quite sure how to answer, so I simply nod my head and clear my stuff out of the way. As Winky sits down, I notice he has a handgun strapped to his belt and a folder in his hands, similar to the one sitting in my lap. It is hard for me to look him in the face at this angle, but I can tell he is not making eye contact with me; rather, he is looking out into the waiting room full of people. I wonder what he plans on doing to me, but as my mind conjures up all sorts of horrible images, the most prominent one being the electroshock machine sitting in a concrete-holding room at MicroCorp headquarters, he being talking again in a quiet, measured voice.

"Mrs. Smith, my name is Agent Bright, and I work for the CIA." At this, I try to interrupt him, my mind going into a thousand directions at once. He brings his hand up to silence me and continues talking as if what he said does not totally change everything. "I know you probably have a thousand questions." Wow, can he read minds too?

"But I don't have a lot of time. I came here for two reasons. First, I came to check on Dr. Smith's progress, and I see his surgery went well with no complications." Since this is more information than I have, I try to interrupt again, hoping to get more details about the surgery, but Winky, or Agent Bright, puts up his hand again to stop me, and I settle for a relieved sigh. "Secondly, I came to give you your real file—the one from our organization." When he says "our" organization, I'm not quite sure what he means; but before I can ask, he turns in his chair to face me. "Yes, Mrs. Smith, that's right. You are also an agent for the CIA but in a different capacity than me. I am not going into great detail, but let's just say your job for the agency could be classified as 'Intelligence Gatherer.'" I shift my gaze from his honest brown eyes to the folder lying in his lap.

· ·

I find my voice to ask, "So the information that Dan Childs has is completely false?"

"Not completely but about 98 percent is false." I feel both relief and regret hearing that fact: relief even though the "Relations" line was blank, that might not be the case, and relief Dan Childs does not know the real me. The regret sets in when I realize I still have no clues into my past.

"Agent Bright, I have a few questions of my own if you don't mind." Agent Bright nods his head in agreement. There are so many questions flitting through my mind I can only think of one that sums everything up. "What is going on?" I ask with all the exasperation I feel.

Agent Bright gives a little chuckle, and now it is his turn to sigh. I'm not sure if the sound is good or bad, so I wait patiently for his answer. It seems to take him a long time to arrange his thoughts, but when he starts to talk, I silently wish I could pull out my memory journal and take notes.

"As I said before, your job at the agency is as an intelligence gatherer, in which you do exactly that—gather intelligence. I'm not sure how much you remember, if any, but MicroCorp was not your first assignment." I feel my head nodding along, and Agent Bright takes notice of it and waits for me to elaborate.

"Yeah, I have had a few strange memories where my hair is a different color and cut, and sometimes I am wearing different uniforms." He nods like he knows exactly what I mean.

"I am not exactly sure how many assignments you have been on, but I think there's been more than ten." *Ten?* I must have a dumbfounded look on my face because the agent nods once again.

"Yes, it does seem like a lot of assignments for someone so young. Usually a person is on an assignment until the agency acquires the information they want or need. So you might work as a housekeeper for a government official for a few weeks or a waitress for a year or more. Your job is to retain large amounts of data in different situations and report everything you hear and see to the agency."

Even though I had a hunch that my job was exactly what he is describing, I am still surprised to hear the truth: I am a government spy. Agent Bright turns back to the crowded waiting room and continues.

"Of course, you can find all this information in your file. I'm going to have to tell the rest of this story in very general details because, after all, it was your assignment, not mine." He throws me a quick smile and launches into how I came to be a spy at one of the most prominent companies in the country.

"Because we are just lowly agency workers, we don't get too many details about the job we are assigned to do. You were sent to Hawaii to gain employment in MicroCorp's new offices as a computer analyst. Your objective was to recover a file known as 'October' and send it to the agency. As soon as you found it and sent it, you were supposed to walk away from the job and leave Hawaii. I have no doubt you had a strict and detailed escape plan, but once again, it was not my assignment, so I am unsure of the ins and outs."

When Agent Bright finishes talking, I see the file name "October" flash across my computer screen at MicroCorp once again, and I cannot stop the shiver which runs down my spine, knowing what happened after I downloaded that file. The agent sits there and lets me process the information for a couple of minutes and then glances at his watch. I can tell he wants to leave, but I still have so many questions for him I grab his arm as he starts to stand.

"Please, Agent Bright, tell me how you found out Andrew and I were here. I cannot stand the idea of Dan Childs walking in any moment." He just smiles and hands me the folder.

"I'm an agent of the CIA," he says, giving me another wink. "But don't worry, Dan Childs has no idea Dr. Smith is a patient in this hospital. The agency has erased any traces of his admittance. As far as Mr. Childs knows, you two have headed back to your house in Carmel. And don't worry, there is already surveillance on the Smith family property."

I am only partially put at ease Mr. Childs does not know where we are—he still knows where to find us. Agent Bright nods toward the two folders in my lap and says, "I hope you find everything you are looking for. I know these folders don't contain your memories, but maybe reading them will bring you some comfort as well as help you decide what to do next."

I don't have time to ask him what he means because at that moment, the doctor walks up to me and extends his hand, "Mrs. Smith, your husband is out of surgery, and everything went just fine. He will need some physical therapy in the following weeks, and you can expect to stay in DC for at least a few days while he recovers. But I see a full recovery in Dr. Smith's future with only minimal scarring and maybe some muscle stiffness. You will be notified when he is placed into a room, and you can go see him."

"Thank you so much, doctor. I am so grateful." As I shake the doctor's hand, I turn to address Agent Bright, but he is no longer next to me. I quickly scan the room and see his retreating back walking out the waiting room door. I have a pang of sadness seeing him leave, but I have a feeling this will not be our last meeting. I also have the feeling Agent Bright and I were not simply coworkers but friends as well.

****

Andrew

I swore when my feet touched American soil for the first time after being in war for three years, I would never put myself in another situation in which I would get shot at. But here I am, lying in a hospital bed with a gunshot wound to my right shoulder. Only a woman could have made me throw that promise out the window in so short a time!

I am so happy to be here, alive, and in a reasonably comfortable bed I cannot seem to muster up enough anger toward Elle for putting me in such a predicament. When I saw her jump into the backseat of that car, I felt like my life was speeding down the road with it. For a split second I could not think of anything—I was stunned, in shock Elle would leave me behind. But I remember the shake of her head, like she was trying to will me to stop and let her go. If I did not go after her, the past several weeks of my life, all the time I spent caring for this beautiful woman, learning what made her laugh, the softness of her skin, the determination which radiates from her, would have been for nothing. But most importantly, my future was in that car, and I knew I could never rest until Elle was safe in my arms again.

Chapter 28

Eleanor

It takes longer than I would hope for the waiting room attendant to notify me of Andrew's floor and room number. I have to keep myself from running to the elevator and down the hall of the surgical ward. As I reach his door, I hesitate out of fear, I guess. I am terrified of what might await me in the room. I don't think I have ever seen anyone in a hospital bed before, let alone anyone just getting out of a two-hour surgery. I remind myself Andrew took that bullet to protect me, and the least I can do is walk into his room with a smile on my face and all the support I can muster.

As I crack open the door, there is a nurse standing at the foot of Andrew's bed checking the machines and typing notes on a rolling computer. She smiles cordially when she notices me and beckons me further into the room. I wasn't sure what I expected, but I am relieved when I finally see Andrew. He has on a hospital gown that is pulled up on his left side while his right shoulder is exposed, showing his bare skin and a large white bandage which already has a tint of blood on it. His eyes are closed, and his breathing seems normal to me.

The nurse walks to the head of Andrew's bed to fiddle with the IV bags hanging on a tall pole. Her movements must wake Andrew because his eyes flutter open and found mine instantly. A smile so beautiful it melts my heart spreads across his face, and tears of relief spill from my eyes. He motions me over with his left hand. I notice there is an IV line taped onto the back of it, but besides this and the two pads on his chest monitoring his heartbeat, he is fairly untethered.

My shoes squeak on the shiny floor as I make my way to his bedside. I reach down and gently hold his right hand as the nurse finishes her task. She tells us it will be a while before the doctor will check in again, and if we need anything, we are to press the nurse's button located on the TV remote. I thank her and watch her walk out of the room before I turn my full attention to Andrew.

"I love you" are the first words out of his mouth, and I soak them up like a sponge. I lean down and kiss his forehead, then his temple, and even his cheek. I am so glad to see him awake and seemingly in good spirit I forget for a moment I could have lost him for good. My answering "I love you too" sounds weak even to my ears, and I shake my head, hoping to express to Andrew how inadequate I know the words are. He feebly squeezes my hand, and I smile at him.

I'm not sure how long I stand there just happy to be touching him before my feet start to fall asleep, as does Andrew. I regrettably let go of him and place myself in a very uncomfortable chair and allow him to rest. I pull out his cell phone and send a text message to Joshua and Nicole informing them Andrew is out of surgery and doing fine. Nicole quickly texts back, saying how relieved they are to hear it and explaining in short sentences where they are and when they are planning to arrive. I assured her I would let them know if there are any changes, good or bad, and wished them a safe trip.

As I finish the last part of the text message, I catch my eyelids drooping too; and after failing miserably at trying to get comfortable, I finally pull my chair up to Andrew's bed and lay my head next to his hand.

I barely register the coming and going of nurses and other hospital staff. When I finally become fully awake, I sit back in the chair and rub my eyes, wondering how long I have been asleep. I hear a soft chuckle and turn to see Andrew's smiling face looking at me.

"Andrew," I sigh his name with relief. "How long have you let me lie here and take up your bed? You should be the one resting."

"It's ten on Tuesday night. I think we have been here a day. And don't worry, love, I only just woke up a few minutes ago."

"How are you feeling?" I ask.

"Not too bad, just really sore, of course, and a little hungry."

"Let me get the nurse for you." As I reach for the call button, Andrew grabs my hand.

"Don't call the nurse yet. We need to talk." That is never a good sign. But there has always been the chance that this discussion was coming. As I sit back down, I will myself not to cry or beg for him to keep me. I must appear strong, and then I can bawl my eyes out later.

I force my back straighter in the chair and make eye contact with Andrew. "Don't look so worried, love. I'm not going to break up with you." At this he laughs, really laughs, and I feel the tension leaving my shoulders.

"I was just thinking about our situation. Ever since I met you, or found you I should say, both of us have been so focused on finding your true identity we neglected mine." I'm not sure how to respond, so when I open my mouth, nothing comes out. Andrew holds up a hand and continues.

"I don't want you to think I have not considered the search for your past of upmost importance because I have. It's just that our last experience made me realize if I had not been conscious when we reached the hospital Monday night, you would not have known anything to tell the doctors. I know that feeling of helplessness. I described it to you when I explained why I never took you to a hospital. And I hated having to put you in the same position. So I have decided, just now, to remedy both of our ignorances and tell you the story of my life."

•••

I am so happy to have Andrew offer to share his story with me that I say, "Andrew, this is the best gift you could ever give me. I am honored to be trusted with your past."

•••

Chapter 29

Andrew

"I was born and raised in Carmel, on the compound we call home. As I have said before, my family has always lived on the same plot of land, for as far back as I know. It was my grandparents who started the overseas shipping business, and when my father became of age, he and his brothers took over the business. All of them had attended different colleges around the country. In fact, that is where my father met and fell in love with my mother. I think they were at a mutual friend's party when my father heard some girl telling off some guy for trying to feel her up. My father said, in that instant, he knew she was the girl for him. 'Someone to keep me grounded and on my toes, someone who wouldn't take any of my crap. It didn't hurt that when she turned around, she was the most beautiful girl I had ever seen!' They married right out of college—my mom's major was finance, while my dad's was business. It just happened to be a perfect pairing of knowledge for taking over a million-dollar company.

"As you already know, I am the middle of four children, so you can guess they started having children right away. My childhood was very normal, sports on the weekends—basketball and baseball—family vacations to Disneyland and the Grand Canyon, and many fights among us siblings. We never wanted for anything, and although my father was away on business a lot or in the office or at the shipyard, I never felt neglected or forgotten. Actually, it was my parents' policy to take each of us for one-on-one time every month. I always chose to go to a sporting event, which thrilled my dad but made my mom cringe. When I was a little guy, I loved school, loved my friends, and my dream was to become a professional baseball player. But everything changed on my ninth birthday.

"I had always begged my father to take me to work with him at the shipyard. He would go there once a week, when the big ships were scheduled to set sail and go over the inventory and any last-minute changes. My mother never wanted me to accompany my father, saying it was too dangerous, and the men were too 'rough' for an eight-year-old to be around. But I had a plan. I asked my father for one thing on my ninth birthday—to take me to the shipyard. 'But it is too dangerous and too rough for an eight-year-old.' my mother started to say. I quickly interrupted her, 'But, Mom, I'm not eight anymore. I'm nine now!'

"I remember my father's booming laughter at my revelation, and the next words out of his mouth filled me with joy. 'He's got you there, hon. He's a big guy now. I think he can handle it.' My mother just rolled her eyes at me. I think she was secretly pleased with my ability to best her, and she allowed me to go with my father that Friday.

"The shipyard was everything I had imagined. There were a large number of huge ships docked at the port, and as we made our way toward my father's ship, I tried counting the number of crates stacked on top of one another. The piles were so high I had to shield my eyes from the sun to see the ones on top. There were machines everywhere—cranes and front loaders. Men were yelling and cursing, which my mother would not have approved of, and I felt a shift inside my head as I watched the hustle and bustle. My dream of being a professional athlete was slowing, being replaced by the dream to follow in my father's footsteps. I could see my future life as one in shipping.

"Because of the nature of my father's shipping business, my family's company was known to ship everything under the sun. I remember once as a kid hearing my parents discuss a freight of circus animals and equipment. I was unable to contain the excitement I felt as I ran to tell my siblings. My father heard me and scolded me pretty good. When I asked him why I had gotten in trouble, he replied, 'Because, son, we make our money in discretion.' When I asked him what that meant, he replied, 'That means the people we work for choose us because they know we can be trusted. Imagine if a different circus heard our clients were planning to start their American tour in San Francisco. The competition could arrive the night before, set up their tents, and steal our client's customers right out from under them. That wouldn't be very fair, would it?'

"I shook my head slowly, not really understanding what he meant. What I did understand was that we did not talk about the freight in our family's shipping business. So that hot day in August, as I overheard my father say the word 'explosives', I let it flow in one ear and out the other, never letting the danger of the word seep into my consciousness. The next thing I knew, my body was flying through the air, like some magic trick. All I could see was fire and smoke. I could hear only silence, and all I could feel was pain."

I have to stop and take a deep breath. Telling this story is wearing me out, both physically and mentally. When Elle suggests I stop and rest a little while, I wave her off, saying, "I want to get this out. I want you to know." Elle nods, and I start slowly again, this time, pausing more from exhaustion than for effect.

"When I woke up in the hospital, my parents were standing by my side. I could see immediately they looked haggard. My father's hair seemed to change from golden-brown to gray overnight, and my mother, who never left the house with a hair out of place, was hovering over me without a stitch of makeup on. I remember thinking I must have been pretty bad. When I tried to move, my body was instantly wracked with pain, and I cried out. My mother started sobbing, and my father gently patted my hand.

"'It's okay, son. Just try to lie still.' He called for a nurse, and a pretty blond lady walked in with a syringe full of a clear liquid. That's the last thing I remember for some time. The next time I woke up, only my father was there, and he was asleep, like you were just now, with his head resting on the hospital bed. I tried calling for him, but my voice came out as a croak. However, he sat up and smiled—it was a painful expression.

"'What happened, Dad?' I asked.

"Still to this day, I can't remember the exact words he used to describe the horrible accident. I'm not sure if it was the morphine or the shock of hearing such tragic news. The gist of the story is an explosion occurred when a front loader dropped a container filled with explosives—what kind, I still do not know. We were so close to the explosion it threw me twenty feet into the air, and I went through a metal container that had been blown to pieces by the same explosion. That is why I have these scars on my torso. I also have them on my legs, if you haven't noticed. I was stuck in a metal death trap for several hours while the rescue crews tried to cut me out. My father was also thrown backward, but he only hit the concrete ground. His foreman, however, was killed by the explosion, and the man driving the front loader had lost a leg. The first question I remember asking was, 'Is that why I cannot feel my legs, did I lose them like the other man lost his?' My father started weeping, and I found myself comforting him, laying my hand on his graying head and telling him it was going to be okay.

"When the doctor came into the room later that day, he described in detail the extent of my injuries. No, I had not lost my legs or any other appendage. No, I should not be paralyzed—my body was just recovering from the trauma of the accident. Yes, I had significant nerve damage and some ghastly scars—which I would probably have my entire life. And yes, I should completely recover from all my injuries, but it was going to be a long, tough process. The doctor was so straightforward with me I liked him instantly. Plus, he was the only one who did not look at me with pity in his eyes. He also told me the types of things I was to expect in the months and years to come. I would have to learn how to do almost every type of motor skill again—eating, walking, tying my shoes, brushing my teeth, getting dressed, going to the bathroom. I had the capabilities of a toddler with a much larger vocabulary.

"'Are you ready to get started?' he asked me immediately.

"'Yes,' I answered.

"And then he made me do exactly what I made you do that first night—he lifted me out of bed, had me support my weight on a walker, took my hospital gown off, and stood me in front of the mirror hanging on the back of the bathroom door. I remember thinking I should be embarrassed to stand naked in front of a stranger. Seeing the damage to my physical body hit me so hard I staggered a few steps back. My doctor was there to catch me and straighten me up again.

"'Take a good look, Andrew. This is your body now. If you don't confront it, you will be plagued with fear for the rest of your life. Look at yourself and take in every inch of hurt and damage. Make your eyes see the things you don't want to see. Take control of your situation and it will never control you.' So I did just that, and I still do every morning when I look in the mirror."

****

Eleanor

When he stops talking, I notice a silent tear running down Andrew's cheek. I reach over to wipe it off and let my hand linger on his face, gently tracing his eyebrows, his lips, and his cheekbones. He catches my hand with his and holds it against him.

"I'm so sorry I am the reason you are in a hospital bed again. I cannot imagine the feelings it must bring back."

He just shakes his head and says, "This time, it is worth it."

I want to argue with him and tell him he is wrong, but I think back to the second I dove into Dan Childs's black car. The only thought I had was to protect Andrew and keep him safe. I understand now he has done just that for me.

Throughout the day, nurses and doctors are in and out of our room checking monitors, discussing physical therapy options, and prescribing medications, which Andrew ardently refused. The only one his doctor could get him to agree to was an antibiotic to decrease the chance of infection. I am surprised at how quickly the staff had Andrew up and moving around the room, insisting he use his right arm at much as possible—getting in and out of bed, dressing himself, pushing buttons on the TV remote control, going to the bathroom.

During every exercise, Andrew's face has a constant grimace, and he even breaks out into a sweat when pulling on his shirt. I voice my concern to the nurse, feeling a little stupid because, of course, they wouldn't have him doing this if they were not certain it would be beneficial. I sometimes forget Andrew is also a doctor, and he would not follow through with their requests if he thought they were not sound.

During a very intense therapy session in which Andrew is having to comb his own hair with his injured arm, a man dressed in a very official black suit enters the room with his arms full of what I recognize as our luggage from the Four Seasons. I can see Andrew's eyebrows raise, and he looks to me. I stand and greet the man, hoping to stop him from potentially making a scene.

"Ma'am," he says, "Agent Bright had me bring your possessions from your hotel. The room was fully checked, and no item was left behind. He also told me to inform you the police have been notified of the situation, and everything is in place for your and Dr. Smith's immediate departure whenever his doctor releases him." He hands me the two suitcases and the two carry-on bags, turns, and walks out of the room.

The nurse comments, "That was very nice of the local police to send someone to bring your luggage."

I simply say, "Yes, it was nice."

Andrew throws me a quick questioning glance and then returns to his task. He knows I will explain everything later when we are alone. When his therapy session is over, he asks the nurse if he is allowed to walk around the hospital, and she suggests he make a trip to the ground floor to really stretch his legs,

"Only if your wife accompanies you, in case you need an extra hand." She winks at me, seeming to say, "You know how men are." "Take some time to visit the gift shop or get some ice cream or go into the cafeteria. As you know, it is good for you to stay as mobile as possible. You need to be back by four so I can give you some more pain medication, but other than that, you are free to walk around." Andrew looks truly excited, and I hate to see his disappointment when he realizes how horrible the hospital food tastes.

Because Andrew's injury is to his shoulder, his legs are just as strong as before, and we make pretty good time getting down the stairs, which he suggested we take instead of the elevator.

"I'm just glad to be out of that room. Even after just one day, I am beginning to hate it." Now that I know his story; I completely understand.

"I'm afraid you are going to be seriously disappointed when you taste the cafeteria food. It's awful."

He laughs and says, "I'm used to hospital food, remember. I cannot wait to taste some bland food and drink some watered-down tea." I laugh along with him as we make our way into the cafeteria. I carry his tray along with mine and use his debit card to pay for the food. Andrew insists I let him retrieve his own wallet and push the buttons on the card machine.

"I have to start doing the small things for myself," he says when I give him an exasperated look. We sit at a corner table, and he begins shoveling his food into his mouth. I can only pick at my grilled chicken because, as I told him, it is awful.

When he finishes off his glass of watered-down tea, he looks at me and asks, "Who was that man that brought our luggage? He looked like someone pretty official. And did he mention someone named Agent Bright?"

I nodded in response to his questions and tried to explain everything; beginning with Agent Bright's startling wink as I entered Dan Childs's car and ending with his hasty exit from the waiting room, leaving out nothing, especially the fact I now was the owner of the CIA version of my life.

"That's great, Elle!" Andrew seems genuinely happy, even though he must know there could be some information in the folder that could seriously complicate our relationship. He continues, "Have you looked over the folder yet?"

I pause, thinking of a way I can describe to him my hesitation about reading the information, and the only thing I can do is shake my head. Andrew gives me a puzzled look, and I try to explain. "I'm scared of what I will find in there, not only about my personal life but about my professional life as well. Agent Bright already told me he thought I had more than ten assignments. Who knows what kind of intelligence I have gathered in the past. Or what I had to do to obtain that information." I let out a long sigh, and Andrew reaches his bad arm across the table to squeeze my hand. I smile and say, "You have no idea how happy it makes me to feel your warm hand on mine again. There were a few moments there I was sure I would never get to feel you squeeze my hand again."

"I know what you mean," Andrew says. "By the way"—his voice becomes urgent and a little angry—"what were you thinking getting into that car? As healthy as I am, or was, I almost had a heart attack when you drove away." I chuckled a little bit.

"Don't you know—I was saving you, just like you saved me." Andrew shakes his head but doesn't say anything.

When we walk into Andrew's hospital room, we get a great surprise— Joshua and Nicole are sitting on the hospital bed and look up when we enter.

"Oh, thank God," Joshua says and runs toward Andrew, throwing his arms around his brother. Even though Andrew winces, he stands there and lets Joshua envelope him into one of his usual bear hugs. I can see Joshua's shoulders shake with small, quiet sobs, and I step away to give them a little privacy. Nicole is standing with her arms open to me, and I practically run myself into their welcomed embrace. Soon, I find myself sobbing. If anyone walked into the room at this moment, they would assume that we had just received some very bad news.

I pull away from Nicole. "Thank you so much for coming and getting here so fast. I wasn't expecting to see you all until tomorrow at the earliest."

Nicole smiles. "When it comes to family, there is no stopping us."

Joshua steps away from Andrew, not even trying to hide his tear stained face. "All I could think about was coming to rescue my little brother, but I see you have taken care of that already." He gives me a look of awe, and I have the feeling I have just won Joshua's respect forever.

Andrew makes his way to the bed and sits down heavily. I think he overdid it with our walk to the cafeteria, but I know he will never admit it. As he fills Joshua and Nicole in on his surgery, diagnosis, my visit to MicroCorp, and Agent Bright, I content myself with sitting close to him on the bed, closer than we have been in a long time. When I think about our last kiss Monday morning, the last time we were so close, my face starts to flush with the memories and embarrassment of having such thoughts in front of his family. Nicole must have asked me a question because the three of them are looking at me curiously.

"Elle, are you okay?" Andrew asks. I clear my throat and try to clear my head too.

"Yeah, I'm fine. What did you say, Nicole?"

"I asked you if you found out anything interesting from Agent Bright."

"Oh yes, he gave me my file from the CIA. I haven't looked at it yet, though."

Joshua spoke up, "Wow, to think that you are married to a spy, how cool!"

Nicole interjects harshly, "Joshua, they are not married."

You could hear a pin drop in the room following Nicole's statement. I feel like I have been punched in the gut—I'm not sure if it is because I thought Nicole was a friend and was starting to think of me as her sister or because I was starting to think of her as mine.

Andrew reaches for my hand and speaks in a tone I have never heard before, stern and angry. "Nicole, you know I love you, but if you ever say anything to that effect again, our relationship, yours and mine, is over."

I stare at Nicole, hating that my presence in their lives has possibly put a rift between her and Andrew. But when she speaks, I hear nothing but honesty and kindness in her voice.

"Andy, I am sorry. I never meant anything negative by what I said. It was careless of me." She turns to address me.

"Elle, please forgive my error in judgment. Of course I know how you and Andy feel about each other. Heck, the two of you have been through more in the last month than most married couples go through in a lifetime."

I feel like I should say something, make it look like I took no offense in what she said, but before I can, Andrew speaks again.

"Nicole, I'm sorry I was so harsh. You must try to understand what I've, what we've been through in the last two days alone. I just don't want there to be any doubt about my feelings for Elle and my intention to marry her as soon as we return to Carmel." I am shocked to hear Andrew say this, and I turn slowly to face him.

"Are you sure about this? I haven't even looked through my file yet. We don't know what it will say about my past—I could already be married, to someone who I love, or used to love, and who loves me and is worried I am dead right now." The hysteria in my voice causes it to get louder and shake. I can't keep the fears from spilling out of my mouth as tears spill out of my eyes. "What then? How will I explain to my husband that since I last saw him, I have married someone else? What if I am a murderer or thief? What—" Before I can finish my line of questions, Andrew stops me by putting his finger to my lips.

"I've told you once, Elle, and I will tell you again—no matter what we find out, I will love you. There is nothing in that file that could change my feelings for you." I lean into his chest, being careful to not put pressure on his right side. He cradles my head and strokes my hair. The silence that surrounds us would make it easy to forget there are two other people in the room, but the nurse walks in to give Andrew his pain medication, and the spell is broken.

It's Wednesday morning, so I am surprised when the nurse comes into Andrew's room and informs us we will be allowed to return home today.

"The doctor will want to have one more checkup with you, and then you can head back home." I am thrilled to hear that word. *Home.* Andrew must be as well because he is a lot more chipper than he was after his brother and sister-in-law left. When the confrontation between Andrew and Nicole was over, Joshua announced they had reservations at a local hotel.

"We should probably let Andrew rest, Nic. Just call us if you need anything tonight." He grabbed Andrew's shoulder, thankfully not the injured one, and gave it a squeeze.

"Once again, thank you all for coming. I can't imagine trying to get us to the airport by myself," I said.

"It's no problem," Joshua assured me. Nicole picked up her purse, gave the two of us a small smile, and headed silently out the door. As she walked by Andrew's bed, he grabbed her hand, causing her to turn and face him. Neither one of them said a word, but in the few seconds, they stood there staring at each other. I could tell whatever damage the argument had done to their relationship, it was being mended in those soundless moments.

The rest of our night was spent watching bad TV and taking small trips down the hall. The only notable thing that happened was an unexpected phone call from Andrew's parents. When Andrew answered the phone, all I could hear was a long string of squeals, cries, and I think a few curse words.

He just rolled his eyes and said, "Mom, I'm fine. I promise. Yes, Joshua told you right. Eleanor and I were mugged the other night as we walked around the city. I had surgery . . ."

I tuned out the rest of the conversation; I just couldn't hear it again. The CIA folder lying on the empty food tray across the room caught my attention, and I could feel it pulling me like a magnet. While Andrew was trying for the one hundredth time to reassure his mother he was, indeed, okay, I walked to the tray and picked up the folder. When I turned to let Andrew know I was going to step out of the room, his eyes were already on me, and he nodded his head. I didn't have to go far before I found a group of vacated chairs near the elevators. As I drew my legs underneath me and opened the folder, I knew my life would never be the same again, so I took a moment to gather some mental strength:

You can do this.
You are strong.
If you don't confront it now, you will be plagued with fear for the rest of your life.
Make your eyes see the things you don't want to see.
Take control of your situation, and it will never control you.

PART 3

Homecoming

Chapter 30

Andrew

If I never fly on another airplane, it will be too soon. Unlike the last several flights, though, the main feeling I have is not nervousness but nausea. Every bump or jolt wracks my body with pain, and I am reminded of the explosion. At first, I was hesitant to tell Elle my past simply because I did not want to see the pity in her eyes over something I struggle with each day. After all I saw in war, the fear of lying in a hospital bed at nine years of age still haunts me.

On the other hand, the best part of this flight is finally knowing the truth about Elle, her past life, and knowing I get to be a part of her future.

****

Eleanor

When the plane lands at the small Carmel airport, it's like a huge weight is lifted off my shoulders. A smile creeps onto my face, and I turn toward Andrew who is gently snoring in the seat next to me.

"Wake up, honey. We're home." Without opening his eyes, his face mirrors mine, and I lay my head on his shoulder trying to get as close to him as possible.

"Those are the best words I have ever heard in my life." I assume he is talking about finally being home, but when he sits up and makes eye contact with me, he says, "You have never called me 'honey' before. And your beautiful Southern accent makes it that much sweeter." I feel the blush creep into my cheeks, but I soak up the look Andrew is giving me, secretly wishing that his shoulder was not injured. Joshua and Nicole are seated in the row behind us, and I turn to address them.

"I bet it feels like you just left here, doesn't it?"

Nicole laughs and nods her head. "No matter how long I am gone from home, whether a few hours or a few days, I am always happy to come back to the compound." Joshua reaches over and rubs her leg with a goofy grin on his face.

"It still kills her to admit that, to this day." He must notice my confused expression because he quickly explains. "I don't know how much you know about mine and Nicole's relationship, but we met in middle school. The moment I saw her, I told my buddy, Dave, I would marry her." When he says this, I am reminded of Andrew's father's same declaration about his wife. "Luckily, we had one class together, and when a test was coming up, I invited her to come to the compound to study." I nodded, letting him know I had heard this part of their story. "Well, when she heard me call my house 'the compound', she laughed the most beautiful laugh I had ever heard and said, 'I would never live in a place called the compound. What does your family do, imprison and starve people?' I let her joke all she wanted, as long as she agreed to the study date. I knew I would win her over eventually with my charm and good looks, so I wasn't too worried about her aversion to the name of my home."

Nicole speaks up, "You always have been a cocky somebody." They both laugh, and I find myself joining in wanting to hear more about their past. Now that I know mine, I can allow myself to wonder about others' pasts too.

"Well," Joshua continues, "as you can guess, Nic fell in love with the place the moment she walked in the front doors, and she has never looked back. I can't remember all the times she stayed the night, sleeping with one of my sisters, of course, because she couldn't stand to be away from me for too long."

At this, Nicole smacks Joshua's hand off her leg, saying, "You wished that was the reason. The real reason was I couldn't stand to leave his house with its happy energy and loving parents. My home life was not all that great. But I won't bore you with that sad tale." She turns to look at the window, and I notice Joshua puts his hand back on her leg, this time, comforting her and keeping her tied to her pleasant present life.

Andrew's parents and Annie are waiting for us when we exit the airplane, and I am pleasantly surprised when his sister and mother give me a warm hug just like the rest of the family.

"Oh, my dear," his mother says, "I am so glad you all made it home safely. I cannot imagine how exhausted you must be both physically and mentally. We are so thankful you were with Andrew. How lucky it was you were there to care for him." She pats my hand, and at this moment, I am so glad she doesn't know the truth—that I am the reason he got hurt in the first place. Andrew walks to my side and wraps his arm around my waist.

"You're right, Mom. Eleanor was a lifesaver, literally." He gives me a sly wink, and I push the horrible memories of his shocked face in the elevator out of my mind. Mr. Smith informs us they are going to drive us straight home so we can get some rest.

"But be warned," he says, "the family is anxious to see you all and check about how you are feeling. Fortunately, I have discouraged the aunts, uncles, and cousins for now and just your brother and sisters are going to attend dinner tonight." Knowing that Andrew is the middle of four children, I am instantly worried the large crowd will wear him out even further.

"That sounds fine, Dad. I just hope Mary is fixing my favorite meal since I did get shot a few days ago." Andrew laughs when he says this, but I cringe, and so does his mother, I notice.

"Don't joke about it, Andrew. It's not funny. You're lucky that you are alive . . . again," she adds quietly.

"Your mother does have a point, son. After the shipyard accident and Afghanistan, aren't you running out of lives by now?"

I am so shocked to hear his father say "Afghanistan" that I drop Andrew's hand and stop walking toward the waiting car. Andrew also stops and turns to face me with an expression on his face that I have not seen since our first encounter. He is giving me a look, almost like he is trying to let me know what he is thinking. He walks to my ear and pulls me close.

"Don't freak out, okay? I just haven't had the chance to tell you about my time in the service. I was going to, but I didn't know how to bring the subject up." I pull away from his embrace to look in his eyes.

"Afghanistan, why didn't you tell me? I saw your dog tags before we left, but I never guessed . . . My brother was stationed in Afghanistan. Maybe you knew him. Did you know him? Do you recognize his name?"

Andrew shakes his head. "No, Elle. I'm sorry, I don't.

With my hopes dashed, I say, "I'm getting tired of being the last person to know everything about you."

"You're not the last person to know everything," he says. "You were the first person to know that I love you."

"One of these days, Andrew, I'm afraid that is not going to be enough."

Walking into the house, I have come to know as my home has a physical effect on both Andrew and I, and we silently make our way to the bedroom that was mine before our "Trip around the World." We leave our bags at the door, along with the tension between us, for now, at least. I can't bring myself to press Andrew any further about his lack of honesty. If it was anywhere but Afghanistan, I might not be so upset. I remember the horrors that were shown on television.

Every night, there would be a report of how many lives were lost fighting the "War on Terror", and I would scan any kind of report I could get my hands on to see if my brother's name was listed as deceased. It sends a shock through my body to think Andrew could have easily been one of those casualties. The wear of the trip has finally caught up to us both, and we collapse on the bed, not bothering to remove our shoes.

The next thing I know, it's five, and we have to be at dinner in an hour. Andrew's prostrate body is motionless next to me. I try not to disturb his much needed sleep as I make my way to the bathroom. The hot water in the shower is one of the best things I have ever felt, and I let it wash away all the fears of the past week: my horrible memory "episode"; the sight of Dan Childs standing at my table in the coffee shop; the long concrete hallway in MicroCorp headquarters; the electroshock machine; Andrew's face in the elevator and the sound of Jones's handgun firing; and our rushed trip to the ER all wash down the drain along with the grime of traveling. When I come out of the bathroom, Andrew, who is now sitting on the couch, looks up at me.

"Can you help me get in the shower? I really need a shower, but my arm is bothering me more than I care to admit." He gives me a small smile, and at that moment, I can't seem to stay frustrated with him. I cross the room and sit next to him, being sure to keep off his injured shoulder. I take his hand in both of mine.

"Of course, I'll help you. It's my turn to take care of you now."

"Elle, I know you are upset with me . . ." I stop him with a small shake of my head.

"Andrew, I am not upset with you. How could I be upset about not knowing everything about you when we just met a month ago? It was wrong of me to have the expectation I would be on the same familiarity level as your parents and siblings. I was just shocked, that's all. I will consider it an honor if I get to learn something new about you every day, from now until we're ninety years old."

Getting Andrew into the shower was both harder and more embarrassing than I thought it would be. During our flight and long nap today, his shoulder has really tightened up with disuse.

"I guess that's why the nurse had you doing all those exercises the first day, to prevent this?"

"Yes, I was afraid my mobility would be impaired on the trip home, but I had no idea I would be this sore," Andrew says as he tries to maneuver into the shower. Even though Andrew has seen me nude, it's a little bit different when the situation is reversed. I get the feeling he is embarrassed, but I'm not sure if it is because of his nudity or his need for assistance.

He closes the shower curtain and manages to wash himself pretty good, considering his injury—I am only called in when he can't reach his back. As I am scrubbing, I can't help but get a good look at his scars. I find myself tearing up at their depth and prominence, remembering the trauma that caused them.

Unfortunately, getting Andrew out of the shower was even more difficult than getting him in it. Because he is wet, my grip on his uninjured arm and torso is shaky at best. After several touch-and-go minutes which were spent trying to figure out the right placement of his hands and feet, Andrew is now sitting safely on the toilet seat wearing jeans and a cotton T-shirt.

As he brushes his hair, I run to grab our bags from in front of the door when there is a knock on it. I jerk the door open, expecting to see one of the family members but instead find a man dressed in a navy blue suit. Since my first encounter with Dan Childs, I have been very leery of men in suits, and I freeze. He extends his hand and introduces himself as Agent Shield of the CIA. I ask to see some identification, and as he is pulling out his wallet from his inside jacket pocket, Andrew walks into the room.

"Elle, I can't find my . . ." When he sees the man standing in the doorway, Andrew quickly puts himself between me and the stranger.

"Ah, Dr. Smith. I was just acquiring my identification your wife has asked me for." He hands his ID badge to Andrew, and I peek over his shoulder, trying to get a glimpse of his credentials. "As you can see, I am an agent of the CIA, and I have been assigned to your case, Mrs. Smith. My job is to watch out for you. I will, of course, maintain a reasonable distance, and you will have your privacy. Here is my card. If you notice anything or anyone strange, please contact me." He stops his rather rehearsed speech, and Andrew speaks up.

"Agent Shield, thank you for your willingness to help us, but I think I can look out for Eleanor and myself." The agent looks from Andrew's face to his bandaged shoulder, and even I notice the incredulous look he gives Andrew.

"I'm sure you are as capable as you say, Dr. Smith. But I have been assigned to your case, and I will fulfill my duties until I am notified by the CIA that my job is done." At this, he turns and heads to a nondescript government vehicle and starts down the long driveway, heading toward town. Andrew and I stand there in the doorway for a little while, watching the dust settle from the agent's retreating car.

He turns to me and asks, "What do you think about that?"

I just shrug. "I have to admit it makes me feel a little better knowing there is someone on our side keeping an eye out for Dan Childs."

"Well, if it makes you feel safer, then I'm fine with it. After all, being in the military prepares you for the feeling of having someone constantly watching you." He grabs his wallet of the table next to the door, reaches my hand, and asks, "Shall we?" I enjoy the feeling of his slightly calloused fingers as we make our way to the main house.

As his father had warned us, Andrew's brother and sisters and their families were there to greet us when we entered the large living room. I had only passed through this room when Andrew and I attended Sunday luncheons what seems like eons ago now. I met so many people then. When I enter the very noisy living room, I recognize a few of the faces, mostly adult faces, as they approach Andrew and me, giving us both hugs and words of concern and offers of "If you need anything, just let us know."

There are several children present, ranging from infants to middle-school-aged. I count six in all and wonder at their names. Andrew's mother claps her hands, and everyone comes to attention. I get the feeling she has had to command rooms full of noisy children her whole life because as she clears her throat, the room falls into a quick silence.

"We are so thankful to have half of our family back home tonight, some of them a little worse for wear but home safely all the same. Let's say a prayer of thanks for such a wonderful homecoming." At this point, she looks to Andrew's father, and his rich baritone voice sounds as commanding as it did at the Sunday luncheons:

"Let us pray," he begins, and I bow my head along with the rest of the family. As he thanks God for our safe return and the blessing of having his family altogether, I consider how this is the first time I have observed Andrew doing anything religious. Ever since I woke up in that strange bedroom, I have been sure of God's presence in my life—one person does not have my good luck in bad fortune and not believe there is someone looking out for them. I find it comforts me to think that Andrew also believes in a higher power.

As the prayer ends, Andrew's mother once again speaks up and ushers everyone into another large room, this one being the formal dining room. The long table seats at least twenty, and everyone hurries to what seems to be their regular seat. Because this is my first family dinner here, I follow Andrew around the table and seat myself next to him. During the course of our meal, I am told the ins and outs of the Smith family. Joshua is the oldest sibling and is married, of course to Nicole.

"We have no children," she says quietly. I get the feeling that is a very sad subject. Andrew gives me a pained look, and I know it is not for Nicole's sake but for mine—he is remembering my doctor's diagnosis that children are also not possible for me. Lily, Andrew's oldest sister, is married to Bob, and they have six children, the oldest being thirteen and the youngest being nine months.

"Yes," Annie speaks up. "I see all the fun Lily is having trying to balance her seven children, and I can't wait to get married and start popping out babies!"

I am genuinely confused at this point, so I speak up. "I thought Lily only had six children, but you just said seven."

Andrew answers me, "Yes, well, it's seven if you include Bob!" The entire table laughs, especially Bob.

The meal was wonderful—several courses of very rich foods: soup, salad, breads, meats, vegetables, potatoes, and even three different kinds of desserts. I could definitely get used to eating like this—not just the great food but the great company. I cannot remember laughing so much, and by the end of the night, my stomach and face muscles are sore. There are a few times I notice Andrew wincing with pain, but when I bring up getting him some medication, he waves me off.

Just like in an old-time movie, when the last plates are cleared off the table, the men go outside for an after-dinner cigar. I am once again surprised when I see Andrew lighting up on the patio. The women of the family make their way into a small parlor, and the children run to a game room that is located upstairs. I plan on sitting quietly and listening to Andrew's sisters and sister-in-law talk about their families, but I am bombarded with questions about mine and Andrew's trip.

Because it ended so badly, I forgot it started out so fun. I sit there and tell them everything I can remember, from our trip to the aquarium in Atlanta to our stroll around DC. They ooh and aah in all the right parts, some of them even comment on how romantic the trip sounds. I have never thought of our trip in that way before—it was mostly research for Andrew and me, but now that it has been brought to my attention, it does seem a little romantic. Parts of it, at least.

By the time the men finish their cigars, I have passed the floor on to Lily who is talking about the joys of potty training her three-year-old daughter. I throw a quick glance at Nicole who is sitting there just as attentive as the rest of the group. Is it just me, or does no one else notice the sadness in her eyes? I excuse myself to the restroom while I hurry out of the room with tears prickling the back of my eyes. Andrew sees me running to the guest bathroom and excuses himself. I am already in the bathroom when he knocks on the door. I reluctantly open it and let him inside.

"What's wrong, love? Did someone say something to upset you?" I shake my head.

"It's nothing. I guess the stress of the past month is still catching up to me." Andrew seems content with my answer, and I don't have the heart to tell him seeing Nicole's sad face had scared me—I know one day, I might have the same mask of sadness when hearing people talk about their children.

As Andrew and I say our good-byes, the walk to our house feels good, stretching my legs as the cool air brushes my cheeks. I am so curious about Nicole's past but feel a little intrusive wanting to know. When I bring the subject up to Andrew, he looks uncomfortable.

"You don't have to tell me. I simply noticed how sad she looked tonight while Lily was talking about her children. And she said something on the plane about her life not being great. I just feel like there is a story there I might need to know."

"You're right, of course," Andrew says. "I've always felt wrong about knowing all of Nicole's story to be honest with you. However, because of her medical history, her and Joshua included me into their very private life several years ago. And I have never felt the same about Nicole since."

We are lying in bed when Andrew finally tells me the sad story. "Nicole is the oldest of five children. She and her siblings do not share a father between them. Her mother was always working different jobs, usually several at a time, and not all of them respectable, especially for a mother of five. Nicole never knew her father only that he worked on an oil rig somewhere in the Midwest. Each time her mother would get a new boyfriend, he would move into the house with them. Looking back now, she does not blame her mother or hold any resentment toward her. I believe Mrs. King thought she was doing what was best for her children by bringing in a male, father figure, even if they did not have the best personality.

"Nicole had to take care of her younger siblings from the time she was really young because of her mother's many jobs. She would get them ready in the mornings, feed them, make sure they got to school and did their homework, not to mention cleaning and cooking—things a young girl should not have to worry about. Mrs. King was always good to her children and did her best to make sure they were provided for and loved. But bottom line, she relied heavily on Nicole."

Andrew pauses. "I know this story doesn't sound too depressing, and so far, it's not that different from thousands of other children living in the

United States. However, everything changed when Nicole turned twelve. Her mother had started a new job working for some pretty shady people. To this day, I'm not sure what their whole operation was about. But anyway, Nicole's mother started messing around with the big boss and brought him into her home—nothing she hadn't done before. Only this time, Mrs. King had no idea who she was introducing to her children.

"He started with Nicole first, raping her and then beating her if she refused or struggled or cried. Anything he did not like resulted in a bruised and broken Nicole. She tried to tell her mother several times, and I'm not sure if she didn't believe Nicole or if she was so scared of her boyfriend she didn't know what to do. After he got his fill of Nicole, he moved onto her younger sisters, all the while treating her younger brothers like slaves, making them do dangerous or illegal things for him while he sat back and reaped the benefits. Nicole went to the police, and they took her testimony, promising to follow up. However, the next day, the detective she spoke to was found murdered outside his home. From that point on, Nicole was too scared to report the abuse again. And that is when she entered our lives."

I roll onto my stomach and place my chin on his scarred chest. I can tell from the tone of his voice that he is getting tired, the physical and emotion demand of the day finally catching up to him. "Andrew, rest. We can always talk tomorrow."

"No, you need to hear this," he says with his eyes closed. "I can still remember the thinness and severity of Nicole the first time she came to the big house. She seemed too tough for Joshua, especially for me, and I was scared for her to even be in our house. But when she kidded me about my name, I thought she was brilliant. I began to see her in a different light. Instead of tough, I saw brave. Instead of scary, I saw strong. Instead of shifty, fierce. Even at such a young age, I could tell Joshua was crazy about her, and I was beginning to be myself. Every time she left our house, she would cry. I never saw her, but I could hear her in Joshua's room telling him she could not explain why she was so scared. I can still hear her say, 'I don't want you to get hurt.' I begged Joshua to tell our parents, and when he finally did, they were beyond concerned for not just Nicole and her siblings but for us as well.

"You see, my parents knew all about Nicole and her family. They knew who Mrs. King was involved with and what he was capable of. A month after Nicole's first visit to the big house, the creep was put in prison, serving a life sentence for manslaughter and several counts of child abuse and child rape. I never asked how the creep was found out and caught. But there is no doubt in my mind my parents had a hand in his incarceration.

"Unfortunately, things only went from bad to worse for Nicole and her siblings. Mrs. King was so furious with their now destitute situation she took it out on her children by neglecting them. She stayed gone, not being able to bear coming home to five needy kids who were always needing something washed or cooked or cleaned. The next month, Nicole found out she would never be able to have children because of the damage her body sustained during those months of abuse. Not unlike you, my love." Andrew strokes my hair softly as he takes another break.

"After that, Nicole moved in with us on a semipermanent basis while her other siblings were dispersed to other family members. They are mostly grown now, the youngest around the same age as Annie. Nicole still talks to her mother who has since sought help for her mental and emotional issues. Mrs. King now holds down a steady job as a bank teller here in Carmel. She's come to Sunday lunch a few times over the years, so has Nicole's siblings." I run my fingers up and down the scars on Andrew's stomach, lightly tracing each one. I see Nicole's sad eyes and feel pity for her.

The next morning when Andrew wakes up, he walks to the bedroom window and begins looking around the yard, straining his neck, this way and that. He looks so funny I ask him what he is doing. "I'm just wondering where Agent Shield is hiding himself." I join him at the window and take a quick look around too, having completely forgotten about our visitor from last night.

"I don't remember very much, if any, from my days as a CIA agent, but I'm pretty sure Agent Shield won't be sitting outside our windows with a pair of binoculars held up to his face." I reach up on my tiptoes and plant a kiss on Andrew's neck. He pulls me into his body with a grunt of pain.

Suddenly, I am hit with another memory flash, which stops my roaming hands. Andrew freezes along with me, whipping his head back and forth, looking for the immediate threat. The vineyards in front of me are replaced by an ocean view. I scan to the left and then to the right, and all I see is endless beach. The sun is high in the sky, and I feel the heat on my skin. Sweat is trickling down my arms and behind my knees; the bench I am sitting on is also hot.

****

"Becca, did you hear what I said?" I turn to my immediate left and see Lauren staring at me.

"Yeah, I heard you, but it doesn't matter. This is my job, and I have to follow through." Lauren makes an irritated noise, and I smile to myself.

It's nice to know someone so well that I understand all their little noises. I reach over and lightly slap her shoulder. "I know you are worried about me, Lauren, but you don't have to be. I have done this dozens of times before, and there is no risk involved." She rolls her eyes, but I continue, "If it will make you feel any better, we can go over the plan again."

She nods without further argument so I start, "We are going to eat our usual Saturday lunch at the corner deli at noon and then go our separate ways. When you hear me leave my apartment at nine thirty, you will unlock my door and get my bags ready for me." I pause to look at her. "You remember what you are supposed to pack, right?" Lauren nods and I continue.

"When you finish, place my bags next to the door and lock up when you leave. I should be back no later than ten fifteen, give or take a few minutes. I should be able to get a taxi pretty easily that time of night, especially in that part of town." I turn my whole body to face her and make sure she is looking into my eyes.

"What are you going to do if you hear me return for my bags by ten fifteen?"

"I'm going to be extremely sad but look forward to your phone call on the following Wednesday at 11:30 a.m. at the phone located outside our corner deli." I nod my head.

"Now, what are you going to do if I am not back by ten thirty?" Lauren looks like she is about to cry, which is a feat in and of itself.

"I am supposed to wait until eleven thirty, and if I still haven't heard you come back, I should leave my apartment, hail a cab, make my way to the corner store, and call the number on the business card in my pocketbook." I nod again as she describes her part of "Operation You Suck", which is what Lauren decided to call it when I told her I would be leaving Hawaii after my assignment was complete.

When I was given this assignment and told my new neighbor in Honolulu was supposed to give me inside information into MicroCorp, I didn't give it another thought. The first time I saw Lauren, I have to admit it was refreshing to have someone so young and vibrant compared to my usual contact people—cranky, slightly paranoid older men and/or women with a chip on their shoulder and curiosity-laden attitudes. She seemed bright and honest, not to mention well educated in all things MicroCorp. I never asked her where she got her information; I just trusted the CIA would not put her in my path unless she was the best.

At first, our relationship was only professional. Per instructions, we were to act like we were new neighbors, getting to know each other. At our first Saturday lunch, we talked about very general topics, our names, our families, jobs, likes, dislikes, etc. In the course of a month, we had covered all the basics and had established a very good working relationship.

I had started my job at MicroCorp and was beginning to learn my way around the city. But after that first month, every Saturday, Lauren and I would meet at the local deli to discuss the inner workings of MicroCorp. I was curious about every detail she could give me simply because it was my job to know all and never be unprepared. I learned several important things, but I was especially interested in Dan Childs. I had seen him several times at the office and was wondering why, as CEO, he seemed to be so involved.

"Don't CEOs of large companies, such as MicroCorp, usually deal with only the higher-level problems? I would think with such a large company, Mr. Childs would delegate some basic operations to general managers, or something?" Lauren dipped a french fry into the pile of ketchup and didn't look up when she answered.

"Dan Childs has been with MicroCorp since they opened the doors. He is actually one of the founders. From the beginning, he has always been 'hands-on'. And to this day, he has been present for the hiring of every MicroCorp employee, but of course, you know that."

I think back to my interview at MicroCorp, and it amazes me that, after all these years, and the dozens of fake interviews I have had, I still get nervous. I guess it makes a little sense, knowing I am not only trying to gain employment but gain important information as well.

In the small and sparsely furnished office, I was joined by a man who would be my supervisor, Mr. Kelly, and Dan Childs himself. When introduced to Mr. Childs, I made sure to make eye contact and seem a tad bit flustered.

"Mr. Childs, wow, what an honor. I see you on television all the time. Just wait until I tell my mom!" Mr. Childs smiled briefly and thanked me. Taking a seat in the back of the room, he nodded to Mr. Kelly who began the interview. Throughout the following forty-five minutes, Mr. Childs did not say a word but sat and listened intently. I thanked my stars my new neighbor Lauren had provided me with a list of questions they would ask, giving me a chance to study. When I asked her later where she got the list, she simply shrugged her shoulders, and I learned then not to ask too many questions about her sources.

At the end of the interview, Mr. Kelly told me I would be contacted within the week, and then both men shook my hand and preceded me out of the room. After that day, I saw Dan Childs multiple times in the office. He never spoke directly to me, but he made himself known. Coming back to the present, I ask Lauren, "Well, who is over Dan Childs? I mean, who does he report to?"

"Basically, no one. Of course there is a board of directors, but they are all old men who are just there to take up space at the table. As CEO, Mr. Childs is the one who runs the show."

From the coldness of Lauren's voice and the fact she still had not looked up from her plate gave me a strange feeling. I can't put my finger on it, but I feel like there is something she is not telling me. And I get it—the entire life Lauren thinks is mine is made up, a fake; in my line of work, people's secrets are their salvation. On that point alone, I will never ask Lauren what her real connection is with Dan Childs and MicroCorp. But now that I consider her my friend, probably one of the best I've had in a long time, I wouldn't ask her out of respect.

There are many things I have learned in this business, some of them extremely valuable in my particular line of work, things I can take from one assignment to the next, like how to properly apply a wig to make it look natural or how to speak in over twenty dialects. Other skills are not as easily transferred from one job to the next. I once learned how to prepare almost every recipe in Julia Child's cookbook when I was employed as a cook at a governor's mansion. Although it is nice to have a lasting knowledge of French-Classical cuisine, more than likely I will never need to cook Lobster Thermidor again.

In Mississippi, I learned how to change the oil and repair flat tires when I worked for a twenty-four-hour auto emergency service. And now, even though I know how to work on my own car, I always take it to a shop for maintenance or call AAA when I have a flat. Very few things are the same on every mission, but no matter where I go or who I meet, one thing is the same—everyone wants to be heard; people are dying to have someone listen to them, someone they think they can trust.

This is no different in my current mission. It is apparent Lauren is craving someone, a friend, and in this instance, I find myself wanting to fill that position. So I will be patient and kind, and one day, she will tell me her secret. As I look at my friend, I am reminded of the daunting task ahead and say, "That's great. You just forgot a couple of things—when should you return to your apartment after you make the phone call?"

"I should not go back to my apartment for three days—that way, I won't run into any 'bad guys'." She tries laughing, but it comes out weak and strained. Before I turn back to face the beautiful ocean, which I will miss more than I can say, I notice a Volkswagen Bug parked behind us in the public parking lot. *I am definitely being followed.*

In the last two months, I have noticed the same car over twenty times. I don't dare say anything to Lauren. That will only freak her out even more. I continue quizzing Lauren because the next part of the plan is the most important. I don't usually—no, I never share my plans with any one, especially a civilian. But since I started noticing the Volkswagen, I decided to involve Lauren even more into my mission, only as a backup plan.

I wasn't sure what she knew and what she had guessed or if she believed a word of it. But when I explained everything, she said, "I could tell there was something more to this whole setup. I just couldn't put my finger on it. I knew you worked for the CIA of course, but I didn't know you were sent here to steal something from MicroCorp."

There was no question of my honesty; she said she would never lie to me, and I would never lie to her. From that point on, Lauren began acting more serious around me, making less jokes, and our Saturday lunches began having a doomsday quality. After years of espionage work, situations have become less scary. But Lauren, being on the outside looking in, sees only danger—the chance of capture or death seems too scary to be real life.

"Okay, last question. Where will I hide the file in case of an emergency escape?" She sounds serious, like she understands the importance of the information I am allowing her to know.

"You are going to hide it under the loose brick on the southeast side of Treasure Street, about one-third of the way down the wall." I simply nod my head, and I hear her relieved (or depressed) sigh. I hate not being totally honest with her. Now she will have a plausible answer to give someone in case she gets approached. *They will never think to look in my shoe.*

Chapter 32

Andrew

"But we just got home!" Elle and I have been arguing for the past hour, but this is the first time I have raised my voice above its normal, measured tone. As soon as her memory flash was over, she ran through the house and started pulling everything out of our suitcases. I followed quickly behind.

"What are you doing?" I asked, perplexed.

"My shoes, my shoes, where are the shoes I was wearing when you found me in Hawaii?" Elle was hysterical and started running around the house, looking under the couch and coffee table and then under the bed in my room and in all the closets.

"Elle, would you please calm down and tell me what's going on?"

"That's where I hid the MicroCorp file—inside my shoe. Where are they?" I was silent for a few moments, and when she looks at me, I just shake my head.

"You didn't have any shoes on, Elle. You didn't have anything on but your underwear, and even that was so torn it was hanging off you." I'm not sure if it was the sudden remembrance of her abuse or the realization she might never find the file that makes her collapse on the floor. At this moment, I don't know what to do.

I will never understand why Elle wants to return to Hawaii; all her excuses have fallen flat: "I feel like I have to do this"; "I have to let Lauren know I'm okay"; "The agency expects me to finish the job, Agent Bright said as much." With each reason she has given me, I have a reason for her to stay: "You have risked enough"; "You don't need to fly hundreds of miles to see Lauren, you can call her on the telephone"; "The agency can send someone else."

I know I am running out of excuses, and she knows it too, but I am so desperate for her to stay she is having a hard time standing her ground. Finally, she looks at me where I am standing across the room. I notice she looks exhausted again, holding on to the counter for support.

"Andrew, I love you—you know that. And I don't have to give you a reason for going back to Hawaii. I could have left in the middle of the night, but I have more respect for you and the sacrifices you have made for me to do that. I am going back to Hawaii. I am going to find the file that belongs to Dan Childs, turn it into the agency, see my only friend from my past life and let her know I am alive, and finish this assignment. I am not doing this just for me but for you as well. Mr. Childs will never leave us alone—we will never be rid of him unless I can turn in some kind of intelligence that will get him busted. I'm sorry you are upset, but I will do this, with or without your blessing."

When she finishes, I can only say, "I'm sorry too, Elle. But I will never give you my blessing." I walk into the guest bedroom and shut the door. I don't see her for a whole day.

Chapter 33

Eleanor

I decide now is as good a time as any to contact Agent Bright with the news of my return to Hawaii. I can't imagine making this phone call with Andrew sitting next to me. I'm sure there are numerous details which have to be arranged, such as plane tickets, accommodations, false identifications, etc. To my surprise, Agent Bright does not sound one bit surprised to hear from me.

"I always knew I would be getting a call from you, but I never expected to hear from you so soon."

"Well, I have had a breakthrough in my recovery, and I think it would be pertinent to return to Hawaii. Can you have it set up?" I hope he understands my cryptic statement, and he seems to.

"Yes, I believe I can. When do you want to leave?" The sooner I can get this assignment done, the better.

"What about Saturday morning?" I ask.

"Sounds great. I will have Agent Shield bring by the details tonight. And, Mrs. Smith, I look forward to seeing you again." I feel a swell of hope in my chest at the possibility of not having to do this alone.

I ask, "Will you be accompanying me?"

I can tell Agent Bright smiles on the other end of the phone. "Yes, I am. I have never been to Hawaii before, and I am looking forward to it."

I am nervous as I hang up the phone and decide I need to review the information in my personal files again before I head back to Hawaii. As I retrieve the folders from my bedroom, I take a moment to walk into the guest room where Andrew slept last night. Just like before, the room is a mess, and I don't notice any difference in the junk on the floor. But as I turn to leave, I do notice that Andrew's dog tags are no longer hanging on the closet door. I look around for them, even move some things, but they are nowhere. Why on earth would he move them?

With the folders in my hands, I realize their presence no longer fill me with nervous anticipation but instead, a kind of relieved happiness. When I first opened the CIA information in the hospital seating area back in DC, I could hardly focus on the content. My vision was blurry from the tears in my eyes, and there was a loud pounding in my ears. It took me a few minutes to get a hold of my senses, and when I did, I dove into the information, reading as fast as I could. Now I have the time and ability to slowly read each line and process what it means for my future life.

- Name: Eleanor Elizabeth Wright
- DOB: October 1, 1984
- SSN: 555-07- _ _ _ _
- Height: 5 feet 4 inches
- Weight: 150 pounds
- Body Markings: no birthmarks, one tattoo located on right shoulder blade, "Eleanor"
- Hometown: Featherton, Tennessee
- Family: Parents, Bill and Judy Wright, deceased, killed in car accident; one older brother, Robert—enlisted in the army, stationed in Afghanistan
- Childhood: attended local schools, graduated with honors; Extra Curricular; track and field, shooting club, basketball, swimming.
- Adolescent Relationships: regularly spends time with friends from school, no steady boyfriend
- Higher Education: attended two years of community college
- Adult Relationships: keeps in contact with brother via the U.S. government, makes a few friends on each assignment, and keeps in contact with them through e-mails and phone calls; new friend in Hawaii, Lauren Price
- Permanent Residence: none
- List of Assignments:

  o Washington DC
  o San Antonio, Texas
  o Jacksonville, Florida
  o Denver, Colorado
  o Boston, Massachusetts
  o Seattle, Washington
  o Williamsburg, Virginia

- ○ Phoenix, Arizona
- ○ San Francisco, California
- ○ Indianapolis, Indiana
- ○ Nashville, Tennessee
- ○ Cheyenne, Wyoming
- ○ Salt Lake City, Utah
- ○ Honolulu, Hawaii

Looking back through the files and information, I am once again disappointed when I read that my parents are deceased. As I read the line again, "killed in car accident", I feel the same sadness I did in DC. At least I still have my brother. I say his name aloud, "Robert Wright", and an image comes to mind of a tall boy with brown hair and brown eyes. He is sitting on a creek bank with his jeans rolled up, hanging his legs into the water. He smiles at me and calls me Squirt, and then the memory is gone.

This has been the pattern since DC. Every line brings pictures from my past: I see my parents retreating figures holding hands; Casey, my friend from elementary school, is letting me braid her hair on the playground; I can taste the cake from my eighth birthday party; I feel the sting of the tattoo needle; I feel the tears running down my face as Robert boards the bus for basic training; a man I now know as Agent Bright approaches my lunch table at school and introduces himself—on and on the memories came. On the flight home from DC, it took me hours to write it all down in my memory journal.

After rereading the information in each folder, CIA and MicroCorp, and deciding none of it will help me in Hawaii, I start doing some normal things around the house. Because Andrew and I have been out of town, the house has not had the chance to get dirty, but I take out the cleaning supplies and begin the task of wiping down all the kitchen and bathroom counters.

As a load of laundry is being washed, I clean the entire bathroom as well as throw out the expired food in the fridge. When that is done, I put all my attention into getting the rest of the laundry washed, dried, and folded. I put away my clothes in the dresser in my room but simply stack Andrew's on the bed in the guest room. After what seems like hours of loading, unloading, and folding, I check the clock, which only reads eleven. I remember Andrew saying once that there is always something going on at the compound, so I get dressed in a cotton tank top and blue jeans and head out the door, hoping to get my mind off the fact that Andrew is still MIA.

Chapter 34

Andrew

I cannot stand to be in the same house with Elle today. I know the second I see her sad eyes, my resolve will crumble, and I will be offering to escort her to Honolulu myself. Instead of putting both of us in that situation, I get up extra early to avoid another fight. The thought of spending even another minute begging her to stay with me causes my injured shoulder to ache along with my head. I call my mother, charging her with the task of keeping tabs on Elle, and I head out the door without a second look back.

At first, I had no idea where to go; but as I drive toward the downtown area, there is only one place I can envision a trip to. Walking in the doors gives me a sense of homecoming. After all, this place has been my home away from home for the past three years. The front desk attendant, Clara, smiles so big it looks like her face will crack.

"Dr. Smith, it is so nice to see you again. We have heard all about your, um, exciting past couple of months—marriage, mugging. My, you have been busy." Clara is quite a talker but a sweet lady nonetheless.

"Yes, Clara, you know me, always a man of surprise. I hate to run, but Dr. Adams is waiting for me. It's always nice to see you."

I quickly walk away, hoping the last few floors I have to traverse before getting to my office will not be filled with the other "Claras" of the hospital. After forty-five minutes of curiosity seekers and genuine well-wishers, I finally reach my office door and hastily put the key in the lock, checking to my left and right and then opening the door to my solitude.

My office is small and sparsely furnished, kind of like my house. There are exactly two pictures hanging on the walls—one of my entire family, and the other is my diploma from medical school. On my desk is a stack of mail fairly small, a nameplate, and a container of pens. As I look around this room for the last time. I get emotional thinking about my past patients and fellow doctors and nurses, people I will no longer have the privilege to work with. A knock on the door brings me out of my daydream, and I gladly welcome the friendly face on the other side of the door.

Dr. Adams is not a big man; most would classify him as average in both height and weight. But his personality definitely qualifies him as a stand-out guy. The first time I saw him was when he entered my hospital room at the age of nine after the explosion. I remember feeling instantly at ease. His large smile and bright blue eyes were both reassuring and strengthening. His graying hair gave the impression he was much older than forty-one.

Since our first meeting, Dr. Adams has become like a second father to me—supporting me in my recovery, even coming to my sporting events, and finally helping me get my job at this hospital. Because of our close relationship, I dreaded telling him more than anyone I was planning to leave. When I finally got in contact with someone at the hospital from my Washington DC hotel, it was Dr. Adams who insisted on taking my phone call. I explained hurriedly that my current situation was taking me away far too much to properly do my job. And even though he sounded understanding on the other line, I knew Dr. Adams was secretly disappointed.

"So you're leaving us?" He says this as more of a statement than question, but I get the sense he is giving me the opportunity to change my mind in the next few seconds. However, I have to disappoint him again.

"Yes, sir, I am. I feel like I can no longer do this position justice. My head and my heart are somewhere else these days."

Dr. Adams just nods, and I know he is remembering our conversation at my house, after my violent outburst toward a patient, in which I said these exact same words.

"You know, Andrew. The first time I saw you, I knew you were strong. No little boy survives an explosion like the one you did and lives to become such a full-functioning member of society. When I first asked you if you were ready to get started and you answered with such a definitive yes, I knew you would go far. And you have, son. There is always restlessness in young men who have completed military service, and you are no exception. But over the last year, I have been noticing a sort of disconnect between you and your work. And even though you plan to take some time off from the hospital, be sure not to stay MIA for too long." I have a strange feeling he not only means from the hospital but from my personal life as well. "And one thing is for sure. I do not want you to continue doing this job when your heart is somewhere else." I sit there quietly as Dr. Adams stands up and heads for the door.

"Oh and, Andrew, there is no shame whatsoever in allowing that 'somewhere else' to be with the woman you love."

I speak up before he leaves the room. "Dr. Adams, I can never thank you enough for all you have done for me." He smiles and then closes the door behind him.

I'm not sure how long I sit in my small office, but when I get up to find a cardboard box to place my few possessions in, my legs are cramping, and my shoulder is screaming with pain. I fish out a bottle of Advil from my desk drawer before making my way toward the custodian closet. The clock in the hallway reads four forty-five. I can't believe I have been lost in thought for so long.

For the past several hours, I have reviewed my entire life from start to finish, following one event to the other and making small connections between them. There were times the connections were easy to see: the explosion setting me on course to desire a position in the medical field; the unthinkable injustice of 9/11 sending me into the military; the love of my family driving me to stay close to home after returning from Afghanistan. But other connections are harder to see like my desire to help Elle because of the knowledge of Nicole's tragic past.

Elle . . . I wonder what she is doing right now.

But even as I begin to picture her beautiful face, I feel the anger rising. How could she even think about doing this? How can she throw away everything we have, everything we have worked for, just to finish this "mission"? She is putting her life in danger, and she expects me to give her my blessing—no way!

I pull my cell phone out of my pocket and start dialing the number of the only person I know who can understand how I feel and make me feel better.

"Joshua, it's Andrew. Can you meet me at O'Leary's?"

****

Eleanor

It was 12:45 p.m. when I heard Andrew come home. It took every fiber of my being not to run to him. The fact he spent all day avoiding me did not make a difference in the slightest—I missed him and regretted our fight the night before. But when I heard the guest room door close and realized Andrew had no intention of checking on me or, heaven forbid, apologize, I could feel my hope plummeting to the floor. I spent the rest of the late night crying myself to sleep.

There is no way I can make him understand my desire, my need to see this mission to completion. Seeing how Andrew is acting, I'm not sure if I want to try to make him see my side of things. It would serve him right if I left tomorrow morning, without a word of explanation. However, I know the second the thought crosses my mind I would never do that to him. Regardless of his childish attitude and actions, Andrew has done too much for me to treat him like that. I just wish he could see his safety is the most important thing to me; it is the main reason I am making the trip to Honolulu.

Chapter 35

Andrew

I deliberately avoided Elle last night when I got home from the bar. It's not that I didn't want to see her. Actually, it was the exact opposite—I am dying to see her. However, on my way in, Agent Shield stopped me at my front door.

"Dr. Smith, I was informed to give this material to your wife. I just received it, and seeing how it is so late, I thought it would be better to give it to you. I did not want to scare her by knocking on the door so late."

I hated to ask the question because I was pretty sure I already knew the answer. "What is this, exactly?"

"Your wife's itinerary for her trip to Hawaii," he answers. "Flight times, details on the Hawaiian investigation, etc. Everything she will need to complete her assignment."

Because my mood was so dark to begin with, I rudely grabbed the folder out of his hands and squeak out a quick "thanks." I'm not sure how I refrained from slamming the door on my way inside, but I did, and I promised myself I would not see Eleanor until I could give her only my love and not my anger.

However, she will be gone again in a few hours, too far away for me to do anything. I'll be here helpless and alone again. I think back to my flight to Honolulu. I was so desperate to get a handle on my life. My dispassion with being a servant of the people, so to speak, was growing daily. But as I saw the sunset that first night from my hotel room, I took it as a sign of good things to come. I never would have guessed that those "good things" would be in the form of a naked, dying woman.

****

Honolulu: Over Two Months Ago

That first sound I heard coming from the alley gave me a knot in the pit of my stomach. Being unfamiliar with Honolulu, I should have kept walking. But years of following my gut and learning to trust its instincts drive me further into the darkness. Thank goodness for the bright moonlight because the farther I journey into the alley, the less streetlight is visible. The sound which caught my attention on the street has ceased, and I am starting to wonder if in my distracted state I had imagined it all.

I call out quietly, "Hello? Is anyone there? My name is Dr. Andrew Smith. Can I be of any assistance?" There is no one here; I'm probably talking to myself like a crazy person. The second I decide this was a very dumb thing to do, I hear another sound. Not the gurgling noise I heard before but the unmistakable sound of someone dying. I stop midstep and face the back of the alley again.

"Hello! Is someone there?" The sound of struggled breath comes from the dead end, and I race farther into the darkness once again. Even with the lack of good lighting, I can tell there is a body positioned face up on the concrete. When I finally reach it, the first thing that catches my attention is the fact the body is female. The second is the victim's lack of clothing. The third is the beauty of the woman. I pause for a split second, and then my training kicks in. This body is one of the worst, if not the worst, case of abuse I have ever seen. There is not an inch of skin that is not covered in either a bruise or bleeding cuts.

I take the woman's pulse, *barely alive*, and then place my ear to her chest, listening for anything that will give me a clue into her prognosis. I never realized how dependent I have become on technology. Start using your instincts, I command. Bottom line, she needs immediate medical attention. Attention I cannot begin to give her in this dark and dirty alley.

Remembering that the nearest hospital is not too far away, I race back toward the street to hail a cab when I spot something suspect. Sitting across the alley's entrance is an old Volkswagen Beetle. It's the kind that comes to mind when one conjures up an image of the 1960s and 1970s. Am I imagining things, or was that car not there when I entered the alley?

From my place in the shadows, I can see two men sitting in the car, both of them staring at my hiding place. Their windows are down, probably because of the warm weather, and I shrink into the darkness to remain unseen while they loudly and somewhat heatedly have a discussion.

"I told you, she's as good as dead. There's no need to hang around here. If someone finds her, we will be the first suspects."

"We need to make sure, though. Do you really want to tell the boss you *think* she's dead? I sure don't want to feel his wrath."

"There's no need, Jones. It will be a miracle if she survives the beating we gave her."

"Still, I would feel much better if we dumped her body in the ocean. That way, there is no question of her survival."

"Nah, let's head back. I'm tired and ready to get drunk. Trust me, will you?"

I can see the other man, Jones, shaking his head in disagreement. But the other one speaks up, "If it makes you feel any better, I will personally check the hospitals later to make sure no one finds her. If, by some chance she is alive, she won't be for long. Deal?"

The engine starts, and I can't hear what Jones replies, but my guess is he agrees because they drive off without a second look to the alleyway where they left a dying woman.

I have never told Elle about the conversation I overheard from her attackers or told her the real reason I chose not to take her to a hospital. I have often wondered if I made a mistake not being completely honest with her. But every time I would second-guess my decision, the knowledge that I was protecting Elle just a little bit more by withholding my information got the better of me. I guess I am the only person who really knows how lucky Elle is to be alive . . . except Dan Childs.

The thought of her possibly running straight back to his violent clutches makes me want to cry. But ever since our fight, I know nothing I say can or will change her mind. I just have to trust Elle and her instincts, the way I trusted my own to keep her alive. I also have to prepare myself to embrace the fact that after she wakes up, I will be alone again.

****

Eleanor

Andrew is awake when my alarm goes off seven. I only gave myself an hour to get ready for my trip, which should be plenty of time. However, seeing Andrew's pathetic attempt at a smile, it becomes hard for me to have any motivation. He is sitting at the kitchen table. I approach him and reach over to stroke his face, filling the stubble which has grown since last night. He catches my hand and places a kiss on my palm and then takes my face and kisses me unlike ever before. After the many kisses we have shared, I thought I knew how each one would feel, but not this one. I have never been kissed so sweetly.

Andrew rubs his thumbs along my cheekbones and moves his mouth all over my face, kissing my forehead, temples, and even my chin. He clumsily stands up, and we move toward the bedroom. We fall to the bed in unison. The knock on our door breaks the moment, and I jump out of bed to race to the shower. Andrew pulls me back down onto him, and I prepare for another fight. Instead, he wraps me in his arms and just holds me. I let his warmth and love seep into my bones, hoping they will stay there the whole way to Honolulu. Another loud knock on the door draws my attention away.

"Can you get that please?" I ask. "I don't imagine the CIA is used to being kept waiting." He simply nods his head, and I run to the bathroom. When I emerge, I expect to see Agent Bright waiting for me, but the only one in the house is Andrew who is sitting on the couch, my packed suitcase sitting beside him.

"The least I could do was pack your suitcase since it was my fault you're going to be late." His sad smile breaks my heart, and I long to reach out to him. But I stand my ground.

"Thank you, but you aren't the only one to blame for my delay. Where is Agent Bright?"

"He's meeting you at the airport. Agent Shield is waiting outside to escort you there."

I nod and spot my CIA folders lying on the kitchen table. As I go to retrieve them, I make a point to stop in the kitchen and remember the first time I saw Andrew. It was here, at this very sink the man I now call my husband first saw me, first talked to me, and first kissed me. The fact I may never step foot in this kitchen again gets me choked up, and I quickly grab my folders and walk away.

Andrew stands by the door, my purse, suitcase, and sweater in his hands. When I reach him, I try smiling to reassure us both that everything is going to be fine. He nods again and then opens the door. Agent Shield is, of course, standing at attention by a nondescript government car. He makes his way toward us and issues a short "Good morning, Mrs. Smith" and then takes my things from Andrew, places them in the trunk, and then places himself in the driver's seat.

These are my last few seconds with Andrew, so I want to make the most out of them, but all I can say is "I will call you as soon as I can."

"Okay. Please be careful."

"I will. I love you."

"I love you too."

Andrew doesn't stay outside to see us make our way down the driveway. His retreating figure in the car's side mirror is the last glimpse I have of the man I love. Who knew saying good-bye would be so hard?

Chapter 36

Eleanor

The car ride to the airport was pretty embarrassing for both me and Agent Shield. I cried the entire way, and it wasn't just any cry; it was a body-shaking, gut-wrenching one. The agent didn't say a word, didn't even try to console me. But I did notice how his foot pressed a little harder on the gas pedal, and the trip, which should have taken thirty minutes, took only half that time.

When we did arrive at the airport, he practically threw my bags at the pilot and bid me a hasty "good luck." Before I could say anything, he was in his car and gone. I stand at the bottom of the airplane's steps for a minute trying to dry my eyes and steal my nerves. Agent Bright is waiting for me inside the plane, and as I place myself across the aisle from him, he picks up a telephone located on the side panel of the plane and informs the pilot we are ready to take off.

This aircraft is not too different than the Smiths' private jet. It is definitely as luxurious as theirs; however, the main difference is the amount of technology on the government plane. I see four flat screen TVs built into the cabin walls and can only guess what their screens would show if they were turned on. Along with Agent Bright's telephone, there are two more in the small cabin which seats about sixteen, one on my side and one on the front wall.

Agent Bright hangs up the phone and turns his attention to me. "Lateness is not tolerated, no matter what the excuse. Do I make myself clear?"

I look him in the eyes and respond timidly, "Yes, sir. It won't happen again."

"Good, because I hate being the bad guy." He gives a small smile, and I am instantly put at ease. He continues, "I understand these past few weeks have been hell, but let's face it, that is par for the course in this line of work. I can't tell you how many of my months could be classified as 'hellish' since I started with the CIA twenty years ago. My best advice to you is to put them behind you and allow them to make you stronger. If you can do that, then you can live a seminormal life."

I think about Andrew back at home and realize he is my new normal. I crave more lazy days surrounded by family and mornings filled with caresses. This business about "hellish" months only quickens my desire to be done with this assignment. I nod my head, not wanting to give an answer and change the subject.

"Agent Bright, I wanted to thank you for giving me my folder. Since I received the information, I have had more memory flashes than ever before."

He nods his head. "It wasn't my decision either way, but I'm happy I could be the one to deliver it. So you say your memories have started coming back?"

"Yes, I have been able to remember my brother's face. The knowledge he is in the military is, I have to admit, rather scary. But at least I know how to contact him. I even remember you, Agent Bright, our first meeting in particular."

He nods again. "Yes, I also remember our first meeting. I was instantly impressed with your maturity and your willingness to not take my BS"

"I knew immediately you were there to get me into some kind of trouble, and I was right. Here I am, over ten years later, barely escaping with my life every time I turn around." I meant it as a joke, but Agent Bright becomes very quiet, and a worried look plasters itself on his face.

"Of course I have no control over your assignments, let alone what happens to you on those assignments, but you have to know I hated hearing about your . . . accident."

"Like you said, it's just par for the course." I wave a hand dismissively with the attitude of someone who is not bothered by being beaten and left to die.

"We only have a couple of hours before we reach Honolulu, so we should probably review the details of our itinerary. Have you looked through the information that Agent Shield dropped off for you?" I didn't want to admit my fight with Andrew and our following reconciliation took most of my time away from studying the details the CIA put together for me, so I skirted the truth.

"Yeah, I looked at it," I said with little enthusiasm. He could tell I wasn't being completely honest with him.

"Why don't we spend the rest of our time looking at it again? Shall we?"

I nodded in agreement, secretly pleased Agent Bright didn't audibly call my bluff. And that is just what we did; the two hours of our trip were spent fine-tuning each and every detail:

- 11:00 a.m. – reach Honolulu airport
- 11:15 a.m. – rendezvous with contact at predetermined location; debrief on investigation in the city
- 11:45 a.m. – appointment at local police office; determine further steps
- 12:30 a.m. – agent's previous residence; retain all important information

By the time the plane lands, I am practically bouncing off my seat with anticipation. I wonder if this is what I felt like before each mission. Anticipation mixed with excitement and even a hint of fear. One thing I am sure of—my fear level has increased because now I know what can happen when a mission goes wrong.

We meet our contact at a pier stretching out from the city. I'm not sure what I expected, maybe someone similar to Agent Bright—tall, muscular, cropped haircut, black suit, authoritative air about him. Instead, our contact in Honolulu ended up being a shrimpy young guy with glasses and greasy long hair. His name is Mike, and when I ask him what his job is, he simply answers, "This and that."

The three of us grab a soda from a nearby vender and sit at one of the six picnic tables. There are people everywhere, 95 percent of them tourists, so our strange little group of three—one business man, one hippy, and myself, a very normal-looking twenty-something—don't draw any strange glances from the passersby.

"So," Mike starts out, "you're the one who caused Dan Childs so much trouble a few months ago. Man, you must be a handful I've never heard so much chatter!" When I ask him what he means by "chatter", he answers, "Like I said, I do this and that. And one of the 'that's' is keeping my eyes and ears open. Let's just say you were a very popular subject around town for a few weeks."

I'm not sure if I should feel flattered, so I don't say anything, just shrug my own shoulders and look out at the radiant blue ocean.

Agent Bright speaks up. "Mike, what can you tell us about the investigation into Agent Smith's disappearance on this end?"

"Well, it was pretty standard, really. When Agent Smith didn't return to work for a few days, her supervisor at MicroCorp called in a Missing Person report to the police. From there, the standard procedure was followed by the Honolulu Police Department."

I interrupt Mike at this point. "Can you tell me what the standard procedure is for a missing person report?" He gives me a curious glance, which I don't understand but begins again.

"The responding officer gathers an initial description and information, such as: facts and/or details of the incident; description of the missing person, height, weight, race, age, clothing, and other unique features; name; last known location; name of last person who saw or had contact with the individual; possible leads and/or known locations frequented by the individual; means of travel available to the person, i.e., foot, bicycle, vehicle. I have personally reviewed the report pertaining to you, and it is, sadly, sparse. Your employer knew only the basics about you. The police couldn't find anyone who knew more than your name. Even your neighbors knew nothing of importance to tell the police." *Thank goodness Lauren listened to me and got out of here.*

Mike continues with an expression of boredom on his face and in his voice. "Until quite recently, the case was still ongoing, but I have a feeling our friends in Washington had it taken care of." At this, he gives a pointed look to Agent Bright who acknowledges Mike's statement with a nod of his head.

"I did my own digging, which I am sure is why you are really here. I have friends in both high and low places, and those low-placed friends were able to share with me just a few pieces of information. You heard me say a few moments ago you were the talk of the town," he addresses me with a bit of some emotion playing in his eyes. "The word on the street was you were left to die in some back alley by some of Dan Childs's goons. Evidently, one of them gets a tad bit talkative after having a few drinks, and he was bragging to another patron how he 'took care' of you. In a bar not far from here one of those 'low-placed' friends I mentioned overheard his speech. He also indicated his boss, the very important and well-known CEO of MicroCorp, was going to be pleased with his work. It seems like he was expecting some kind of reward for the great job he did on you."

Mike must notice me wince with revulsion because he quickly adds, "Sorry, I meant no offense." I wave him off, and he continues. "I didn't hear anything for a couple of weeks, which was strange because I had feelers out all over the city. But after three or four weeks, the man entered the same bar one night with bruises covering his face and one eye swollen. When prodded about what happened, he hesitantly and gruffly answered he hadn't done as good of a job as he had thought. Other than that, he wouldn't say anything else. That's when I began doing my own digging."

It is such a relief to get some information about what happened while I lay unconscious across an ocean. It is also comforting to know I had several people looking out for me, even if I didn't know it. The whole time Mike was talking, Agent Bright took notes, and now he spoke up, asking him to clarify a few things. When asked who his informant was, he shook his head and grinned really big.

"Nuh-uh, Agent, you know that is not how this works. The saying is, if you name your friends, they won't be your friends anymore." Agent Bright must be expecting this answer, so he moves onto other questions regarding the dates and times of these interactions.

As Mike answers his questions, I let my eyes look around the beautiful scene surrounding me. The beach is packed with families—mothers and fathers try to wrangle their children who are kicking and screaming, fighting against the placing of extensive sunscreen across their chests and faces. A few other groups are clearly college kids throwing Frisbees or footballs and laughing loudly with cans of beer in their hands. I can even see a tour group full of retired older men and women. Their impractical outfits cause me to stifle a laugh. They are all wearing tennis shoes and socks, large straw hats, sunglasses, and I even spot a fanny pack or two. How blessed am I to get to enjoy this beautiful place well before retirement age. I mentally add this to my "Lucky List."

Mike and Agent Bright have finished with their question-and-answer time, so I address our informant once again. "You were saying you did some digging for yourself?"

"Oh, yes. I went to your apartment and hung around for a few days. I have to admit that the place was a dead end. I learned nothing. I even pretended to be interested in renting your apartment, hoping that would stir up some good gossip. The only thing I did learn was your next-door neighbor, Lauren, I think, had also taken off the day you disappeared. That piece of news led me to believe you might still be out there somewhere. The next week is when I received a call informing me to narrow my search to talk about Dan Childs."

The next question Agent Bright asks Mike is the most important one— the one that will determine if our trip to Hawaii was all in vain.

"Do you know if the local police recovered any of Agent Smith's possessions?"

"In all honesty, you'd be better off asking them. Like I said, I got a phone call telling me to cease tracking Agent Smith, and so I did just that. But there is one thing I do know. A couple of days ago, I heard Agent Smith's neighbor returned to her apartment about a week after she disappeared."

I am thrilled to hear Lauren is safe and back in Honolulu and am suddenly ready for our meeting to be over. Thankfully, Agent Bright seems to be anxious to make our appointment with the police, so we stand and thank Mike. He shrugs, like it's commonplace for him to have rendezvous with undercover CIA agents. He heads the opposite way down the street, gets on a bicycle, and pedals out of site.

At the local police station, we meet with the police chief who seems entirely unhappy to be hosting us. As he shuffles us into his cramped and hot office, a deputy yells something that sounds a lot like "What about the Donovan case? The coroner hasn't called back with the results."

"Call Johnson and have him drive by the hospital and stay there until I get those results!" He slams the door and then maneuvers himself into his office chair, while Agent Bright and I take the other two chairs in the room. "Well, what can I help the CIA with?"

I look to Agent Bright, and he begins smoothly. "Chief Richards, first of all, we appreciate you taking the time to meet with us. We know you are a very busy person with a lot of responsibilities, so we appreciate your valuable time." I look back toward the chief and notice the redness of his face fading, and his frown is replaced with a more genial look.

"Well, it's my pleasure to be of assistance." He focuses his attention on me, and I squirm in my seat. "You seem very familiar. What did you say your name was, miss?"

I clear my throat and try to sound like a confident government agent instead of a scared girl in trouble in the principal's office, which is truthfully how I feel. "My name is Agent Eleanor Smith, but you probably know me as Rebecca Greene." When I say this, the chief's eyes widen, and he looks over my shoulder. I follow his gaze and turn around in my seat to see a large wall outside of his office that is covered with "Missing Person" posters. I feel my own eyes widen as I catch an eerily good sketch artist's rendering of my own face. I catch Agent Bright's attention, but he doesn't acknowledge me. When I turn back around, the chief is giving us both a questioning look. Agent Bright sits silently at my side, so I take initiative and speak up.

"Yes, sir, that is me. I was on assignment here in Honolulu and was reported missing by my supervisor at MicroCorp. I understand some of your detectives carried out an investigation into my disappearance, and both I and the CIA appreciate that. However, as you can see, I am not actually missing, which is why Agent Bright and myself have come here today." The chief sits silently, and Agent Bright begins talking.

"Like Agent Smith said," Agent Bright starts, "we have come here today to share some information into the CIA investigation of Dan Childs." The chief interrupts Agent Bright.

"Dan Childs, the CEO of MicroCorp?" His tone of surprise and sudden interest causes me to give him a questioning look, the same look, I notice, is on Agent Bright's face. Chief Richards continues talking, "I had a lot of dealings with the man when he decided to build the MicroCorp facility here in Honolulu. I have to admit I am surprised that he is under investigation. He seemed like such a powerful man with plenty of connections in the government. But I guess that doesn't matter if you're doing something illegal." His last sentence is phrased more like a question than a statement, and I realize he is trying to get more information out of us, but Agent Bright stops him in his tracks.

"Of course, Chief Richards, you know I cannot divulge any information that may hinder our ongoing investigation. I can tell you, though, the CIA involvement will not cause you or your department any more trouble. As Agent Smith said, we appreciate your speedy and thorough investigation into the Missing Person's report."

The chief nods his head and asks, "Is there anything I can do you for you? I assume your trip to the city was not merely to have this meeting. A simple phone call would have sufficed."

Agent Bright answers, "Yes, we were wondering if your detectives ever found anything belonging to Agent Smith in their search—personal property, clothing, anything outside of her apartment?"

Chief Richards stands and makes his way to the office door, opening it to yell across the police station to a young officer. "Hey, White. Did you all find anything in regard to that Missing Person's case a few months back for a Rebecca Greene?"

A man, whom I assume to be Detective White, yells back almost immediately, "Yeah, someone turned in some clothing found behind a dumpster we believed could belong to the woman. I think Marks checked with her neighbor, and she confirmed our theory. Last I heard, he left the clothing with her." Agent Bright and I exchange a curious look.

"Do your deputies usually turn over evident to a civilian?" the agent asks.

"No, of course not. However, the deputy that was assigned the case was new, and well, needless to say, he no longer works here."

A thrill I have never felt courses through my body, and I am already on my feet by the time that Chief Richards turns back around. He seems startled by my sudden flight from the chair and stumbles a little as he bumps into a large filing cabinet. "Thank you so much for your time, Chief Richards," I say, thrusting out my hand. He takes it questioningly but gives it a firm shake, and then I'm out the door. I don't wait to hear what Agent Bright is telling him, but as I take one last look over my shoulder, I see the chief take down my Missing Person poster from the wall and thank my lucky stars for that inexperienced and now-unemployed deputy.

Our cab ride to my old apartment is agony as my mind runs through all the "what-ifs" that could have happened in the few weeks Lauren has had my clothes: What if she no longer lives there? What if she threw them out? What if my shoe is not among the clothing that the police recovered? What if Dan Childs has already gotten to her and found the disk? I am driving myself crazy thinking all these negative thoughts, so I focus my thoughts on Andrew. If I can just retrieve the disk, my obligations to the CIA are fulfilled. Or are they?

Now that I have gotten a taste of this sort of life, the danger and excitement, can I really give it up? In one way, I cannot imagine the rest of my life being consumed with so much uncertainty. And after what happened in Washington DC, I never want my job to put Andrew in harm's way again. But would I be happy in some mundane job: sales manager at Smith Shipping, Incorporated? I don't think so. There is no doubt in my mind Andrew would never allow me to continue my life as an intelligence gatherer for the CIA if we stayed together. As I picture his face from this morning, and I hear his question in my ears, I am more confused than ever.

****

We lay in a huge heap in the middle of the bed with our fingers intertwined. Neither one of us wants to say anything and break the spell of the moment. I silently wonder what he might be thinking. Does he hate me for leaving? Will he ever understand? Tears sting the backs of my eyes when I think about leaving him here alone. He rolls over onto his good elbow and gives me a serious look.

"Marry me," he says quietly.

"What?"

"Marry me, Elle. For real. Marry me. You would make me the happiest man on the planet."

"Andrew, I can't think about this now."

"What is there to think about? I love you, you love me. It's simple, really. The simplest decision you will ever have to make."

I sigh. "Andrew, I do love you. But there are things about both you and me which are not easily remedied with a simple declaration of love. And you know that."

"Whatever comes our way, I know we will get through it, just like we have so far."

I look into his beautiful green eyes. They are filled with love, compassion, gentleness, respect, everything and anything I could ever want in a husband. But something still holds me back. I can tell my silence is starting to bother Andrew because he lies back down on the bed.

"I can't believe it took you all two seconds to decide to go back to Honolulu, but you can't give me a simple answer."

I'm not sure how to respond. He is right, and I know it, but there is no way for me to explain my hesitations to him without causing hurt feelings.

****

As I wonder what Andrew might be doing, the cab stops in front of a very ordinary apartment complex—concrete and windows reaching about ten stories into the air.

I can feel Agent Bright's eyes on my face, but I take a couple more seconds to steel my nerves before turning to face him. "You don't mind if I have a few minutes alone with Lauren, do you? I just don't want to overwhelm her. I know she'll be confused and probably mad too."

Agent Bright must hear the desperation in my voice because he nods. "Sure, I've actually got to make a few phone calls and let headquarters know how our meeting went at the police station. I'll be waiting for you out here. Good luck, and I hope she has what you are looking for."

As I step out of the cab and onto the sidewalk, I turn back to ask Agent Bright if he can give me some advice for the situation I am about to get myself into, but he has already pulled out his smartphone and started dialing numbers. I give him a small wave and then shut the door. As I face the apartment building, I can't decide which emotion is the strongest: fear or joy.

The elevator is small and rundown; the air conditioning is struggling to meet the demands of the cramped space, and I can feel the sweat rolling down my back. When I pushed the button for the seventh floor, it was completely out of habit, or what would be considered habit since I haven't pushed that particular button in almost three months. A slideshow of memories begin at the same time as the elevator.

I remember the first time I rode this very elevator; it was the morning I moved into the building, and the temperature in Honolulu was reaching into the high nineties. I have the same thought today as I did that day—I wish I would have taken the stairs. When I reach Lauren's door, I take a few calming breaths before knocking a little too forcefully and wait with baited breath for the unknown type of welcome my old friend will give me. I hear, "Just a minute" and some hurried footsteps, and then the door swings open, and I plaster on what I hope is a friendly smile.

Lauren stands there looking like someone has just punched her in the gut, and I have to admit I am a bit disappointed she doesn't look even the least bit happy to see me. I hold up a hand in a shy salutation, and Lauren hastily says, "Becca, oh my gosh, it's so good to see you." Her words are friendly, but her tone is not, and there is a hushed quality to her voice.

"I'm sure it's a surprise to see me after so long, but you have to understand there was no way I could contact you. You see, I've been suffering from—"

My words are cut short when Lauren frantically looks over her shoulder toward the approaching footsteps I have also just heard. I start again, "Oh, I'm sorry," I whisper, "I didn't know that you had company. I can come back later."

When she looks back to me, Lauren's face is one of indescribable sadness. She mouths a simple "I'm sorry," and I give her a questioning look. At that same moment, I hear another voice coming from the inside of Lauren's apartment—a voice I hoped I would never hear again.

Dan Childs swings the apartment door the rest of the way open. "Well, look who we have here. Ms. Greene, what a pleasant surprise."

Chapter 37

Andrew

I've spent the morning lying in bed, which is something I never do. But after Elle left, I had no strength, let alone desire to do anything else. I wonder if she found the disk and silently pray she has. *Maybe this will be it—the end of such uncertainty. Maybe she will come home, agree to marry me, and we can forget all about this horrible time.* I find myself almost willing her back, imagine her taking each step in reverse, away from the plane and the terror Honolulu holds.

Unbidden, the image of her broken body in that alley plasters itself into my brain, and I physically cringe from the memory. I wonder if this is what it's like for Elle when she has one of her flashbacks. Do some of them cause her physical pain, or are they just a picture, a snapshot of something she has seen or done? For her sake, I hope they are the latter. Knowing now the life she has lived—the sadness of losing both parents, the feeling of abandonment when her only brother went into the military, not to mention her career with the CIA has to carry with it a feeling of despair and pressure so great—I know I will never understand.

As I hear a knock on the door, I once again pray she has found what she needs and, at this moment, is returning to me. I can feel the tightness in my injured shoulder as I drag myself out of bed.

Nicole is standing there with her arms full of Tupperware dishes when I finally swing the front door open. She looks a little putout but smiles and says, "You are the last stop. I decided to take the leftovers from our office picnic to everyone else on the compound before I bothered you and Elle. I figured you guys wanted a little privacy this morning."

At the mention of Elle, I can't find it to return Nicole's smile, but I wave her into the kitchen. "Is this all leftovers?" I ask as she dumps the containers on my counters. There has to be about fifteen different sizes of Tupperware, and at a quick glance, I can see sweet-and-sour chicken in one and spaghetti in another.

"Yes, can you believe there is so much? You should have seen the back of my car when I started delivering them this morning—the trunk was full of Tupperware containers. I looked like I sold the stuff!" I chuckle, and the two of us begin an assembly line of sorts, packing the containers into the fridge, wherever there is room. I see Nicole glancing toward the bedroom door, so I decide to speak up.

"Elle's not here, Nicole. She left for Honolulu this morning." With her back to me, I'm unsure if Nicole heard what I said; but when one of the containers falls to the ground, spilling some variety of crackers all over the floor, a sense of dread consumes me, and I grab Nicole's shoulders and spin her around. Her eyes are as round as saucers when she finally looks up at me, and I can tell that she is about to cry.

"What is it, Nicole? What's wrong?"

All I can hear before she bursts into horrible sobs is "Oh, Andrew, I am so sorry."

I know my pacing across the floor is neither beneficial to me nor the carpet, but I cannot seem to stop. I don't know how long I have been doing it—it seems like hours, but it's probably more like minutes. Any time spent in this house doing nothing is time Elle does not have on her side. By my calculations, Elle has been in Honolulu for about thirty minutes, which is a lot of time in which something could have gone terribly wrong.

When I finally got Nicole calmed down enough to tell me what she meant by her apology, I wasted no time in contacting Agent Shield. Within ten minutes, he was knocking on my door, and we had a game plan. The plan, which seems spotty at best, requires us to go to Hawaii, a place I swore I would never return. Just like in the hospital after I got shot, I think to myself, only a woman could have made me throw that promise out the window in so short a time! If it was anyone but Elle, I would probably let the government agents responsible for this mess retrieve her and bring her back, but I no longer trust anyone but myself to take care of her.

Nicole's crying from the couch snaps me back into the present, and it's all I can do not to lash out at her. *How could she do this to me, to my family, to Joshua?* But I have to stop myself from going any further because truthfully, I should have seen this coming—I should have figured this out a long time ago.

When Elle told me about the folder that Dan Childs gave her at MicroCorp headquarters with notes pertaining to our relationship and the intimate details contained within, I gave it more thought. Who could be spying on us? What would they have to gain by giving Dan Childs information on Elle? It seemed nearly impossible at the time to give an answer to a question which has infinite possibilities. Both Elle and I have come into contact with dozens of people since returning from Honolulu. Beside the staff here on the compound, there have been people we've seen on the street, at doctor's appointments, in restaurants, not to mention my coworkers at the hospital and the Smith Shipping employees. It seemed like anyone and everyone could be one of Dan Childs' informants.

But never, not for one single second, did I suspect someone in my own family to betray me like Nicole did. I mistook her standoffish attitude toward Elle as her ability to distrust outsiders. I never would have guessed her cool indifference was hiding the fact she was in Dan Childs's pocket. With each visit into our home, she was gathering information. With each sentence we spoke, she was analyzing what to tell Dan Childs. Because I blame myself for not putting the connections together, almost just as much as I blame Nicole for being a traitor to our family, I have avoided even looking at her. However, I can't help from glancing toward Joshua who is standing in the opposite corner of the room, staring at his wife as though he doesn't know her at all.

I hear Agent Shield continue his questioning of Nicole, and I stop my pacing to hear how all this started. "Mrs. Smith, when did Dan Childs first contact you?"

"It was the day before Andrew returned from Honolulu with Elle. I was sitting at a café downtown, and a man in a suit approached me. He introduced himself as Dan Childs, and I instantly recognized him from television. I thought at first he was just flirting with me, but when he pulled a folder out of his briefcase, I noticed it had my name on it. He told me he knew this meeting must seem strange, but he needed my help in stopping a dangerous person. At that point, I thought I might have been set up on one of those practical jokes shows. I imagined Joshua jumping out at any moment, saying, 'You're on candid camera!'" She stops and looks up to Joshua who is looking at the floor. In a pitiful voice she says, "That just seems like something you would do. You've always been a joker."

When Joshua neither moves nor speaks, Nicole gives a little sob, and Agent Shield brings her back on topic. "You were saying he had a folder?"

"Yeah, he had a folder and told me Andy was bringing home a woman from Honolulu who was a very dangerous person. He told me she had stolen some important information from his company, and she had tricked

Andrew into helping her. When I finally realized he was serious, I asked him why I should help him. I distinctly remember what he said because it was in that moment I decided to help him. He said, 'If you help me, Mrs. Smith, I can help you. I have your information here, and I see your home life growing up was not a bed of roses. I can guarantee your mother and your siblings will never want for another thing again. If you provide me with details of this woman's whereabouts and goings-on, I can provide you with the peace of mind that your family will be taken care of.'"

I feel my heart breaking just a little bit, and I look at Joshua. I can tell it is taking every bit of his strength to not reach out to Nicole. And honestly, I would not blame him if he did. Out of the whole family, he, I, and our parents are probably the only ones who know the sad truth of Nicole's past—she only trusts a few people with the knowledge, and we just happen to be two of those people. But before I can dwell on her explanation, Agent Shield continues asking her questions. "How did you contact Dan Childs, Mrs. Smith, and what sort of information did he want on Agent Smith?"

"He gave me a card with his cell number on it. I would call him every couple of days. At first, all I could tell him was that Elle was unconscious. I don't think he believed me because he said, 'Mrs. Smith, I cannot follow through on my part of the bargain if you don't follow through on yours.' I assured him I was telling the truth. The day Elle finally woke up, I was relieved to have something of note to tell him. I called him as soon as we returned from Andrew's house, and then that night, my mother called and said a check was delivered to her house that day. She was so happy I could hear her sobs over the phone. After that, he wanted to know everything— what she did, where she went, everything I could tell him."

Agent Shield asks, "When was the last time you talked to Dan Childs?"

"The day Andrew got shot in Washington. I had been telling him where Andrew and Elle were stopping on their trip. When I talked to Elle that day and she told me she was at some little coffee shop, I immediately texted him. I had no idea he was in Washington. When Elle called that night and said Andrew had been shot, I knew I had screwed up. I never called Dan Childs again." She looks at me and says, "I never meant for you to get hurt."

Nicole stops and begins sobbing. I look away, not wanting her to see the tears in my own eyes. It seems like it should be easy for me to hate Nicole after everything she has put me and Elle through. But if I am honest with myself, what would I have done if the situation was reversed? What if someone told me I could be saving both of my families, the one that raised me and the one that took me in? Without a doubt, my answer would have been "Yes, I'll do whatever it takes."

At the moment, though, I feel too betrayed to think rationally. If Nicole had just been honest with me, with us, then Elle would be safe, and Joshua would not be faced with a future married to a woman he doesn't trust.

Nicole speaks up through her tears, "Andrew, I am so sorry. I thought I was protecting you, protecting the whole family. I thought she was a dangerous person. You have to believe I thought I was doing the right thing."

I look at her, the woman I have loved as a sister for most of my life, and say the only thing I can think to say, "I love you, Nic, but you betrayed me, and you betrayed Joshua. I'll never be able to trust you again."

She looks me straight in the eye. "I can't believe you would listen to a stranger over me, that you would choose your relationship with her over your relationship with me."

I just shake my head. "No, Nic, you're the one who chose to listen to a stranger. You're the one who made the wrong choice." I turn and walk out the door, not wanting to see her sad face anymore.

In two minutes, Agent Shield meets me outside, and we make our way to the small airport just thirty minutes down the road. I don't even want to think about what is going on in my living room. If I know Joshua, I'm sure he is not saying anything; and if I know Nicole (which I'm not sure if I really do), she is probably begging Joshua to say something. I can't imagine what will happen to them, but I don't have the time to right now.

"Why don't we just call Agent Bright, tell him what we know? Surely, he can protect Elle until we get to Honolulu, and we figure out how much Dan Childs knows."

Agent Shield seems frustrated when he replies, "Don't you think I've tried that? I cannot get a hold of him. He's not answering his cell, and the pilots aren't either. Have you tried to call Agent Smith?"

"No, she doesn't have a cell phone. I assumed being on a government plane, with a government agent, I would be able to reach her. How silly of me!" I blow a frustrated breath of my own out and instantly regret my sarcastic comment. "Look, I'm sorry."

"No harm done," Agent Shield says. "Let's just get there as fast as we can."

I couldn't agree more.

Chapter 38

Eleanor

Seeing Dan Childs standing in the doorway is like seeing the figure of death coming to steal away my future. Lauren stands meekly behind him, and all I see is panic in her eyes. With the two of them standing there, side by side, I am hit with the realization they look very similar—same straight nose, same high forehead, and the pieces of some unknown puzzle start clicking into place. Didn't I wonder once how Lauren knew so much about Dan Childs and the inner workings of MicroCorp? Didn't Lauren seem to get more serious when I showed any interest in the CEO? And when I told her I was going to steal a document, didn't her personality take on a more ominous quality? I look back and forth from father to daughter and wonder how the reality of the situation never smacked me in the face like it is now.

Dan Childs smiles and says, "Yes, you're just now figuring it out, aren't you? Ms. Greene, I would like you to meet my daughter. Oh, but silly me, you two have already met. Haven't you, dear?"

As he turns to address Lauren who is standing behind him, I make my move and lunge toward him, wrapping my hands around his throat. I have the element of surprise, but he regains his footing rather fast and pulls my hands free of his windpipe. I am astonished at his strength, and the last thing I hear is Lauren letting out a scream and then all goes dark.

When I open my eyes, I am reminded again how every moment of waking up for me is a new adventure. Each time I open my eyes, I'm not sure if I will see something good or bad. Unfortunately for me, the situation I am in is about as bad as it can get. I am sitting up against something soft and warm, which moves a little at a time. Trying to keep up the appearance that I am still unconscious, I barely move my head around in both directions, and I see Dan Childs standing directly to my right with a gun pointed at me. His attention is focused elsewhere, and he is on his cell phone. I try to make a move toward him, but I hear Lauren's voice behind me.

"Don't be stupid, Becca. You're in no shape to take him down now." I whip my head around to face her, and I am instantly wracked with nausea. My head screams in protest as I give a little whimper. "See, I told you," she says with a note of satisfaction in her voice.

"You always did love being right." I try to joke, but it just comes out hoarse.

"Well, in this case, I am right." Lauren moves a little, and I can feel her spine against my back. We are sitting against each other on the floor, and I can tell she has been supporting my weight by the way she repositions herself. "You've been out for about twenty minutes," she whispers. "I was worried at first, but I could tell you were still breathing, so I knew you would be okay."

I slowly raise my left hand, trying not to draw any attention to us, and I inspect the knot on my head. I wince as I find a large bump, and when I bring my hand down, there is a little bit of blood on my fingers.

"Are you okay?" Lauren asks, her voice heavy with concern.

"Yeah, I'll be fine."

"He slammed your head against the door frame pretty hard," she says, matter-of-factly. I try to steady my breathing and consider our options. Agent Bright must realize how long I have been gone. But I'm sure in his mind, Lauren and I are just catching up, and he is giving us some privacy. I look around to see if there is anything I can use as a weapon, and Lauren speaks up. "I'm so sorry, Becca. I didn't think I would ever see you again. I never meant for you to get hurt like this."

The sadness in her voice pulls me from my weapons search, and I reassure her, "Don't worry, Lauren, we'll be okay. I'll get us out of this mess somehow. Oh, and by the way, my name is Eleanor, but you can call me Elle."

I feel her back move in a little laugh. When I ask her what is so funny, she replies, "Neither one of us have been going by our real names—mine is Haley, Haley Rose."

I laugh a little too and say, "Nice to meet you, Haley."

Her body sags a little bit when she says, "I guess this makes us the worst friends in the history of the world."

And I answer her with all the emotion I have felt since the first time I remembered her face, "I don't care if your name is Daffy Duck—I'm just glad to have you as my friend. You will never know what that means to me."

She simply answers, "Dido."

Dan Childs shuts his cell phone and focuses his attention on us. "Well, well. It's good to see you have finally decided to join us, Ms. Greene. I'm sure you are wondering how all this came about, aren't you? I'm not usually for giving thieves and liars what they want, but you have been such a good sport about all this I think I'll let you in on the details.

"You see, after I found out that my men had not really killed you like they had said, I tried tracking you down. I checked your apartment, the hospitals, the police department, and even the Internet. It occurred to me since there was no trace of you here in Honolulu, you might have left. A search of departing flights on the night of our little encounter showed an unscheduled takeoff of a private jet owned by the Smith family. From there, it was easy to find someone to help me spy on you. Their family is so large, and Nicole Smith was the perfect person—a woman with a troubled past and a struggling family. Like I told you in Washington, when you are me, anything is possible. And you wouldn't believe how far a little cash will go."

I can feel the shocked look on my face, and it must be pretty obvious because he looks at me with a little smirk. "Yes, Nicole was more than willing to help when I told her you were a dangerous criminal. My promise of taking care of her mother and siblings didn't hurt either."

I know I should feel hurt and betrayed, but my first thought is of Joshua and his open smile. He is going to be so devastated when he learns the truth, the whole family will be, especially Andrew. I think back on the times I thought Nicole was just shy or distrustful of outsiders, and now I know the truth—she was just distrustful of me. She must have hated me because she thought I was corrupting Andrew. I notice Dan is still talking, so I bring my attention back to the present.

"I really should be thanking you, Ms. Greene. If it wasn't for you, I would not have been reunited with my daughter. We haven't seen each other for some time, you see, with me being so busy and her being so . . . difficult."

I wish I could see Haley's face. Dan's is nothing but a mask of pleasantness, but I know hers is saying something totally different.

He continues, "I had no idea she was in Honolulu until I came to check your apartment for the second time, after our run-in in DC. Of course I was thrilled to learn my very own daughter had been your neighbor for months before you decided to disappear." He turns his focus to Haley, and I stiffen at the malice in his eyes.

"I hate to admit my dear daughter hasn't changed a bit since the last time I saw her. A few things are different, of course, like her name and hair, but her pure hatred of me is still the same, as is her desire to completely ruin me. I just don't know what I ever did to make her hate me so."

The concern in his voice is complete mockery, and Haley takes the bait. I feel her body shaking with rage as she begins yelling, "You know exactly what you did. You ruined my life. You ruined my mother with your lies and abandonment. She loved you so much, and you never cared one bit for her. She died with your name on her lips, and you didn't even bother to come to the funeral. You left me an orphan, with an empty bank account and an empty heart. You will never know what I had to do to survive. And I might have forgiven you if you had apologized and made me feel loved, but you never gave me another thought. I hated you then, I hate you now, and I will always hate you."

For a second after her tirade is done, I think Dan Childs might actually apologize. He looks genuinely sorry, but when he opens his mouth, nothing but indifference comes out. "Don't you think, Ms. Greene, it is pitiful how much my only child hates me? What a waste of time and effort, my dear. You could have put all your hard work into becoming a normal functioning member of society instead of a basket case with daddy issues. I should have had you killed the same time I had your mother killed. Look at all the headache I would have saved myself."

Before I know it, Haley is on her feet and is rushing toward her father. She slams into him, knocking the gun from his hand, but he grabs her by her hair and throws her to the ground. I make a move toward the gun, but he is quicker than me, picking it up off the floor and pointing it at Haley who is curled up on the ground quietly crying. I raise my hands in submission but scoot closer to my friend and lightly put my hand on her back.

"Okay, this has gone on long enough. Ms. Greene, I am going to ask you a simple question, and for every time you refuse to answer me, one of you will pay the price for your unwillingness to cooperate. Since my daughter has clearly decided not to tell me anything, it's your turn. Where is that file?"

I silently stare at him, almost daring him to hurt me, which is exactly what he does. I feel the butt of the gun across my face, and I see stars in my eyes. I cry out and shake my already sore head to clear my eyes of the tears that have begun to form. Mr. Childs stands there with the gun pointed at me and says, "Okay, it's my daughter's turn."

At this, he kicks Haley in the ribs, and she screams. The sound pierces my resolve, and when I open my mouth to tell him what he wants to know, Haley shouts, "No!" I look at her bloody face, made that way from hitting the tiled floor, see her clutching her ribs, and wonder to myself how long I will let this go on.

Mr. Childs turns the gun back on me and asks again, "Where is my file?" I look once more to my friend curled up on the floor, but before I even get a chance to answer, Mr. Childs fires. A burning pain shoots up my leg, and I fall backward on the floor. I never would have imagined a gunshot wound would burn like a fire out of control. I look down and see a neat hole in the top of my foot, similar to the wound on Andrew's back. A small amount of blood is trickling out of the hole, but the bottom of my foot is a different story. Where my strappy sandal used to be, there is a hole twice the size as the one on top.

However, the amount of blood pouring out the bottom of my foot is unsettling. I feel a little woozy but make myself stay calm. I have to protect Haley and myself. I struggle to sit up before answering.

"It's under the loose brick on the southeast side of Treasure Street, about one-third of the way down the wall."

As I help Haley stand up, I notice the look of triumph in her father's eyes. He seems more relaxed, and even his grip on the pistol in his hand has slacked some, which is exactly what I wanted. I'm not really sure what I am going to do now, but I knew I had to get me and Lauren out of the situation we were in.

I think back to mine and Andrew's mantra, *Take control of the situation*, and that is exactly what I'm going to do. Unfortunately, even though Mr. Childs's grip has slacked, his focus has not, and he herds us out of the apartment and into the tiny elevator. As he pushes the down button, I keep a steady grip on Haley's waist as I try to take pressure off my right foot. She is weak, too weak to be a part of any plan I might conceive, so I keep my thoughts focused on trying to take down her father by myself.

On a positive note, I know Agent Bright is downstairs on the street waiting for me to return with the disk. I can only hope the gunshot has alerted him, and he is fast enough to assess the situation before Mr. Childs can force Haley and me into a car. Because once we arrive at Treasure Street and he finds out I lied to him, all hell will break loose.

The elevator *bings*, and we step into the lobby. Mr. Childs looks around and then motions for us to walk ahead of him out of the doors and into the street. My eyes immediately scan the road for the government car which brought me to the apartment building, but I don't find it. I start to panic as I whip my head from side to side. Mr. Childs is focused on getting his keys out of his pocket when all of a sudden, I see a cop car speeding around the corner. The lights are on, but there is no siren.

Mr. Childs quickly pushes the unlock button on his keys and throws Lauren and I into the backseat of his own car. When he closes the door, I see him look up and spot the police cruiser. Instead of looking panicked, he looks determined. He tries to make his way around the car and into the driver's seat, but the sounds of gunshots stop his progress. He backtracks, running to the back door, and drags me out by my feet onto the pavement, banging my head against the concrete curb.

Pulling me up in front of him, I struggle with all my might to break free of his hold. He points the pistol to my temple and makes me face the police car. All four of the cruiser doors are open, and there are three men with guns pointed at me and my captor. My hazy mind recognizes the men standing behind the front doors as Agent Bright and Chief Richards of the local police, both of them pointing their own guns. However, I must have injured my head harder than I thought because behind the driver's side passenger door stands Agent Shield with his pistol trained on Mr. Childs. *That can't be right; Agent Shield is in California.* I have the funny feeling I already know who is standing behind the passenger side back door. Making my gaze shift across the top of the car, I see the beautiful green eyes I have come to love staring back at me.

✳✳✳

Andrew

Seeing Elle with a gun pointed to her head is the most horrifying thing I have ever witnessed. Her face is bloody and already bruising. I notice her holding her right foot off the ground, and as I examine it more closely, I can see a tiny bullet hole on the top. After countless battles and countless wounds, I could never have imagined the terror I feel in this moment.

Putting yourself at risk is one thing, but seeing someone you love at risk is another. It takes everything I have to stay cowered behind the car door. When I make eye contact with Elle, I try to run to her, but Agent Shield catches my movement out of the corner of his eye and orders me to stay where I am. "You could put her in more danger if you make any sudden movements," he calmly tells me.

I want to scream at him, scream at Dan Childs, but I know it won't make any difference. The situation is completely out of my hands, and I have never felt so helpless. Agent Bright is yelling at Dan Childs to put his weapon on the ground and step away from Elle with his hands up, but he is not moving. My brave girl is holding her own, not shaking with fear but standing tall with determination in her eyes.

"Drop your weapons, or your agent dies right here, right now!" Dan Childs yells back.

"Shoot him!" I hear Elle say, but none of the agents take a shot. Unlike her, I don't have confidence in their ability to hit Childs and not her, and I am grateful they don't follow her orders. She wriggles in his grasp, and he forces his pistol harder into her head.

Agent Bright talks low so that only the four of us can hear. "We're going to have to do something fast before this turns into a hostage situation. We could end up chasing him all over this island. But one thing is for sure, if we allow him to get in that car, we might never see Agent Smith again."

His words, although true, are debilitating, and I sag into the door frame. I can't imagine losing her forever. Knowing I need to be strong for Elle, I straighten my stance and make eye contact with her. In that instance, she winks at me and falls to the ground.

The sudden shift of her weight throws Dan Childs off balance, and Agent Bright takes the opportunity to fire. In less than a second, Childs is lying dead on the ground, and Elle is half running, half hopping across the road toward me. I am vaguely aware the other agents have rushed toward the body, but all I am focused on is reaching my wife. We crash into one another, and she collapses. I sweep her into my arms and begin carrying her unconscious body to the car.

Chapter 40

Eleanor

I dread opening my eyes. The hardness of the bed and the roughness of the sheets only confirm my suspicions I am not at home. The awful sound of medical equipment beeping somewhere makes me give an audible sigh, and I can feel warm fingers pressing into my wrist.

"You know, I'm sure one of these machines I'm hooked up to does a fine job of taking my pulse. You don't have to do it for them." My voice is scratchy and dry, so the joke I was trying to make falls flat, and I sigh once again.

Standing directly above me is Andrew, and his smile is the most welcome sight I can imagine. Because of the angle of my bed, I struggle to sit up, but Andrew quickly finds the remote control and pushes the incline button. I wince when the movement causes blood to rush to my bruised and battered head. Andrew reaches for me, but I wave him off. "I'm fine, really. Just a little sore."

The hospital room is pretty bare, no generic pictures on the wall or deceivingly uncomfortable chairs in the corners. To my left, I see a drawn curtain and hear someone snoring behind it. Andrew sees me looking around and answers my unasked question.

"You just got back from surgery. The doctors tried to repair some of the damage done to your right foot. The good news is the bullet missed anything important, and with a little therapy, you should have full use of your foot."

I just nod my head and he continues. "Your other injuries are also not serious. The bump on your head has already reduced in size, and the CT scan shows no permanent damage. The bad news is you do have a broken nose, and although it looks pretty rough now, it should heal in a couple of weeks."

I don't even ask for a mirror—I would rather not see what "pretty rough" looks like at the moment. I close my eyes and lay my head against the pillow.

"Why did you come, Andrew?" He knows I don't mean to the hospital. "You don't know how terrified I was when I saw you behind the car door. You could have gotten hurt."

Now it's Andrew's turn to sigh, and I open my eyes to see him shaking his head in exasperation. When he begins speaking, his tone has a harshness I have heard only once before.

"Do you really not know why I came, Elle? Because if you don't, I have done a poor job of showing you how I feel about you. When I found out what Nicole had done—"

I stop him there and quickly ask, "How did you find out? Does Joshua know? Is he okay? Where is Nicole?" I am sitting up now, and Andrew forces my shoulder back down to the bed.

"Calm down, Elle. I found out because Nicole told me. When I mentioned you had returned to Honolulu, she broke down and told me everything. Yes, Joshua knows, and no, he is not okay, not at all. As for Nicole, I'm not sure where she is. Agents Bright and Shield made it clear what she did wasn't technically illegal, and it is up to you and me to press charges against her if we wanted to."

"Of course we don't want to!" I quickly add.

Andrew raises his eyebrows. "Well, I was going to wait and ask you what you thought."

Feeling a little offended, I say, "Andrew, I can't believe you would think I would want that. Nicole messed up, but we all have." I look into his green eyes which have held such warmth, acceptance, safety, and love. "I've messed up, Andrew. I messed up when I left you standing on the street in DC., I messed up when I told you I was coming back to Honolulu, I messed up when I walked out our door, and I messed up when I didn't give you an answer earlier today."

Andrew takes my hands in his. "You're right. You have messed up but only because I failed you first. I never should have let you get into that car in DC. I should have thrown myself onto the bumper before letting you drive away. I never should have let you come to Honolulu by yourself. I was hurt and mad. I never should have let you walk out our door without me right beside you holding your hand. And I should have told you every day since the morning you woke up, that from the first time I saw you, I've loved you. You are the reason I am the person that I am today. You give me a new hope and a new purpose in life, and I will be forever grateful."

Silent tears stream down my face, and even though my head is pounding and my foot is throbbing, I decide now is the time to tell the truth. "Andrew, it feels so good to hear you say these things. I cannot imagine a proposal more romantic and heartfelt. However, I can't accept your offer of marriage."

Andrew seems stunned. "What did you say?"

"I said, I cannot marry you." He stands up quickly from the bed, putting distance between us.

"Please, tell me you are joking." His voice holds a quiet anger, and I reach out to him, not being able to stand the look of devastation on his face.

"I want to try to explain why I cannot marry you," I say hastily.

"I wish you would," he replies tersely.

And this is the point I realize nothing I will say to him will ever get through. The second I gave Andrew an answer of no, I caused a rift which could never be crossed. Knowing my case is hopeless, I decide my lame excuses would cause him to hate me more than I would be able to stand. That is why I lie.

"I never loved you, Andrew. Sure, I was grateful for what you did for me. You have to realize in my line of work, deception is part of the game. I wouldn't have survived as long as I have without it."

Andrew's face is a mask of shock and anger. "No, you wouldn't have survived as long as you have without me saving your life."

"You're right, and I thank you for it. However, that does not erase the fact that I simply don't have the same feelings for you as you do for me." I try to make my voice sound casual and nonchalant.

"I don't believe you," he spits out.

"I am sorry things had to end this way. The truth of the matter is, I used your skill as a doctor, your family's wealth, and your compassion as a human being to help me regain my memories. I will forever be in your debt, of course."

"Just stop with the bullshit, Elle. Just stop." Andrew takes a deep breath. "Am I supposed to believe every kiss we shared, every touch, every secret I told you, even the most intimate details of my life meant nothing to you? That is simply not possible."

"Actually, it is possible. I used those things to my advantage. Your feelings for me were the perfect incentive to finding my identity."

"Why are you acting like this?" he suddenly bursts out. "Quit pretending you don't have feelings for me." He takes a calming breath. "I don't know why you are choosing to hurt me like this, but I simply cannot and will not take it. I swore I would never walk out on you again. I promised to do everything in my power to protect you. I even took a bullet for you."

The pain in his voice is almost more than I can bear. "However, if this is how you truly feel, if you have only used me and my family as a way to complete your mission, then I must congratulate you."

The change in his tone and the choice of his words take me by surprise. "What do you mean, 'congratulate me'?"

"You should be congratulated for being the most convincing agent the CIA has. Not to mention, the biggest bitch." With this, Andrew walks out of the room.

I hear a knock on my door. I look up to see Haley peeking around the door frame. I wave her inside, and she walks in, carrying a shoebox. I feel a slight sense of dread knowing what is in there, but I don't protest when she sits it on the foot of my bed.

"I'm so glad to see that you are all right." Her face seems a little paler, and her movements are very rigid.

"Thanks. The same goes for you. I wasn't sure if we were going to make it there for a while. I was actually getting depressed thinking we might die in your crappy apartment." She genuinely laughs at my joke but stops short and begins to cry.

"If I had just been honest with you from the beginning," she starts, but I hold my hand out to stop her.

"I'll hear none of that. Neither one of us was totally honest with the other, and that's just the way the game is played. I wouldn't have lasted in my line of work if I was truthful to each person I meet. No offense, but if I had known you were Dan Childs's daughter, I wouldn't have trusted you as much."

She gives me a questioning look. "It's not you, really. It's just in my nature to distrust anyone with so much information *and* a personal connection to the case." Haley seems to accept my answer. She shrugs her shoulders and points to the shoe box.

"Agent Bright told me the truth about the disk—that you hid it in your shoe. I understand why you couldn't tell me. But I hate knowing it was right under my nose this whole time, and I could have turned it in months ago."

"Oh well, it's just one of those things." I reach to pick up the box.

"Oh no, you don't. You're not supposed to be moving at all." Haley rushes to get the box before I can make another move and hands it to me.

"How are you feeling?" I ask as I notice the pain in her eyes.

"I have a bump on my head and some bruised ribs but nothing serious. It seems you got the worst of the injuries." Once again, I wave her off like it's nothing for me to have a gunshot wound to the foot and a concussion.

I look down at the shoebox. Haley wraps her warm hands around mine, which gives me the courage to open the box. Inside is a pair of torn and dirty tennis shoes. I can tell they used to be white, but now the mud and what looks like dried blood is caked on so thick hardly any of their original color remains. I cannot stop my hands from shaking as I pull out the left shoe and reach my hand in slowly to pull back the sole and reveal a small dug-out area, only big enough to hold the disk which lies within it.

As I pull it out, I look at Haley, and we breathe a sigh of relief. I stare at the small plastic disk that has caused so much trouble in my life and briefly wonder what would have happened if Dan Childs had never stopped me that night in the lobby of MicroCorp. I would probably be working on my next assignment, living who knows where. I might still be in communication with Haley, but I would most certainly never have met Andrew. I would continue living the life of a government spy—no real friends, no real family, no real connections. Everything would be fake, fast, and failproof, a life that seems less appealing to me now that I know how it feels to belong and be loved.

I place the disk on the food tray, not wanting to touch it any longer. Haley speaks up, "Seems sort of ridiculous, doesn't it? The fact something so small had such a big effect on so many people."

In that instant, I know what I have to do. I pick up the remote control and smash the corner of it into the disk. Over and over, I drive the remote into the disk until it bends from the force. It's like the action broke some kind of lever loose in us because when I look into the face of my friend, she is on the verge of laughter. Once we start, there is no getting us to stop, and I find myself feeling better than I have in days.

I have been in the hospital in Honolulu for a week now, and I am dying to leave this god-awful place. Haley has been to see me every day. We have spent the time getting to really know each other. I have been pleasantly surprised to find out, although the details of Haley's life are completely different from what I had known from before, her personality is not. She is the same spunky, funny, brutally honest person I used to eat lunch with every Saturday. Something else which has not changed is the fact she worries about me. Haley would never say it, especially after I explained why she would not have the pleasure of meeting the man who saved my life; the pity in her eyes says enough.

One afternoon, we were having a discussion about our favorite television shows when Haley abruptly changed the subject.

"How did you do it, Eleanor?"

"How did I do what?" I asked, genuinely confused.

"How did you wake up in a strange house with no recollection whatsoever of who you were or where you were or how you got there? I don't know if I could handle the sudden realization that I was completely alone." I think about her question while she continues. "I've known I would be alone ever since my mother passed, and I made it my life's mission to destroy my father. I was able to come to terms with loneliness and sacrifice, but those things were thrust onto you."

I take a deep breath before answering her, knowing the confession I am about to make should be to Andrew and not my friend.

"When I woke up that first morning, I was beyond confused and, I won't lie, scared. It's so hard to explain to someone the thoughts that go through your mind when you have amnesia. The whole world doesn't make sense. I remember finding a magnetic calendar on Andrew's fridge and being excited to find out the date. Things you take for granted like the day of the week, the faces of your parents, even your name are taken away from you. I can't describe it now, but I had the strongest drive to find answers. That is the only reason I was able to pick myself up off the bedroom floor and walk out. And then I saw Andrew, and I swear, Haley, he was like an angel. I immediately trusted him. His crazy story about finding me in an alley was terrifying, but I believed him." I pause to gather the courage I'm going to need to finish my admission.

"After that, everything revolved around him. I ate with him, slept with him, laughed with him, cried with him, fought with him, searched with him, lied with him—it was all about him. I didn't think about it like that at the time. It was just the way things were. He was my ticket to everything. Without him, I could do nothing, both financially and emotionally. But something changed when I left for Honolulu with Agent Bright. I realized I did not need Andrew to live my life. I could take care of myself. Reading my folder and remembering things about my past just reassured me that I was capable of being my own person, independent from anyone, and I suddenly craved that freedom and responsibility. I knew if I accepted Andrew's proposal of marriage, I would forever regret not taking the chance to reconnect with myself and my independence."

Haley just sat there, looking a little incredulous. And I continued. "I know that sounds really, really selfish and ungrateful, but it is, in fact, the opposite. I gave a lot of thought to marrying Andrew, and at first, I couldn't imagine anything better. My love for him is unlike anything I have ever felt before. However, when I realized how I truly felt about him and what I truly wanted to do with my life, there was no way I could commit halfheartedly to someone who had committed totally to me. It would not have been fair to either of us. I just pray Andrew will one day find it in his heart to forgive me and understand why I chose to refuse him."

"Yeah, I don't see that happening" was her only response.

Agents Bright and Shield have been in and out of my room all week checking on my progress and going over final details of the case. My little disk-bashing episode did nothing to actually damage the information contained within the quarter-sized component. The CIA was now in charge of "October", and I found out really quick how low I am on the totem pole of CIA intelligence. When I asked Agent Bright what the disk I risked my life for contained, I was rewarded with a hearty laugh and a shake of his head.

I requested a formal leave of absence from the CIA until I can get my bearings but still have not decided where I am going to go and what I am going to do. Haley offered to let me stay with her in her new apartment, across town from our old building. However, the thought of staying another second in this city makes me sick to my stomach. Too much has happened here; too many bad memories cloak the tall buildings and the perfectly blue waves. I think about returning to Tennessee, the place where I grew up, and wonder if it will be too painful to go back there knowing no one will be waiting for me. I think about returning to Carmel, if only to walk on the beach again. But the fear of running into Andrew or any of his family causes me to banish the thought as quickly as it appeared. It's a tad bit depressing to realize you have nowhere to go, no one to turn to, so I was surprised when Agent Bright walks into my room carrying an envelope along with my suitcase.

"I was asked to give you this."

I give him a questioning look as I turn it over in my hands. The envelope almost falls to the floor when I recognize the handwriting as Andrew's.

"When did he give you this," I ask calmly.

"When he left to return to Carmel earlier this week. I took him back to the airport."

"Did he say anything to you?"

Agent Bright shakes his head. "He thanked me for my help in Washington DC and for looking after you."

I can't find anything to say in return, so I simply nod. "I'll leave you alone." He starts walking to the door and then stops and turns back toward me. "I know it's none of my business, and you have every right to tell me to butt out. However, I feel like I need to say something." He stops and looks to me for permission to continue. Not being sure if I want to hear what he has to say, I don't acknowledge he has even looked my way.

"Dr. Smith is one of the most decent men I have ever had the pleasure of knowing. And you would do well to realize the truth of my words. Whatever your reservations are, you must know you will never find someone who will put up with your shit like he has."

"You know what," I shout, "I am sick and tired of every man in my life cursing me out for trying to keep my head above water. I'm drowning here. Can't anybody see that?" Tears flow down my face, but Agent Bright doesn't make a move to comfort me.

"I am always on your side, Eleanor. But you need to take some time to get your act together. Go back home to Tennessee. See if you can remember the reasons for the choices you have made. Try to contact your brother, get in touch with old friends, and put a lot of thought into contacting Dr. Smith in the future."

I dry my eyes on the bedsheets as Agent Bright walks out of the room. He pokes his head back through the doorway. "I hate to pour salt in your wounds, so to speak. But from now on, you will no longer be known as Agent Smith. See you outside in twenty, Agent Wright."

As he closes the door, I can't help but feel like I've been punched in the gut and slapped in the face.

I slowly open the envelope Andrew left for me and dread the words on the page inside. Instead of finding a personal message, however, I find a poem which I recognize is from the book we bought in Washington DC:

"False though She Be to Me and Love"

False though she be to me and love,
I'll ne'er pursue revenge;
For still the charmer I approve,
Though I deplore her change.
In hours of bliss we oft have met;
They could not always last;
And though the present I regret,
I'm grateful for the past.

Epilogue

Carmel, California

Four Months Later

Annie Smith

The doorbell rings, but no one answers. My family is too busy yelling at each other to hear it. Because it's Saturday, Mary, our housekeeper, is off enjoying the weekend with her grandchildren, so it is left up to me to answer the door. Actually, I'm grateful for the distraction. Ever since Andrew's last return from Honolulu, the usual laughter in the big house has been replaced with shouts of anger, sadness, and bitterness. I never imagined my family would be so separated. It makes me sick to think one person could cause so much turmoil.

I wipe a silent tear which has escaped my eye as I pull open the heavy front door. On the other side stands a man in military fatigues. He is tall, probably the same height as my oldest brother Joshua, with brown eyes and brown hair-cropped short, a style you would expect to see on a soldier. As my eyes take in the full form of his face, I am struck with how handsome he is and also how familiar he looks. I am taking in his erect posture when he clears his throat.

I suddenly find my voice and my manners. "Can I help you?" I ask pleasantly with what I hope is an attractive smile on my face.

"Yes, ma'am," he replies seriously with a strong Southern accent, and I get a strange feeling in the pit of my stomach. "My name is Robert Wright. I am looking for my sister, Eleanor, and was told she lived here."

I am in shock; this has to be what shock feels like. No wonder he seemed so familiar; he is Elle's brother. I'm not sure what look I have on my face, but I suddenly feel shaky. The man thankfully reaches to catch me as I stumble into the door frame.

"Are you okay, ma'am?"

I nod my head and scream over the loud voices of my family drifting from the living room. "Andrew, can you come here, please? Now!"

Acknowledgments

This book has been a long time in the making and would continue to be a file on my flash drive if it had not have been for the following people:

First and foremost, my Creator, who has given me life, love, salvation, and the passion to do something I never dreamed possible. Second, my amazing, loving, supportive, and talented husband, Adam. (The adjectives I could use to describe you, honey, are endless.) Your creativity and your admiration inspire me. Third, my beautiful daughter Caroline who had to endure my constant "just a minute" calls while I was writing. And last, my parents, Jerry and Carol Price. You love me no matter what, and I am blessed to call you mine. 1434!

A huge thank-you to my first readers who, because of their love for me, took time out of their busy schedules to read my story: Carol Price, Joy Rose, Haley Wallace, and Heather Dillinger. Your support means more than you could ever know. Special thanks to Haley Wallace for the expert nursing and medical information. Eleanor would have undergone a lot of unnecessary hardships if it wasn't for you.

I want to say a huge thank-you to Sid Wilson, my publishing representative, for answering all my questions and for helping me through the ins and outs of publishing my story.